Praise for the novels of
Jasmine Haynes

"Deliciously erotic and completely captivating."
—Susan Johnson, *New York Times* bestselling author

"An erotic, emotional adventure of discovery you don't want to miss."
—Lora Leigh, #1 *New York Times* bestselling author

"So incredibly hot that I'm trying to find the right words to describe it without having to be edited for content . . . Extremely stimulating from the first page to the last! Of course, that means that I loved it! . . . One of the hottest, sexiest erotic books I have read so far."
—*Romance Reader at Heart*

"Sexy."
—*Sensual Romance Reviews*

"Delightfully torrid."
—*Midwest Book Review*

"More than a fast-paced erotic romance, this is a story of family, filled with memorable characters who will keep you engaged in the plot and the great sex. A good read to warm a winter's night."
—*RT Book Reviews*

"Bursting with sensuality and eroticism."
—*In the Library Reviews*

"The passion is intense, hot, and purely erotic . . . Recommended for any reader who likes their stories realistic, hot, captivating, and very, very well written."
—*Road to Romance*

"Not your typical romance. This one's going to remain one of my favorites."
—*The Romance Studio*

"Jasmine Haynes keeps the plot moving and the love scenes very hot."
—*Just Erotic Romance Reviews*

"A wonderful novel . . . Try this one—you won't be sorry."
—*The Best Reviews*

Berkley titles by Jasmine Haynes

TEACH ME A LESSON

THE NAUGHTY CORNER

THE PRINCIPAL'S OFFICE

WHAT HAPPENS AFTER DARK

PAST MIDNIGHT

MINE UNTIL MORNING

HERS FOR THE EVENING

YOURS FOR THE NIGHT

FAIR GAME

LACED WITH DESIRE

(with Jaci Burton, Joey W. Hill, and Denise Rossetti)

UNLACED

(with Jaci Burton, Joey W. Hill, and Denise Rossetti)

SHOW AND TELL

THE FORTUNE HUNTER

OPEN INVITATION

TWIN PEAKS

(with Susan Johnson)

SOMEBODY'S LOVER

Specials

LA PETITE MORT

UNDONE

TEACH ME A LESSON

Jasmine Haynes

HEAT
New York

THE BERKLEY PUBLISHING GROUP
Published by the Penguin Group
Penguin Group (USA) LLC
375 Hudson Street, New York, New York 10014

USA • Canada • UK • Ireland • Australia • New Zealand • India • South Africa • China

penguin.com

A Penguin Random House Company

This book is an original publication of The Berkley Publishing Group.

HEAT and the Heat design are trademarks of Penguin Group (USA) LLC.

Library of Congress Cataloging-in-Publication Data
Haynes, Jasmine.
Teach me a lesson / Jasmine Haynes.—Heat trade paperback edition
pages cm
ISBN 978-0-425-26624-3 (pbk.)
1. Student counselors—Fiction.   2. School principals—Fiction.   I. Title.
PS3608.A936T43 2014
813'.6—dc23
2013036556

PUBLISHING HISTORY
Heat trade paperback edition / April 2014

PRINTED IN THE UNITED STATES OF AMERICA

10 9 8 7 6 5 4 3 2 1

Cover photograph: "Girl tied with a bow" © Yarkovoy / Shutterstock.
Cover design by Diana Kolsky.

To Kurt Loesch, a wonderful friend. We miss you.

ACKNOWLEDGMENTS

Thanks to my special network of friends who support me, brainstorm with me, and encourage me: Bella Andre, Shelley Bates, Jenny Andersen, Jackie Yau, Ellen Higuchi, Kathy Coatney, Pamela Fryer, Rosemary Gunn, and Laurel Jacobson. Thanks also to my editor, Wendy McCurdy, and my agent, Lucienne Diver.

1

"HE WANTS ME TO HAVE SEX WITH OTHER MEN." JEANINE SMITH punctuated the admission with a sob and a dab at her eyes with a moist tissue.

Charlotte had heard a lot of strange things within the confines of her therapy office, but this was definitely a first. She'd read of such behavior, men who wanted to loan out their wives, but she'd never personally encountered it. She dealt with relationship issues, performance and satisfaction concerns, self-esteem and body image difficulties, trauma and abuse recovery, and a whole list of other sexual anxieties. Her watchword was *empowerment*, and she believed in a compassionate, sex-positive psychotherapy. To her, no client's problem was greater than another's, and she never allowed herself to make judgments about whatever matter a client brought her. But she was human, and she could still be shocked.

It had taken Jeanine three sessions to work herself up to this revelation. "I mean *he* doesn't want me, so he intends to give me to other men? Isn't that crazy, Dr. Moore?" She sniffled, blotted her eyes, then her nose, threw the tissue away and grabbed another from the box Charlotte kept handy on the table between them.

Charlotte didn't believe in the psychiatric couch. She set two comfortable chairs by the corner windows of her office, with a view of the oak trees separating her complex from the neighboring one. Even at the beginning of November, when the weather in the San Francisco Bay area had begun to change from fall to winter, she found the view to have a calming effect on her clients. She didn't refer to them as patients. She wasn't a doctor, she was a psychologist, but Jeanine didn't listen well and Charlotte had stopped correcting her on the title.

Jeanine also paid in cash and didn't bill her insurance company, all of which made Charlotte wonder if the overly common *Smith* was a false name. Charlotte had decided to let her keep her anonymity; if she'd pressed the issue, she wasn't sure Jeanine would come back.

"Let's discuss the particulars," Charlotte said, her tone neutral. "We can start with how he brought up the subject."

Jeanine blew her nose. Despite the red-rimmed eyes and the slightly smeared mascara, she was a good-looking woman. Wavy blond hair past her shoulders, blue eyes, a neatly dressed woman with a trim figure, she was a well-kept forty-three-year-old. Charlotte didn't even need to add the common phrase *for a woman her age.* Jeanine had a teenage son with her first husband—who, by Jeanine's account, rarely saw the boy because he was often abroad on business—and two more children, a girl of ten and another boy aged eight, by her second husband, David. He was fifty-two, and their sex life had ground to a halt two years ago. Of course, most couple's problems weren't about sex per se but usually concerned issues in other areas of their relationship that manifested themselves in the bedroom, which was why Charlotte would have preferred couple's therapy. Jeanine claimed her husband refused to have any counseling. She believed David was suffering from erectile dysfunction and had even gone as far as to suggest Viagra. He'd refused that, too, telling her there was nothing wrong with his . . . parts.

Jeanine grabbed another tissue and held it crumpled in her hand in readiness. "Well, um, it was about a month before I started seeing you, and, um, I'd tried to initiate sex, and well, um, he wanted to fantasize about me and . . . other men . . ." Her voice trailed away.

"And this incident was the catalyst for you coming here?" It often took people several sessions to work up to revealing the *real* reason they'd sought help.

Jeanine nodded, gulped a breath of air, then everything seemed to rush out. "The worst part was that he actually got hard. He never gets hard for me anymore, but then he starts telling me how sexy it would be if I went out for drinks with the girls after work, and when I got home, he could smell sex on me, another man." She paused, looked at Charlotte, and lowered her voice, saying, "Another man's come. He said he'd put his hand between my legs and find me wet, and then he'd—" Jeanine stopped, swallowed, stared at Charlotte.

"You can tell me whatever is necessary, Jeanine. I have no judgment about it."

Jeanine nodded, her lips working a moment before she spoke. "He said he'd want to lick me clean after another man had come in me. He'd lick me all over."

Very interesting. "What was your reaction?" Charlotte prompted.

"My reaction? I was outraged, horrified—" Her gaze flitted about the room as if searching for another word. She grabbed a tissue, wadding it up with the other already in her hand.

Charlotte didn't push, letting the woman work it through.

Finally, Jeanine let out a long sigh. "The terrible thing is, Doctor, I got turned on. I wanted to have sex right then. I just wanted to climb on top of him and take him."

Well, well, well. "That isn't a terrible reaction, Jeanine. You don't need to feel guilty about a fantasy the two of you had."

"There's more, Doctor. He said it was the perfect solution to our problem. That I wanted more sex, and he was willing to let me have it. He even said he'd want me to call him while I was, you know"—she threw her hands up, her voice rising—"right in the middle of things. He wanted pictures. He even suggested hiding in the closet so he could watch."

Charlotte didn't allow a single facial muscle to twitch. She'd been a psychologist for twelve years, and she'd heard a lot of stories, but while she'd read a bit about this phenomenon, hearing it in practice was, well, quite amazing. She could write a paper on it.

"How do his desires make you feel?" Her job was about discovering her client's reactions to events and dealing with those reactions.

"It's like I'm some sex object. Or his personal porn queen. What if it means he's gay, that he wants to look at other men? Or maybe he wants to have an affair, so he's giving me permission first. Then he'll feel justified in doing it. Or maybe this is a test to see if I'll be faithful." She stared at her hands, wadding and unwadding the tissues. "I just don't know what it means." Her voice was almost childlike. "Well, ultimately, I guess it means he doesn't want me anymore, which is what I've thought for a couple of years. I haven't let him talk about it since that night." She raised her eyes. "You know, it's always been like he has two faces. There's the outer one where he's concerned about his reputation. But at home, he was different, like I was his refuge, a place where he didn't have to keep up appearances." Her chin trembled. "But this whole sex thing began, and suddenly he became tense even at home." Her voice softened into a whisper. "I just want him to be the way he was."

Another thing Charlotte had discovered was that what a client often thought was the inciting incident had seeds in something much earlier. "Tell me, did he ever talk like this before, when the sex between you was better?"

"No." Jeanine tapped her lips with three fingers, then dropped her hand. "Well, okay, yes, in a way. He always wanted to know about my other lovers before him. Not my ex-husband, but any other men. He liked me to describe what we did."

"How did he react to your descriptions?"

She was very still, looking deep. "He'd get pretty worked up. And the sex was, well, he was like a wild man."

"How did that make you feel?"

"It was kind of arousing, actually."

"I'd like to offer an opinion, Jeanine. Is that okay with you?" She nodded her permission.

"His fantasy doesn't sound like it came out of the blue just a few weeks ago. I would venture the possibility that he was subliminally revealing his fantasy when he asked about your past lovers. Now that he's experiencing performance issues, he's resurrected that fantasy to excite himself." And it had worked, at least for him, until Jeanine became upset.

Jeanine pursed her lips. "But it still means he doesn't want me."

Charlotte had encouraged Jeanine to bring her husband to one of their sessions for this very reason. To discuss performance issues. Women tended to see it as an invalidation of their own sexuality, while for men, it questioned their very manhood. However, Jeanine was the client, and it was Jeanine's psyche she needed to work with.

"It's not about his desire for you. It has nothing to do with physical attraction or lack of it. There's nothing wrong with you."

Jeanine began patting her eyes again, ready to burst into another volley of sobs.

"What if you told him you'd do it?"

Jeanine stopped, her mouth gaping. She slapped it shut, stared at Charlotte with narrowed eyes a moment, then said, "That's a joke, right?"

"No. I'm not saying you should have sex with another man. I'm merely suggesting that you play your husband's game. Talk to him about what you'd do with another man. Engage him." She lowered her voice. "Excite him."

"But that's sick." Jeanine shook her head.

"Everyone thinks of sex differently. Diverse activities arouse them. Some people like to watch—"

"You mean peeping toms?" Jeanine interjected.

"No, I don't mean people who do it in secret at the expense of others. I'm talking about consensual voyeurism and exhibitionism. Some like to watch. Some like to be watched. Has your husband ever asked to watch you masturbate?"

Jeanine's face colored. "Of course not."

Charlotte didn't like labels, but she had to say that Jeanine was a bit of a prude. She wanted sex, she wanted to feel desirable, but she expressed no interest in stepping out of the box. Except for admitting that it turned her on when she'd told her husband about her previous lovers. "There's nothing wrong with masturbation. It can be part of a healthy sex life." Charlotte paused, gauged the look on Jeanine's face. Some psychologists didn't make suggestions, never offered opinions. Their technique was to listen and lead the client to his or her own conclusions. Perhaps because she was in sex therapy, Charlotte made a lot of recommendations. Some people wouldn't consider all the possibilities on their own.

"I have a suggestion, and before you discount it out of hand, I want you to consider it."

"Yes, Doctor." But Jeanine toyed nervously with the edges of her tissues.

She was a very buttoned-up woman. She could have insisted her husband join her in therapy to talk about *their* issues. But she wouldn't. She needed to stand up for herself more, but when Charlotte mentioned this, Jeanine tuned out. In a roundabout way, Charlotte's newest idea was designed to help her grow some backbone while at the same time engaging her husband.

"Play his game," Charlotte said, "but make it your own. Indulge his fantasy in the least threatening manner. Prepare an intimate setting, no kids, no distractions. You've already talked about past lovers with him. Take it a step further and talk about a new lover. Ask him what he'd like you to do with this man. Allow him to get turned on by your words. Touch yourself for him. Excite *him* with *your* excitement."

Jeanine closed her eyes as if she couldn't bear to contemplate it.

Charlotte knew it was unconventional, but her therapy techniques often were. She believed couples needed to step out of their comfort zone. As long as they weren't doing anything illegal or harmful to their partner, or becoming obsessive, just about anything could have a positive effect. Masturbation, sex toys, role playing, fantasizing, exhibitionism, voyeurism, even bondage and submission, could all be incorporated into a healthy sexual relationship. These activities only became unhealthy in the ways a couple dealt with them, not in the acts themselves.

She was even willing to try a bit of BDSM herself, if for no other reason than to be able to recommend it. Or not.

Jeanine, however, had a long way to go. "What if he thinks I'm going to do it for real?"

"Make it clear that you don't intend to act on anything. What's important is that you'll be giving him acceptance for his fantasies."

"But I don't accept his fantasies."

Acceptance was the crux of the problem. "Are you sure you don't? If you strip away all the emotion about not being desirable, about him no longer wanting you, and you consider the times you talked about your other lovers, are you *absolutely* sure you don't feel any acceptance?"

"I . . ." Jeanine trailed off, her lips parted.

"You said it was exciting at the time," Charlotte reminded her.

Jeanine continued to fiddle with the tissues.

The light on Charlotte's phone—which was on the desk behind Jeanine—began to flash, indicating her next client was out in the waiting room. She glanced at the unobtrusive clock on the table between them, a business-card holder with a small clock on the side facing her. "Our time's almost up. I'll leave you with this: While my suggestion might not be the right one for you, maybe another will come up when you're reviewing what I've said. The most important thing is for you and your husband to find a place where you can get these feelings out in the open so they aren't festering between you."

"I'll definitely think about it." Quickly, almost in relief, Jeanine leaned down to pick up her purse from the side of her chair.

As she exited, Charlotte had the feeling Jeanine wouldn't even consider the suggestion. She wasn't past the complaining stage. Charlotte wasn't sure the woman ever would be. But that was her job, to move people past rehashing their complaints and into constructive work on their issues.

She shifted to the chair behind the desk, tapping a button on the keyboard to bring her computer to life. She had a couple of minutes before the start of her next appointment, and she wanted to type up a few reminder notes for Jeanine's file.

Fingers poised, an errant thought flitted across her mind. She talked sex all day long, yet she hadn't been with a man in a disgustingly long time. Months. How many? Nine months at least, maybe even more. Far too long. She flipped to her to-do list.

Note to self: Find a man, have some hot sex.

That made her recall her best friend, Lola Cook. And the new man in her life. And the new kinky sex.

Second note to self: Better yet, find a hot man to spank you.

2

CHARLOTTE WORKED TUESDAYS AND THURSDAYS AS A GUIDANCE counselor at the same high school she'd graduated from twenty years ago. She had, in fact, planned her future in this very office, from the opposite side of the desk. Carpeting had been installed over the linoleum tiles, but the desk was the same, its veneer slightly more battered, as was the credenza beneath the window. She'd requisitioned a small conference table and four accompanying chairs, two of which sat in front of the desk, and her chair—she'd bought it herself—was ergonomic.

She spent money when it was necessary—like on the ergonomic chair—and she pinched her pennies on things that didn't matter—like brown-bagging it. Bringing your own lunch could be much healthier and lower in calories because you chose your own ingredients. Pinching the pennies was worth it.

Sometimes she ate her lunch outside, but today, seated at her small conference table, she gazed through the blinds at a sky that was heavy with dark clouds, rain threatening at any moment.

Last week, Halloween had been a gorgeous day, in the seventies, warm enough for short sleeves, but come November, the temperature had dropped and the clouds rolled in. November was typically one of the rainier months, though not always. Sometimes the first two weeks brought a deluge while on Thanksgiving Day you could practically eat outside. That's what she loved about the Bay Area, the variety.

Charlotte had been a part-time guidance counselor at the high school for the past five years. She enjoyed her practice but she'd also wanted to work with kids, helping them the way her counselors had helped her. It also gave her a chance to do something completely different from her therapy work. It was always good to mix things up.

Since she had a student meeting at one o'clock, she should have been studying the file open on the table in front of her. Instead she was thinking about spanking, not the discipline kind, but the fun kind. Lola loved her sex play with Gray Barnett, though even after three months, she was still scant on details. But these days, Lola damn near glowed. Charlotte didn't believe it was *just* the kinky sex. It was Gray. For the first time in ten years, Lola had a real relationship. Charlotte was happy for her friend.

But she kept thinking about spanking. And wild sex. And how long it had been since she'd had sex, wild or not. As a therapist, it was her duty to find out what this spanking thing was really like from an experiential perspective. And damn if the thought didn't make her hot and bothered. And extremely curious. Especially with the lack of sex in her life for the past several months.

All right, enough daydreaming. Flipping a page in the folder, she absently stabbed a fork into her salad. Somehow the plastic tub had moved—God only knew how or when—and her fork almost upended the container. She grabbed at the tub, the utensil clattering on the table, spraying balsamic dressing across another folder, but she managed a magnificent save before the entire salad turned into a mess on the beige carpet. The only casualty was her apple, which tumbled off the table and rolled under the desk.

She went down on her hands and knees, stretching an arm beneath the desk, her face and chest practically mashed into the carpet before she could reach the errant apple. Ah, got it.

"Lose something, Miss Moore?"

Charlotte gave a tiny squeak and banged her shoulder on the underside of the desk. She snapped up straight, the apple in her lap, and smoothed her skirt down over her knees with one hand.

Principal Hutton lounged in her doorway, arms crossed over his white shirt and red tie, shoulder braced on the jamb.

Damn. Busted with her butt in the air.

"Are you all right?" he asked politely. Behind him, the hall was quiet. Her office was in the Administration building several doors down from the principal's.

"I'm fine." Her shoulder only smarted a little. She held up the apple. "A delinquent. Tried to hide from me under the desk, but I found it out."

Principal Hutton raised a brow. "I trust you didn't bruise its fragile ego."

"Oh no, never." She waved the apple in the air. "Absolutely bruise-free."

She was in a unique position, sitting back on her calves. Principal Hutton, at six-one, had always towered over her petite height of five-two-and-a-half—okay, maybe it was a quarter inch instead of a half—but from her vantage point on the floor, he appeared to be a veritable giant, his chest broad, his shoulders wide, his thighs muscled. He was definitely attractive—she'd never questioned that in the three years he'd been at the school—with salt-and-pepper hair, swarthy skin, sharp, aristocratic features. His female students were in awe of him. Not so Charlotte.

At forty-eight, he was ten years older than her. And she liked her men younger. Once, a long time ago, she'd almost married a man who was more than ten years her senior. After a narrow escape, she'd realized that if she wanted autonomy in her life, her career, and in her relationship, she'd be far better off with a younger man, one who would cede control to her.

Yet, from down here on the floor, she was seeing Principal Lance Hutton in a whole new light. Or maybe it was the spanking thing infecting her mind. Whatever the reason, he was suddenly more than merely attractive. He was big, he was strong, he was sexy.

She'd be willing to bet that receiving a spanking from the principal would be incredibly hot. And his age wouldn't matter at all. In fact, it would elevate the experience to mind-blowing. When Principal Hutton spoke, people jumped to do his bidding.

Yes, yes, yes, Principal Hutton was just the kind of man she needed for this new adventure she intended to embark on.

LANCE DIDN'T INDULGE IN INTEROFFICE RELATIONSHIPS, BUT HE was a red-blooded male, alive and kicking, and he'd certainly noticed Charlotte Moore. One couldn't miss her gorgeous red curls, luscious figure, and the hint of fun-loving mischief dancing in her brilliant green eyes.

Yes, he'd noticed her in the three years he'd been principal, but now he was *noticing* her. First, her rather delectable rear assets in the air as she reached under the desk—he should have announced himself long before he did, but the view was too good to pass up—and now her position down on the carpet. On her knees. Her lips plump and succulently red. The imagery that came to mind was spectacular.

"Speaking of delinquents"—because he couldn't ogle her all day—"I need a favor."

She didn't get up, which, though delightful, was making it hard on certain parts of his body—*hard* being the operative word.

"Of course, Principal Hutton. Whatever you need."

Lance didn't demand formality from his faculty, and in this moment particularly, he would have preferred his first name on her lips. Especially if her lips were—

He needed to keep his mind on business. "Ruth Fineman's son became ill at school today, and she had to rush over to pick him up."

"I hope he's okay." Her brow furrowed in concern.

"I'm sure it was nothing serious." He'd asked Ruth to update him. She'd been in his office when she received the call. "Unfortunately, she was my monitor for after-school detention today. I'd appreciate it if you'd fill in for her. Unless you have a patient right after school."

Charlotte shook her head as she rose, one hand on the desk. "Clients, not patients," she said. "And I don't schedule appointments on my school days. In case a student needs me after classes end."

Of the counselors on staff, she was the only one working part-time. She was excellent at her job, the students loved her, and her private practice had never interfered.

"Thank you. Detention is forty-five minutes long, beginning at three fifteen. Your charges will report to the hall, which is the second portable down by the tennis courts. Mrs. Rivers has the key and the list of names."

Despite the fact that she was now standing, his pulse didn't slow, and he could feel his heartbeat against the wall of his chest. Yes, he'd noticed her, but now she was having a physical effect on him. He was sure that tonight he would still see the image of her down on her knees. And what a delectable image it was.

She gave him a saucy salute. "You can count on me, Principal

Hutton." The bit of sky visible behind her had darkened, rain hitting the window in a steady beat.

"Don't forget your umbrella."

She laughed. "I already did forget it."

He imagined her silky blouse wet with the rain. Sticking to her skin. Rendering it see-through. "I'm sure Mrs. Rivers can find you one."

She tipped her head, arching a brow. "Then again, it might have stopped raining by then."

His business done, he should go. Oddly he didn't want to. Odder still that he'd made the arrangements covering Ruth Fineman himself instead of delegating. He had two assistant principals who handled personnel, and technically, neither Charlotte nor Ruth worked directly for him. He didn't involve himself in such day-to-day operations as who monitored detention. Yet when Ruth left, he'd thought of Charlotte. Instead of picking up the phone, he'd taken it upon himself to walk down the hall to her office.

Maybe he'd been *noticing* Charlotte Moore far longer than he'd realized. And after seeing her on her knees, he wasn't going to stop noticing her any time soon. In fact, he had a feeling she'd be playing a very big part in his dreams.

THOUGH CHARLOTTE DEALT WITH HER SHARE OF DISCIPLINARY problems at the high school, her main role was helping kids plan their futures: careers, colleges to attend, trade schools if that was their inclination. She didn't generally get involved in detention, suspension, or expulsion. She preferred to be on the proactive end of things.

So what to do with the eight teenagers—three girls and five boys—scattered about the portable classroom? Formica-topped desks attached to hard plastic chairs were five rows deep and five across. They'd all managed to sit at least three desks apart, except the two girls in the back corner. The overhead lights were glaringly harsh in the windowless room. She would have left the door open to let in some daylight, but with the rain, the outside air was cold. Where windows should have been, the walls of the cheerless portable were plastered with posters declaring what kids *shouldn't* do, warnings about venereal disease, the evils of smoking, and the consequences of drinking and driving. All very good information, but there was nothing of a positive nature. Nothing upbeat.

She'd arrived a few minutes early, and they'd all filed in within ten minutes, leaving their detention slips on her desk. Instead of a blackboard, the front wall of the room was covered by a large white board, with a row of colored markers and erasers.

What was she supposed to do? Make them write fifty times *I will not* and fill in the blank for whatever they'd done wrong? After-school detention seemed a bit archaic. At the very least, it was elementary school.

Charlotte picked up the pink detention slips, thumbed through them. They were in triplicate. The rain beat on the roof, almost masking the whispers of the two girls in the back. The only other female in the assembly sat on the opposite side of the room, her head down, thick brown hair falling forward to obscure her face, arms folded over her chest holding her zippered sweatshirt tightly closed. Her whole body almost curled in on itself as if she were trying to disappear. Charlotte found herself most interested in this shadow girl.

But she wouldn't let any of them off the hook because of her interest in one girl. The slips had places for name, class level, date, time, reporting faculty member, and boxes for the behavior categories, which were anything from disruption to tardiness, lying and cheating, defiance to inappropriate language and electronic device violations. Below that was a handwritten description of each incident. Charlotte ignored those. She wanted to hear what her *charges*—as Principal Hutton had called them—had to say.

"Let's talk about these." She fluttered the stack of pink. The occupants of her detention hall uttered a universal groan.

It wasn't necessarily her intention to embarrass them in front of their peers, but she believed they needed to at least think about what they'd done in order to be sentenced to detention.

"Emma and Brittany. Please describe your disruptive behavior." She finger-quoted the last two words.

As Charlotte suspected, they were the two whisperers in the back. The blonde answered, "It wasn't our fault. Mrs. Lowell ignored the class bell, and we were going to be late for cheerleading practice. All I did was pass Emma a note with a question mark on it."

Emma, an equally slim cheerleader type with long black hair, nodded her agreement vigorously. She gave her hair a sexy toss over her shoulder and leaned her chin on one hand to gaze across the room at the handsome African-American boy seated three rows over. Charlotte recognized him as a football player.

Glancing down at the detention slip, she mused, "So Mrs. Lowell didn't ask you five times during class to stop whispering?"

"She mumbles," Brittany said. Emma nodded. "So I have to keep asking Emma what the teacher said."

"Ah, I get it. Emma's hearing is better than yours. Maybe we need to send you to the school nurse to have that checked."

The lanky, dark-haired boy at the front of the class snickered. Charlotte silenced him with a look that said *Just wait, you'll get your turn.*

"Or maybe you should sit closer to the front of the class so you can hear better." She made a check mark on Brittany's detention slip. "In fact, I'll make a note to tell Mrs. Lowell about your hearing issue so she knows to seat you up front." Charlotte smiled sweetly. Brittany and Emma pasted identical grimaces on their faces.

Charlotte turned to Snicker Boy and smiled. "What about you? Tell us why you're here."

He grimaced and flared his nostrils. "I didn't do anything wrong." Hmm, that seemed to be a common theme. "All I said was that Justin had his head where the sun don't shine. And Miss Brouton wrote me up for *not disagreeing appropriately*." He finger-quoted and Charlotte realized she'd made a small mistake with that gesture earlier. "I mean, I could have said he had his head up his"—Charlotte held up a hand and he cut himself off—"but you can see I used something more *appropriate*," he stressed.

Charlotte fished his detention slip from the stack based on his behavior category and the faculty member. Miss Brouton taught Social Studies. "So, Tyler, tell us why you felt Justin wasn't seeing things clearly"—she smiled sweetly—"which is a much more appropriate way of stating the issue."

"He said the government had no right to intern the Italian immigrants during World War Two. And I said they had as much right to intern them as they did the Japanese. The United States was at war." Tyler's voice rose, and his face turned ruddy with agitation.

Charlotte wanted to enter the debate, but the issue wasn't about internment camps and denying citizens their rights, it was about Tyler's handling of the disagreement. "People don't hear what you're saying when you get angry. They only register your emotion. Have you ever thought about joining the debate team?"

"What?" Tyler stared at her as if she had her head where the sun don't shine.

"The debate team." It would teach him how to argue without being offensive.

"What's a debate team?"

She lowered her head slightly and looked at him from beneath her lashes. "That's a joke, right?" She hoped it was. "I'm putting a note here for Miss Brouton to recommend you join the debate team."

And that debate was over. She pulled out the next detention slip. Michael, inappropriate language. She did *not* ask what word Michael had used. Carlos had been written up for excessive tardiness. Noah was in detention for texting in class (disruptive behavior), as was Jamal, the football player. Noah claimed it was an emergency text about his dog eating his homework—Charlotte didn't allow her laugh to surface—and Jamal had to text the coach, HAD TO, all in capital letters. Everyone had an excuse for why they'd broken the rules. No one took responsibility.

She'd saved the shadow girl for last. Melody Wright. A pretty name that, at this moment, didn't suit her at all. If possible, the teenager had curled even further in on herself, her feet up on her toes, her body hunched over. Charlotte almost asked if she was feeling sick, but she didn't believe the malady was physical. She was loath to question the girl, to even call attention to her, but to leave her out at this point would only make her stand out more.

"Would you care to tell us why you're here, Melody?"

3

"IT SAYS ON MY SLIP" CAME MELODY WRIGHT'S SOFT REPLY.

"All I see is that you had some issues with aggressive behavior." The girl was a freshman, the complaint made by her science teacher, but Charlotte still didn't read the scrawled comment. She wanted Melody's version, just as she had with the others.

"I dumped—" The rest was a mumble of words Charlotte couldn't make out.

"I'm sorry, I didn't hear that."

Melody raised her head, her hair falling aside, and Charlotte saw her face for the first time. Angry, festering acne mottled her skin. It was painful to see, and Charlotte's empathy rose. The bane of a teenage girl's existence, the physical and emotional scars it could leave in its wake. Poor kid.

"I dumped," Melody enunciated, "a beaker of sugar water on my lab partner's head."

Tyler snickered. Charlotte shot him a menacing glare. "Why did you do that, Melody?"

"Because it felt good," the girl answered, a scowl further marring her features.

"You go, girl." Jamal punched a fist in the air.

Charlotte silenced him with a look, too. "Did your lab partner do something to make you angry?" She had a fairly good idea it had to do with her acne.

"He existed," Melody said, then she dipped her head, letting her hair fall back into place to hide her face, like a turtle pulling its head back into its shell.

Emma and Brittany began whispering.

"Brittany, are you having trouble hearing again?" Charlotte called out loudly.

"No, ma'am," Brittany shot back, tucking her hair behind her ear.

"Then don't make me write *another* detention slip."

"Yes, ma'am." The two girls smiled at each other, a knowing, mocking smile that could have been directed at her or at Melody.

Her charges became restless, leaning down to touch their backpacks, adjust their jackets, and Charlotte glanced at the clock strategically placed on the back wall where the teacher could see it and the students could not. Unbelievably, the forty-five minutes of detention hall were up, and some inner teenage alarm clock had gone off in each and every one of them. Except Melody.

"Class dismissed," she said.

Tyler was the first to stand in front of her desk. "You have to sign the slip so I can get back into class."

"Oh." She signed with a flourish, tore off the top two sheets, and handed them back. One for the teacher, one for the student, and the last to be turned in to the Administration office.

She'd signed the slips, and the portable was empty except for Melody. She was still hunched in her chair. Charlotte scrawled her signature on the last slip and split the pages.

"Melody, you'll need this to get back into class."

"I don't want to go back." She spoke clearly despite the curtain of hair draped across her face.

Charlotte rose, strolled slowly down the aisle. "Do you want to talk about it?"

"No."

"Well, I'd like to talk about it."

"I have to go home now. My mom will be worried." Melody was back to mumbling, but Charlotte understood her nevertheless.

"All right. But I'm going to write you down for a meeting on Thursday. When's your study period?"

"Eleven."

"Then I'll see you in my office at eleven on Thursday. I'm in the Admin building."

Melody didn't argue. She simply reached out for the slip and tucked it into her sweatshirt pocket. Sliding out of the desk chair, she circled behind it so she didn't have to push past Charlotte and shuffled to the door at the front of the class. The pant legs of her jeans dragged on the floor, the hems frayed and dirty from the wet ground outside. The door closed with a thud behind her.

Charlotte sat in the chair Melody had vacated. She realized that every detention slip awarded was done so to maintain order in the classroom, and that teenagers, even high school students, needed to respect authority and submit to discipline, but the infractions today were all rather minor. Melody Wright, though, worried her. The girl was battling demons. She was a freshman, her first year of high school, new people, greater challenges, and a skin condition that could scar a young girl for life. *It felt good* held a definite edge of hostility. *He existed* was even scarier. Her lab partner had done *something*. Charlotte needed to figure out what it was. She needed to help Melody.

The door opened. Melody had come back. Maybe she was ready to talk.

But it was Principal Hutton's tall form framed in the doorway. A smattering of raindrops glittered in his salt-and-pepper hair and dotted the shoulders of his suit jacket.

Seated at the student desk, Charlotte could well imagine what it would be like to have him as her detention hall monitor. Her heart fluttered like she was one of his adoring female students. Despite being in the same building, she rarely saw him. Now it was twice in one day.

Oh, Principal Hutton, I've been very, very bad. Whatever will you do to punish me?

She could think of a lot of things the principal could do to her.

CHARLOTTE MOORE'S SMILE WAS PURE CLEOPATRA WHEN SHE saw Marc Antony for the first time. And it made Lance hard.

He needed to take control. Or he'd lose it completely. He strolled down the length of the side aisle to her seat in the back. "I trust your students didn't completely demoralize you and make you sit in the corner."

She laughed, and the musical sound sneaked beneath his ribs. The tiniest of lines at her eyes and her mouth testified to a lot of laughter. She was at least ten years younger than him, if not more, but he was sure she'd done twice the laughing that he had. She made him want to do more of it.

"Oh no, it was marvelous," she said, amusement sprinkled in her voice. "A truly unique experience. I'll have to do it again sometime."

"Don't tell me you've never been in detention before."

"Never." She leaned forward, hands cupping her chin as she gazed up at him.

"Not even in grade school?" From his vantage point above her, he could make out the creamy swell of breast in the vee of her blouse. Charlotte Moore had magnificent breasts. He shouldn't be noticing, but he couldn't help himself.

"My teachers said I was a perfect angel. They gave me gold stars, not detention."

He wagged a finger. "Are you sure you're not exaggerating? I've *never* had a student who was *never* bad."

She placed the flat of her hand to her chest. He wanted to touch his tongue to the skin between her fingers. "You never did anything to get sent to the naughty corner? Never received a spanking?"

"Not even once." She was smiling again. The Cleopatra smile. The one that brought Julius Caesar and Marc Antony to their knees before her. "But I've been thinking," she said in a singularly innocent, angelic voice.

"About what?" he was compelled to ask.

"That maybe I missed out by never being spanked."

Her brilliant green gaze mesmerized him. "Corporal punishment like spanking has been deemed to damage a child's psyche," he advised her.

Oh, that smile. Soon *he'd* be on his knees, too.

"But I'm not a child, Principal Hutton."

"No, you most certainly are not." Not with those breasts. Or the lush curve of her hips. Or the plump, beckoning mouth. Her scent rose to him, the hot, sweet perfume of arousal. It swirled around him, ensnared him, whispered to him. Despite the cold, damp day outside, his temperature was rising. As were other parts of his body. No woman had ever gotten to him so quickly. Especially not an employee. And they were on school property. He had a strict rule. A code.

She made him forget all his rules and codes, where they were, who she was, who he was. Made him *want* to forget all of it.

"Maybe I should do something really bad, Principal Hutton." She fluttered her lashes at him. It was the sexiest thing he'd ever seen. "Something for which I'll deserve a spanking." And somehow *that* was the sexiest thing he'd ever heard.

He'd been married and divorced twice. He'd had lovers before, between, and after his ill-fated marriages. But with her words, every sexual thing he'd ever done seemed vanilla in comparison, damn near missionary. Or maybe it was just her. As if she'd somehow tapped into something he'd never known was buried deep inside him.

Now all he wanted was her delectable derriere beneath his hand.

Lance backed up three steps and turned. At the door, he punched the lock. Then he looked at her.

"So what have you done, Miss Moore, that's really, really bad?"

HEAT FLASHED ACROSS CHARLOTTE'S SKIN. SHE COULDN'T believe what she'd said. She should have been talking to him about Melody. She should have given him the signed detention slips. She certainly shouldn't have goaded him into locking the portable's door.

Actually, she couldn't believe that had worked. Principal Hutton's reputation was sterling. There'd never been even a hint of a salacious rumor. But when his gaze had dipped to her chest, she couldn't help herself. And now she was very glad for the fact that the portable classroom had no windows.

Charlotte rose, strolled down the row of desks to the front of the class, her hips swaying seductively. Then she turned, propped herself against the teacher's desk. And put a finger to her lips.

She could feel his eyes as if he was actually touching her.

"Fuck," she said softly.

"Fuck?" he questioned with equal softness.

"Inappropriate language in the classroom."

Something started to blaze in the depths of his brown eyes. They almost glowed. She wanted his hands on her. She was wet and ready for it.

"Fuck, fuck, fuck," she whispered in the quiet room, the only other sounds being the tattoo of rain on the roof and the harshness of his breathing.

"That is very, very bad, Miss Moore." There was a new huskiness in his voice. "This goes far beyond after-school detention." He was at the desk in three strides, towering over her, his height making her knees buckle. "This calls for drastic measures."

"I'm so sorry," she said softly, pleading. "I didn't mean it, Principal Hutton."

He shook his finger at her. "Too late for apologies, Miss Moore. I'll have to spank you. It's the only way for you to learn your lesson."

Yes, yes, yes. It was exactly what she wanted. "But I've never done anything to earn a spanking before."

"You certainly deserve it now. Turn around, bend over, and put your hands on the desk."

She did as he instructed, her skin tingling, heart racing, legs weak with desire. Going down onto her elbows, she fully exposed her bottom to him. If she was naked, he would surely have seen the dewdrops of arousal on her. Lola was so right; the whole experience was overwhelmingly erotic. She watched him over her shoulder as he unbuttoned his suit jacket, slowly removed it, and threw it across the desktop of the first seat in the row.

Charlotte's gaze dropped to his waist. Lord. The evidence of his desire was outlined against his slacks. He wanted to spank her as much as she wanted it.

"This is going to hurt me more than it hurts you, Miss Moore." He rolled up the sleeves of his white dress shirt, revealing corded muscles and a light dusting of dark hair on his forearms.

"I doubt that, Principal Hutton."

He circled her, coming up on her left. Bending down to her ear, his body heating her to her core, he whispered, "You're right. I'm going to enjoy it."

She scented him like a bitch in heat, the purely male perfume, thick and salty. Her mouth watered for a taste of him. "Oh, Principal Hutton, please—"

He cut her off with a delicious swat right on the juncture of her thighs. Sensation flashed through her, from the site of his touch straight up to her throat and every organ in between. All she could think was that Lola hadn't exaggerated: There was *nothing* quite like a spanking. Especially when it was Principal Hutton. Maybe *because* it was Principal Hutton.

The second time he swatted her, she almost came.

EVEN THROUGH THE WOOL OF HER CAMEL-COLORED SKIRT, HIS palm tingled with the heat of her flesh. With each slap across her ass, he caressed her, learned the feel of her contours. Her moan of pleasure reached deep inside him. He burned for her.

She laid her forearms flat on the desk, flexed her fingers, her head arching back. The action gave him a better angle, and this time his fingers slid along the crease of her pussy. He felt her contract. She balled her hands into fists. A sigh of ecstasy escaped her lips.

"My dear Miss Moore, you're not supposed to be enjoying

this." He swatted her again, his fingers lingering, touching, probing, caressing.

"Oh"—she groaned—"I hate it"—she gasped—"this is awful"—she sucked in a breath—"Oh, Principal Hutton." Her voice rose on his name.

"Liar," he said softly. He cupped his palm and delivered a harder blow.

She pushed back against his hand, her body begging for more.

He wanted to bury himself inside her. He wanted to take her right there on the desktop. Simply roll her to her back and plunge deep. But taking anything more would change the event, distort it. He wanted to savor *this*, the feel of her skin. And his power over her.

"Say it again, Miss Moore." His voice sounded strained even to his own ears.

"Fuck." She groaned. "Fuck, fuck, fuck," she chanted.

He rewarded her with another slap for each time she said the word. Her legs began to tremble, her body quivered, she panted, and despite the wool skirt separating his palm from her bare ass, he felt her heat and moisture, and scented the sweetness of her come as she climaxed. Her cry was long and low, from deep in her throat. He caressed the soft, warm spot between her legs until he felt her muscles relax, her body going prone on the desktop.

She was amazing. She made him feel amazed with himself. She'd come without even skin-to-skin contact.

Breathing in, breathing out, she sighed. "Oh. My. God." Each word was a separate sentence. She turned her cheek to the wood and looked up at him from one eye. "I never knew being bad could be so good." Then she levered herself slowly up off the desk, blinked, and finally smiled. "So *that's* why they're always lining up at your office."

He could have pulled her into his arms, kissed her. He could have demanded that since he'd gotten her off, she had to get him off. But the moment had been spectacular just as it was. He wouldn't alter it. He wanted to fully savor it before he took more.

"You're my first, my dear Miss Moore." Despite her heels, she was still a head shorter, and he wanted to lick the column of her throat as she tipped her head back to look at him. "But that," he said softly, "is *not* going to be the last." He leaned down enough to put his lips to her ear, her hair soft against his cheek. "Because I'm absolutely, positively, one-hundred-percent sure you're going to be very bad again"—he pulled back to lock eyes with her—"and again."

Grabbing his jacket off the student desk, he strode to the door, unlocked it, stood with his hand on the knob. "When you choose to be bad, you have to suffer the consequences."

"I'll never do it again, Principal Hutton." She smiled, her eyes sparkling like jewels.

He knew she was lying. She couldn't wait to do it again. Neither could he.

4

"I'VE BEEN VERY REMISS IN MY DUTIES TOWARD MY CLIENTS BY not checking out other possibilities," Charlotte told Lola at lunch the next day. Sexual possibilities, she meant; spanking in particular. After that announcement, she savored a bite of her pastrami on rye. She didn't regularly indulge in fatty foods, but when she went out for lunch, she savored every bite. The Dutch Bakery had the best pastrami on the San Francisco Peninsula. And the marzipan cakes tempted her from behind the glass-fronted display case, not that she'd allow herself one of those.

Charlotte had a two-hour break between sessions. Thank goodness they'd arrived before eleven thirty because the line at the counter was now ten deep, seating was scarce, and the noise level had risen to mind-numbing. Servers delivering lunch plates dashed to and fro, tossing down crockery, grabbing up empties.

"I wouldn't call it being remiss," Lola said. She was enjoying the other half of Charlotte's pastrami. The sandwich was way too much for one person, so they'd shared. That's what best friends did, divide the fat intake. "You've simply had your eyes opened." She patted her napkin on a wayward dot of mustard at the corner of her mouth.

Charlotte pointed her finger. "*You* opened my eyes." She lowered her voice in deference to the lunch crowd around them, and for Lola, though the noise level would cover anything, she said, "If you hadn't gotten naughty with that hunky coach of yours, I would have discounted the whole spanking business. And I'm a psychologist, for God's sake."

"You're too hard on yourself."

Not really. Charlotte was overdramatizing, but she had to admit she'd only considered the negative psychological aspects of BDSM, as in when a client became obsessed with it or used it to act out childhood traumas. There were, however, a lot of fun, sexy aspects that could be incorporated into a healthy love life and used to add variety and spice.

Lola Cook and her new man were a perfect example. And Charlotte wanted real-world ideas. "So spill, woman. I want details. Everything. What should I do next?"

But she knew Lola. Her friend wouldn't spill much. They'd been best friends forever, having attended the same high school, though long before Principal Hutton's tenure. Despite their friendship, Lola was a much more private person. After a bad divorce in her twenties, this was her first real relationship. She was still feeling her way with Gray Barnett.

"That's your problem, Charlotte."

Charlotte put a hand to her chest. "Me? A problem?"

"Yes." Lola pointed her finger, punctuating. "The best thing is *not* knowing what he's going to do next. The surprise. The anticipation." She leaned forward. "The fact that *you're* not the one controlling everything."

Charlotte liked to control. But she'd also loved the way

Principal Hutton had taken over after she'd suggested she needed a spanking. She closed her eyes briefly, savoring the memory the way she'd savored her pastrami. God, it had been out of this world, over-the-top fabulous. She'd actually had an orgasm. She couldn't define the physical sensation as pain. His hand made her tingle, his touch tantalized. The tingling had gone on all evening. Lola was right, part of the thrill had been the fact that she hadn't known what to expect. She'd bent over the desk and put herself in Principal Hutton's hands. Locked away in the portable classroom with him, she would have let him do anything to her. *An-y-thing.*

She focused on Lola's face. She'd often worn her long black hair pulled into a ponytail, but since this thing with Gray began, she wore it down. Her brown eyes seemed deeper, the way she moved was sexier. Tall and willowy, she was Charlotte's opposite, and somehow, in the last few months with Gray, Lola had begun to exude sensuality. Men looked, stopped, salivated. She'd become a sexual being. Charlotte didn't believe that was a bad thing.

Lola smiled, her gaze sparkling with knowing. "You get what I mean, don't you?"

Looking at her friend, Charlotte wanted to experience what Lola had. She wanted to be at her lover's mercy. She wanted to be tied to a bed for a whole weekend, a man's sex slave. Lola had revealed that much. Charlotte dreamed about it at night.

"You're right," she agreed. "I'll let the principal figure it out. But I'll have to give him some incentive, do something he has to punish me for."

"Your principal," Lola mused. "That's hot. But what about your job?"

"This is an experiment," Charlotte said. "I'm not going to get emotionally attached or anything. He's way too old for me, almost fifty, and not my type at all."

"Personally, I think you need a new type. You've been picking the wrong kind of men up to now. That's why you always seem to get bored so easily."

They were the right kind for Charlotte, young, malleable, and totally different from her former *older* fiancé, Martin. "I was never bored." Though she did have a tendency to start finding things wrong with a man after about six months. "Anyway, it's not like this is a relationship. It's just a sexy fling. No one has to know." Of course, that meant not locking themselves in any more portable classrooms. From now on, they'd need to meet off school property and outside of school hours. "Besides, he's not actually my boss. I report to the assistant principal." After polishing off the last of her pastrami, she munched on her pickle spear. "So how's the counseling going for Gray and his son?" She realized Lola hadn't revealed any new details about her deliciously kinky sex life, but that was fine. Lola had given her excellent food for thought.

"I don't ask a lot of questions, not my business," Lola said, "but Gray says things are better between them. He was disappointed at first that Rafe didn't try out for the football team after camp this summer, but he finally accepted that football isn't Rafe's thing. And I have to admit Rafe tolerates me better than before. Last weekend we went for a hike out at Pinnacles National Monument."

After his divorce, Gray had gone through some trying times with his teenage son, Rafe, and that had caused difficulties in Lola's budding relationship with Gray. Charlotte had been glad to hear Gray decided on family counseling. And that Rafe agreed to it.

"Rafe even invited the twins along." Lola opened her eyes wide to indicate her amazement. "I actually enjoyed spending the day with Harry and William. They weren't obnoxious at all." She lowered her voice conspiratorially. "I think I'm starting to like them." This wasn't the first time she'd included her two nephews in outings with Gray and his son.

"Well, you do owe them big-time." The twins, Harry and William, had spent a good part of the summer with Lola while their parents were in Europe. It was through the twins—and football camp—that Lola met Gray.

Lola pushed her fork through the small bowl of coleslaw on her plate.

It was a sure sign something else was on her mind. "What?" Charlotte prompted.

At the next table, a lady bit into a chocolate-covered marzipan cake. Charlotte salivated.

Lola let out a puff of air. "Gray wants me to move in with him."

"And that's a problem because . . . ?" When it wasn't his weekend with his son, Lola was either at Gray's house or he was at hers. "Ghost loves him." Ghost was Lola's cat, and she rarely came out from under the bed for anyone, but Lola said the cat had started sleeping on Gray's chest when he was over. "And you love him," Charlotte added softly.

"Yeah. I do."

"But?" Charlotte urged.

Lola shrugged. "I work at home." She was a freelance technical writer. "All of a sudden *my* office would be in *his* house, and we'd have to share the spare bedroom that *he* already uses as a home office."

"But he goes to work every day." Gray was CEO of a large corporation. He coached only during the summer, and that was part-time, mornings only, for six weeks.

"But he brings work home. And he uses the spare room."

Charlotte had been to dinner at Gray's. It wasn't a small place, but with three bedrooms, one of them used by his son when he stayed with Gray every other weekend, that left only one for a home office.

"It's just a workspace, Lola. The issue isn't insurmountable. You could even keep your condo as your office."

"I can't afford that."

"Why? Is he going to make you pay rent at his place?"

"Of course not."

"Then maybe it's possible you're making an issue out of nothing because you're afraid of the bigger commitment you'll have by moving in."

"I'm not afraid of commitment," Lola denied.

"Then what's really bothering you?"

Lola chewed her lip. "I don't know."

Charlotte pursed her lips and narrowed her eyes.

"I really don't know." Lola slumped. "He's the best. The sex is the best. Everything's great. But . . ."

Charlotte sipped her water before saying, "He's nothing like Mike." Who was Lola's good-for-nothing asshole of an ex. Charlotte remembered Lola saying something about men being nice when they didn't live in your house and couldn't tell you what to do. That sentiment had its roots in her marriage to Mike the ass, who constantly picked on everything from Lola's clothes to her hair to how she treated his mother.

"I know Gray's totally different from Mike," Lola said softly.

"Is the kinky sex getting too much for you?" Charlotte queried. Lola wasn't a prude, but her experience had been limited. Maybe Gray was pushing her too hard too fast.

But Lola smiled. "Hell, no." She dropped her voice. "It's better than that lady's marzipan cake."

Charlotte groaned. They'd always loved the same sinful treats. "Why did you have to remind me?" Then she raised an eyebrow, smiled a little. "Do you need a session in my comfy office? Free of charge."

Lola waved a hand. "No. I'm fine. I'll probably move in. It'll just be an adjustment."

"If you've got to talk, I'm here." Charlotte didn't want Lola screwing this up for herself. Gray was perfect. Lola was happier than she'd been in ten years.

"Thanks, but I'm fine. When I finally make the decision, I'll probably ask you to help me pack up, though."

Charlotte was sure Lola wasn't totally *fine*. She'd have to watch carefully, make sure Lola didn't freak out, and hold her hand all the way to Gray's house.

LUNCH YESTERDAY WITH LOLA HAD GIVEN CHARLOTTE IDEAS.

Her Thursday appointment with Melody Wright was set for eleven, so at ten o'clock, Charlotte stopped by Principal Hutton's office. His secretary, Mrs. Rivers, was the lion guarding his door.

"Has the principal got a couple of minutes?"

Mrs. Rivers pushed her glasses down the bridge of her nose, perusing Charlotte over the top of the horn-rims. The woman was ancient, having been the principal's secretary when Charlotte was a student, but she hadn't changed one iota. Her gray hair was still piled on top of her head. If her optical prescription had altered in the ensuing twenty years, she'd had the new lenses put into the same frames—or ones exactly like them. She still wore the same second-Thursday blouse. Mrs. Rivers had a different outfit for every day of the month, the same wardrobe she'd worn twenty years ago. The fabric was only slightly faded after all those years of laundering.

"Let me check if he has time to see you." Mrs. Rivers pushed a button on her intercom. "Can you see Miss Moore for a couple of minutes, sir?" Mrs. Rivers was extremely formal. While Charlotte used the title Principal Hutton because it gave her a little thrill, Mrs. Rivers had always called him *sir*.

"Send her in." His deep voice echoed from the office and the intercom.

Permission granted, Mrs. Rivers flourished a hand.

Charlotte stopped just inside the door. His office was by no means ostentatious, simply a desk, credenza, filing cabinets, a conference table, and four chairs, two of which were positioned in front of the desk. The office was perhaps one and a half times the size of hers, but the desk was larger and made of wood, and his computer was an updated model. Framed certificates lined the walls. There were no personal photos. She knew he had no children, but if he had parents or siblings, he certainly didn't display pictures of them.

"I wanted to discuss Melody Wright. She was one of the girls in detention on Tuesday." Her voice sounded normal, but her insides were fluttering. Her eyes had certainly been opened. Principal Hutton was tasty in a dark blue suit, light blue shirt, and striped tie. She had visions of bending over his desk. A psychologist was allowed her fantasies just like anyone else.

"Sure, let's talk. Close the door."

Her breath quickened as if he'd told her to pull up her skirt, but Charlotte didn't let her reaction show. She simply closed the door, took the seat he indicated on the opposite side of his desk, and crossed her legs. She'd dressed with him in mind, a green blouse to match her eyes and a pencil skirt that hugged her bottom. Was he remembering what they'd done after detention? Of course he was. It was in the flicker of his gaze down to the vee of her blouse.

"About Melody Wright?" he asked.

All right, so they weren't going to talk about *it*. "I'm worried about her. The other students in detention were"—*normal* wasn't the right word because it implied that Melody was abnormal—"ordinary. Their offenses were minor and pretty common. Everyone texts when they can get away with it. Or passes notes. Or uses an expletive once in a while. But she was different. Her demeanor was that of someone carrying the weight of the world."

Principal Hutton rolled a pen between his thumbs and forefingers. "I have to admit I don't know who she is." No wonder. He was principal to fifteen hundred students.

"She's a freshman."

He tossed the pen onto the desk and tapped a few letters on his keyboard. "Let me look at her grades and transcripts." The school had gone fully online three years ago. "W-R-I-G-H-T?" he asked for the spelling.

Charlotte nodded.

He read. Charlotte noticed he didn't wear reading glasses. "Hmm," he murmured.

"What's that mean?"

"Her grades are poor this year. But she was an A student in middle school."

"So something changed over the summer?"

"Could be." He tapped a few more keys. "And that was her third detention this year."

It was only the beginning of November, which meant three detentions in two months. "Why didn't somebody send her to me?" Because her main task was career and college counseling, management might very well have bypassed her. "Is she seeing one of the other counselors?"

He shook his head. "Doesn't appear so. Her two other offenses were relatively minor, one for spilling soda on another girl's shoes."

"Was that an accident?"

"No. Says here she admitted doing it on purpose."

Just like she'd confessed to dumping the beaker of sugar water on her lab partner's head. At least the girl didn't dissemble. "Did she say why she did it?"

"Nothing written here."

"What was the other detention for?"

"Inappropriate language." He glanced at her, a slight curve to his lips. "She used *your* naughty word to another student, Miss Moore. But I wouldn't give her the same punishment. That's reserved for you alone."

Her skin flushed at the reminder. "I'm so glad to hear that, Principal Hutton."

The sexy half smile still lurking on his lips, he sat back. "So what are you thinking?"

She was thinking about what she could do to get her next spanking. But he was talking about Melody. "Something happened over the summer to impair her motivation and her attitude." She wondered when Melody had developed the extreme case of acne.

"Are we talking possible abuse?"

Abuse could definitely make a student's motivation and attitude take a nosedive. There was also Melody's attire and the way she hunched in on herself, a defensive posture. But her detention-worthy behaviors were aggressive. Abuse *was* a possibility, but Charlotte would like to see Melody's eighth-grade school picture. She'd be willing to bet she'd looked like a different girl.

"I can't rule out abuse, but I don't feel that's the issue. She's got quite a case of acne, and that can be devastating at her age." She shrugged. "But who really knows at this point? I've got an appointment with her this morning. I'll see what I can figure out."

"You should talk to your assistant principal about this."

"I will. But you were the one who sent me to detention, so I came to you first."

He picked up the pen again, twirling it in his fingers. "You should always come to me first for your detention."

He was giving her the opening she wanted. "Don't I have to misbehave before I get sent to detention, Principal Hutton?"

"With your track record, Miss Moore, I have no doubt you will."

Rising, she smoothed down her pencil skirt, calling attention to her thighs. She leaned both hands on his desk, and his eyes dropped to take in the view down her blouse. Charlotte licked her bottom lip, making her lipstick glisten.

Then she whispered, "Cocksucker."

"Miss Moore, I am shocked." His eyes glittered lecherously. "Are you referring to me? Or to yourself."

"I would never believe that's what *you* are, Principal Hutton."

"But I'd venture to say you are."

She batted her eyelashes. "And proud of it."

The muscles of his face tensed in an effort not to laugh, but he played his part. "Totally inappropriate language, Miss Moore. This requires extensive after-school detention."

"I definitely need to be punished, Principal Hutton."

"It's going to take more than our usual forty-five minutes. We'll need to do it at my house."

"Whatever you say, Principal. I know I've been very bad."

"Tomorrow night."

She almost sighed. She wanted it tonight. Then again, tomorrow was Friday, with no school and no work the next day. The possibilities were limitless.

5

FOR ALL THE SIGNS OF RELUCTANCE—SHUFFLING FEET, SLOW
movements, failure to meet Charlotte's eyes—Melody had at least
been prompt. Wearing the brown hoodie wrapped tightly around
her and the frayed hems of her baggy jeans dragging on the floor,
she hunched in Charlotte's guest chair and hid her face behind
her hair.

Instead of sitting behind her desk after closing the door, Charlotte pulled a chair next to the girl. The position was less formal,
and it also made the meeting feel less like a disciplinary action
and more a friendly conversation.

But Charlotte did jump right into the issues. "I'm concerned
about your grades, Melody. A's in middle school and suddenly in
high school, you're barely passing."

"Classes are harder," Melody mumbled, but Charlotte could
make out the words.

"Not that much harder. I went to high school, too."

Melody shrugged. "Ancient history. Everything's changed.

Not enough teachers. They don't have time for all of us. We need more computers." She sounded like an ad for a bond measure to increase school funding.

"We have tutors and labs after school where you can get assistance," Charlotte offered, but she already knew tutoring wasn't going to help Melody.

"They're just other students working for extra credit. They don't know any more than me."

So someone had sent her to the tutoring labs. "You know, these four walls"—Charlotte held her arms out in both directions—"are sacred territory. Whatever's said inside them doesn't go outside. You can tell me whatever you want. I"—she put a hand to her chest, leaning down to get a better glimpse of Melody's face— "believe that the summer between middle school and freshman year is a very difficult transition period for a lot of people. And sometimes they need to talk about it."

"Summer was summer," Melody muttered.

"So nothing happened that bothered you or made you feel bad about starting high school?" She let her voice rise slightly, making it a question. Enough of the girl's face was visible for Charlotte to note the tensing of her lips and the clench of her jaw.

Melody looked at her for the first time, lifting her chin to reveal the full ravages of her acne. "You mean this?" She stabbed a finger at her mottled cheek. "Well, yeah, Miss Moore, my face bothers me. And I feel bad about it. And I don't like people looking at me. And I *don't* like talking about it."

"Have you been to a dermatologist?"

Melody snorted and shook her head. It was neither a yes nor a no. It was simply disgust. "I'll raise my grades," she said. "And I'll play nice with others. And I'll work on my self-esteem during these trying teenage years. And I'm sure I'll grow out of it." She grabbed her chest. "I'm sure I'll eventually grow breasts, too, so

I don't look like a freak. Can I go now?" Her voice was an ugly sneer.

Melody had already had this talk with someone; obviously it hadn't worked. Charlotte didn't think all the trite phrases about inner beauty shining through and ugly ducklings turning into swans would make any impression either. In fact, they would probably make things worse. But Melody needed help.

"I'd like to talk again," Charlotte said. "I'll schedule you in for next Tuesday at the same time," she added, not giving Melody an opportunity to back out.

"You can't force me to come here."

"Actually, with your disciplinary history, I can." Of course, Charlotte hadn't gone through any channels to do that yet. She would if she had to, but she was hoping Melody would simply volunteer.

"Fine. Whatever. But it's not going to do any good."

"I'd still like to talk to you."

Melody made a face as she left, one that screamed boredom and gave no indication whether she'd return at the appointed time.

Charlotte concocted plans anyway. By next Tuesday, she'd make sure she was armed with more background. First stop, Facebook. People tended to reveal an amazing amount of personal information on social media these days, as if typing it all in while only your computer could see you meant that you weren't telling everything to the world. But Melody was the anomaly. Charlotte couldn't find her on Facebook. Or Twitter. Or Pinterest. She couldn't find Melody anywhere in the social media whirl. It was unheard of. Not only had the girl dropped her friends, she'd dropped off the entire web. There was only one thing for Charlotte to do: She'd have to resort to the age-old world of high school cliques.

So, during lunch period, she headed up to the quad. The school had been constructed on a hill, five long buildings rising up, stairs and walkways in between, lockers along the outer walls beneath overhangs. The first building was Music and Drama, then English, Math, and Science, followed by the student quad, with the cafeteria off to the left, and the Administration building like a sentry just above the quad. Since the rain had stopped yesterday, and the sun was out, most students preferred sitting on the stairs running the length between the buildings. Beyond the quad and Administration were buildings for History, Social Sciences, and the languages. The gym, football field, track, tennis courts, and baseball diamond were down to the right on the flats.

Another person might have gone to Melody's science teacher—and Charlotte would eventually do that—but if you really wanted to know what was going on, you got it from the students themselves.

Since she wasn't a teacher and didn't generally involve herself with disciplinary action, Charlotte had always found herself at an advantage with the kids. She performed more constructive duties with them, course planning, college planning, life planning. And they seemed to like her. She learned a hell of a lot more by listening to what students had to say. So today, she headed for one of her girls. The quad was awash in laughter and young voices as Charlotte approached the steps.

"Hey, Lydia, got a minute?"

"Sure, Miss Moore."

Lydia jumped up from her seat amid a group of four girls. She was pretty, petite, and blond. A junior with a bubbly personality, she was getting her courses in line for medical school. An aggressive player on the water polo team, she was also on the debate team. Charlotte was sure Lydia would run for class president when she was a senior.

"Let's walk," Charlotte suggested. She stuck to the sun, heading slowly back across the quad. "Do you know a freshman named Melody Wright?"

"I'm a junior, Miss Moore, I don't know any freshmen."

Class snobbery. Charlotte wanted to laugh. "Don't kid me. You know everyone, Lydia."

The girl wrinkled her nose. "Well, I might have heard the name. Does she have—" Lydia circled her face with her hand instead of saying the actual words.

"She has acne."

"Yeah, well, poor kid, I know who she is." Lydia's face softened as she pursed her lips. Her sympathy appeared real.

"What can you tell me about her?"

"Nothing." She shrugged. "Well, almost nothing. A few idiots make fun of her. But I don't hang around with kids like that."

"I know you don't. But you hear everything." Charlotte pandered to the girl's ego. "You know everything that happens in this school."

"Well." Lydia smoothed her silky locks. "Some of the worst call her Mudly instead of Melody because her face is like a volcano." She grimaced. "Then there's the fact that she's got the figure of a boy. You just don't know how being flat-chested can demoralize a girl. She's got two big strikes against her."

They were huge strikes. Just when boys started looking at girls and girls started looking at boys—although Charlotte had to admit they started looking a lot earlier these days than they had when she was in middle school. "Have you tried to make friends with her?"

Lydia stopped, looked at Charlotte. "I don't know her at all, Miss Moore. Besides, I don't think she wants any friends. Even if I approached her, she'd only think I was doing it to make fun of her. Like I was going to set her up for a fall or something."

"Oh."

"I've never actually heard anyone calling her names. If I did, I'd say something. This is just stuff you hear. Because, well, she stands out."

Charlotte understood about the soda spilled on the girl's shoe and the inappropriate word. Melody had been retaliating for some cruelty perpetrated upon her.

"Okay. So did you hear anything about science class and her lab partner?"

"I don't listen to *gossip*," Lydia stressed. "But there was something about her dumping a whole beaker of sugar water over his head. They were growing crystals with it, I think. At least that's what Mr. Gunderson had us do in freshman science."

"But you didn't hear why?"

"I only heard that it was her boyfriend from middle school." She widened her pretty blue eyes. "I guess they broke up."

A boyfriend. Now that's something Charlotte had never considered. "What's his name, do you know?"

Lydia shook her head. "What I told you is all I know." She glanced over her shoulder. "Look, I gotta get back."

Charlotte realized Lydia's friends were packing up. So were most of the other kids, crumpling paper bags, heading for the trash cans and recycle bins.

"Okay, thanks."

"If I hear anyone giving her a bad time, I promise I'll give them a piece of my mind, Miss Moore."

"Thank you, Lydia."

Charlotte sat on the edge of a recently vacated picnic table as the quad quickly emptied. The sun's warmth seeped into her skin. Melody Wright actually had three strikes against her: her skin, her shape, and not enough self-esteem to appreciate her inner beauty. Because every child, every girl, every human being had something beautiful and special. Melody Wright just didn't know how to see it in herself.

Charlotte's mission was figuring out a way to show her.

LANCE COULDN'T FIND A STORE IN HIS SCHOOL DISTRICT THAT sold the things he wanted. Which was probably a good thing. A sexual fetish shop probably wouldn't raise any property values.

The store he'd looked up on the Internet after Charlotte left his office this morning—his personal computer, not his school-issued desktop—was along a stylish mall in a newly refurbished downtown only ten minutes along the freeway. He shared the sidewalk with mothers pushing strollers, poodles prancing at the ends of their leashes, teenagers rushing for after-school coffee drinks or pizza parlors, and a few lovebirds holding hands. The place he had in mind didn't advertise sexual toys in the window, but instead displayed a variety of skimpy lingerie. Feathered Halloween masks were on sale now that October was over, although Lance figured the masks could be marked back up for Mardi Gras in a few months.

Stepping inside, he found the front room equipped exactly like the window. Racks of colorful bras and panties, a counter displaying bright jewelry and sparkly makeup, hooks on the walls holding costumes and sexy scraps of lace.

"May I help you, sir?" The salesgirl looked young enough to be one of his students. Or worse, his daughter. But if he'd had a daughter, he would have been against the nose ring, the blue hair, and the black fingernail polish, not to mention the short pleated skirt that barely covered her—

He needed to stop being so judgmental. "I'm just browsing," he said quickly. Under no circumstances would he be able to purchase what he wanted from this . . . girl.

"The garters and bustiers are all on sale this month." She fluttered exceptionally thick lashes at him.

"Thank you." He smiled. Charlotte Moore would have a field day with him on this one. She probably recommended sex toys to her clients all the time to spice up their sex lives. Although he was sure that was probably minimizing what she did.

At that point, thankfully, the shop's door opened again and two ladies entered, providing the diversion he needed to make it to the back room.

He wasn't a prude, but the kinkiest he'd gotten—before he spanked Charlotte—was using his second wife's vibrator on her. The experience had been pleasurable enough, until he'd realized she preferred using it on herself when he wasn't around. Most men would have looked to their own prowess, but Lance had begun to understand that she enjoyed sex in ten-to-fifteen-minute bouts without all the mess and fuss of having to deal with anyone else's orgasm but her own.

It was this kind of thinking that had given him ideas about Charlotte. He could spank the naughty little wench—*cocksucker*, that still had him laughing—or he could up the stakes with something special. The problem: He had no idea *what*. Hence his shopping trip. He was sure something would catch his eye.

The lingerie racks gave way to a narrow hallway filled with shelves of sexual gag gifts: inflatable dolls, inflatable penises, penis joke books, penis eraser heads. Hah, that would go over well at school.

The hallway opened up into a long room that was twice the size of the front area. Well, hell, here was where all the business was done. And here's where all the customers were. Couples, women, men. There were shelves of how-to books, erotica for couples, for women, for gays and lesbians. All manner of vibrators covered half a wall, all shapes, sizes, colors, one-speed,

two-speed, three-speed. Next to that hung cock rings, cock har-
nesses, cock plugs, cock pins—uh, no, thank you very much. He
didn't even *want* to know what they were used for. There were
gels and heating lotions, wands that looked like feather dusters
and would probably cost a hell of a lot less at a discount department store. Leather masks, headgear, hoods, handcuffs, ball
gags, nipple clamps, blindfolds, floggers, paddles, leashes, col-
lars. The assortment boggled the mind. But the handcuffs caught
his eye. Regular police-style metal handcuffs, leather manacles,
fur-lined, silk ties.

"Looking for you or her or him?" A husky voice right next
to him.

He hadn't heard the saleswoman approach. At least she was
long past the age of consent, and attractive in an over-the-hill-
actress kind of way. He preferred the actresses of his own genera-
tion, the ones who played tough, ball-busting executives.

"For her," he said.

The woman fingered the fur-lined cuffs, sheepskin under
leather, with a buckle. "These are comfy." The blond highlights
in her brown hair sparkled in the overhead lamps. She was several years older than Charlotte and had none of Charlotte's
softness.

"She'd probably prefer silk," he said.

The woman fingered those, too. Her nails were a hard red, her
hands unlined, the diamond on her middle finger large. "They'd
be a good choice." She glanced up at him, her eyes an unnatural
shade of violet. "New submissive you're breaking in?"

He gave a wry smile. "More like she's breaking me in."

"*Ahhh,*" she said on a long sigh. "You're new to being a dom."

"I'm not a dom."

"But she wants to turn you into one."

He didn't actually know. But he figured Charlotte for a woman who liked fun and games. And she'd started a new one with him. "We're both new at this."

He wondered why he was telling this woman anything. Because she was a saleslady in a sex shop? There was a certain freedom in that.

"Perhaps you need a class or two to show you the ropes."

"A class?" Oh yeah, this place really did boggle the mind.

"I give personal training. I'll show you how to tie knots on her, how to truss her up, how to apply nipple clamps so they don't do any physical damage." She reached into her purse and pulled out a business card. "We can even dominate her together, if you'd like." She winked. "Just until you get the gist of it. I've worked with a lot of couples. Are you interested in giving her to other men?"

He'd stood in front of an assembly of fifteen hundred students— if you weren't afraid of teenagers, you weren't afraid of *anything*— and he had never once in his life found himself speechless. Until this moment.

She slipped the card into the breast pocket of his jacket.

He took one step back. Discovered his voice. "I believe I'll take the silk cuffs." He pointed slightly behind and to the right. "And the feather duster."

She laughed, batted his chest. "It's a feather *teaser*, silly man. But I like your choices." She lowered her voice, tapped the pocket where her card lay. "Just call if you need any pointers." Then she grabbed one of the cock plugs—a bronze circlet shaped like a snake with a head that would go . . . inside. "And I found just what I was looking for." Carrying her choice, she paid for it at a counter in the back. On her way out, she waggled her fingers at him.

Good God, the woman didn't work there at all.

At the last moment, before going to the counter himself, Lance pulled a simple no-frills vibrator off the wall to add to the red silk cuffs and overpriced feather duster. Maybe he was a novice. Maybe he was even a prude. But he removed the woman's card from his pocket and tossed it in a trash can by the register. Handcuffs, feathers, and a vibrator were as far as he was willing to go. At least for now.

6

THE PRINCIPAL'S HOUSE FORMED A T, WITH THE LIVING ROOM, dining room, and kitchen across the front. The bedrooms were along the length of the T, down a hallway of windows facing a brick patio and a manicured green lawn bordered by a tall privacy hedge.

He'd lit a fire against the cooling November night and taken a seat on the living room sofa situated in front of another bank of windows facing the same patio and lawn as the bedroom hall.

"Now take off your clothes." He flourished a hand.

"You're joking, right?" Charlotte had barely walked through the door. He'd directed her to stand in front of a cherrywood coffee table, the fire deliciously warm at her back, the high heels of her shoes sinking into the thick, patterned Persian carpet.

"Don't argue. Just take your punishment." His face was impassive in the fire's glow. He hadn't turned on a lamp, the only illumination provided by the fire and the light spilling in from the foyer. Dressed in a black pullover sweater and black slacks, he wasn't much more than a dark shape on the leather sofa.

"But—" It was like sex; you wanted a buildup, although there'd been very little buildup in the detention hall. And she'd gotten wet this evening as she'd showered, shaved, lotioned, and primped. "My clothes." She pointed to the tight Lycra top that molded to her breasts and the black leggings outlining her hips and thighs. "I dressed for you."

"So undress for me." He leaned his elbows on his knees, legs spread wide, and lowered his voice to a seductive pitch that set her skin on a slow burn. "Tuesday was for high schoolers. Tonight's detention is for big girls. I want you naked. I want to see your skin turn pink and your nipples get hard." He sat back in his former nonchalant pose. "So take everything off, or I'll have to come over there and strip you down myself."

The firelight glowed in his eyes, the look scorching, and suddenly Charlotte wanted to do anything he asked. Crossing her arms, she grabbed the hem of her Lycra top and yanked it over her head, sending it flying and her curls bouncing over her bared shoulders. Then she slipped her fingers beneath the waistband of her leggings and bent, pushing them all the way to her high heels before she stepped out of the shoes.

"Jesus." There was a new hoarseness in his voice. "Put on the heels again."

Kicking aside the leggings, she did as he bid, once again standing before the firelight, this time in only underwear and high heels. In the window's reflection behind him, the firelight shone like a corona around her.

"Perfect." He rose, skirted the coffee table, and strolled around her to stop at her back. In the reflection, their coronas merged into one, and the warmth of the fire was replaced by the blazing heat of his body. As he loomed behind her, she felt deliciously over-whelmed by his height, her heart in her throat, a throb deep in her belly.

He leaned down. A warm breath whispered across her nape. "Hands behind your back."

The order sent a shiver through her, straight down to her cli-toris. She crossed her wrists at the small of her back and watched him in the window as he reached for something on the mantel. He didn't bind her with rope as she expected, but instead wrapped something silky around her right wrist, then her left.

"Silk handcuffs." A tantalizing breath whispered over her again. "Too tight?"

She shook her head and answered as well. "No-o." Her voice cracked.

She'd asked for a spanking. He was escalating. And drawing her oh-so-willingly along.

He reached to the mantel again. The firelight danced around him as his shadow separated from hers, but she couldn't make out the object. Until he trailed something soft down her spine, leaving tingles in its wake. Feathers.

He tapped the inside of one foot with his shoe. "Spread your legs wider."

Charlotte readjusted. Featherlight, he caressed the line of her thong where it bisected her cheeks. She watched him in the win-dow, his gaze intent on her body.

"You have an amazing ass." He stroked back and forth, up and down. Between the fire and the closeness of his body, her skin was ablaze. She understood what Lola had said, that the words were as important as the actions. It was the whole package that got her blood pumping.

"No spanking this time?" she ventured.

He glanced up, breaking his concentration on her butt. "My

dear Miss Moore, your infraction was so egregious that you will need multiple punishments, one of which may or may not be a spanking, depending on how I feel." His voice dropped to a mere breath of sound. "So stop directing. Stop questioning. And simply do what I tell you."

"Yes, Principal Hutton." There was definitely something to be said for giving up her control. She was nothing more than a mass of nerve endings begging for his attention.

The exquisite torture continued, her spine, her bottom, the backs of her thighs, up along the inner thigh, then the feathery softness between her legs. Charlotte barely trapped the moan inside. Then he trailed the waistline of her thong, following it around to the front until he stood before her.

"I'm told it's called a feather teaser," he said, his head bent as he swished it—three feathers on a wooden stem—across her mound. "Your breasts are definitely a temptation. I don't know how I can concentrate on your punishment." He raised just his eyes. "Perhaps they need their very own punishment."

Yes, yes, please. But Charlotte didn't beg.

The feathers teased their way up to the swell of her breasts above the bra's demicup. "What a blessing your breasts are, Miss Moore," he murmured. "I had no idea."

He surely had, since she wasn't one to button all the way to the top, but she loved the way he talked, the words a stroke as exquisite as the feathers. She would remember everything for her clients, how each mini-event in the evening affected her, the physical sensations, the emotional tidbits.

With a flick of his wrist, the front clasp of the bra snapped open. Instead of pushing aside the cups, he tickled the feathers beneath the lace. Her nipples peaked. This time, Charlotte allowed herself the moan.

"That sounds like you're enjoying your punishment, Miss

Moore." His eyes suddenly gleamed with evil intent and he pinched her. Hard. Electric jolts shot straight to her center.

God. *This* was what she'd counseled couples on when their love lives had gone stale. Make each caress unique. Savor one individual touch at a time. Don't rush. Role play. Drive your partner crazy. The principal was certainly using every technique in the manual.

He pinched her other nipple, stroked the feathers back and forth between her legs. It didn't matter that she wore the thong; he pushed her to the edge. Her limbs trembled, her belly quivered, her breath panted from her lungs. She didn't realize she'd closed her eyes until he was suddenly flush against her body, the hard imprint of his cock on her belly.

"What was your infraction, Miss Moore?" Harsh demand laced his voice.

What had she said or done the other day to make him angry? She couldn't remember. With the state he had her in, she wasn't thinking clearly. But she'd do it again, whatever it was, if this was what he gave.

"Begins with a C," he prompted.

Oh yeah. Now she remembered. "Cocksucker," she whispered.

"Indeed." He smiled like the devil himself. "You shall have your wish."

"BUT FIRST, MY DEAR MISS MOORE, I HAVE SOMETHING ELSE planned for you."

Lance could feel her full-body quiver beneath the feathers he swished back and forth across the swell of her breasts and her tempting nipples. He thought of the woman in the sex shop and her suggestions. Nipple clamps? No, not for Charlotte; he couldn't risk damaging her. And he certainly didn't want to share his domination of her. He had her right where he wanted her, the tantalizing scent of her arousal rising, mesmerizing him, keeping him as close to the edge as she was. He shifted slightly, rubbing the hard ridge of his cock against her belly.

"Close your eyes," he told her.

"Yes, Principal Hutton," she purred sweetly, and closed her lids, hiding the almost feverish glow of her emerald green irises.

He circled her again, trailing the feather, giving the crease of her ass one last tease before reaching for the last item he'd set on the mantel. The no-frills vibrator. Before he forced her to her knees, he was going to make her scream his name.

"Spread your legs as wide as you can go," he whispered, standing close to her once more, his breath ruffling the fine tendrils of hair tucked behind her ear.

She redistributed her weight on her shoes, gasped as she teetered. "I'll fall over."

"I'll hold you up." He pressed flush against her back. The top of her head skimmed his jaw. She made him feel big, strong, and powerful next to her petite height. He rotated his hips slightly, the angle of her hands in the silk cuffs forcing her to cup his cock.

She squeezed his balls. Lance barely suppressed a groan, barely restrained himself from surging into her grip. But he was saving the surging for later.

"Stay still," he commanded as he wrapped his arm around her waist. Holding the tip of the vibrator in one hand, he turned the base with the other, and the thing purred to life.

Charlotte jolted when he touched the whirring device to the crotch of her thong. "Oh my God." She ended the lament on a moan.

"It's Principal Hutton," he corrected, "not God."

"Whatever your name is," she answered with a dreamy note

in her voice, "don't stop." She leaned her head back against his shoulder. She was small enough for him to be able to look straight down to the vibrator between her legs.

"I won't stop until you come for me, my dirty little slut."

As she quivered in his arms, he realized how uninventive he'd been in his lovemaking. He'd rarely used a vibrator on a woman. Never tied anyone up. Seldom employed dirty talk to excite and tantalize. Not to mention the spanking. Maybe it was him, maybe it was the partners he chose. Safe, unimaginative women who never required much from him. He was reminded of what the woman in the sex shop had said. He wasn't leading Charlotte; she was leading him. Charlotte Moore was a whole new breed of woman.

And he fucking loved it.

Pulling back the elastic, he slid the vibrator inside her panties. The device slipped in all her moisture, and he allowed his fingers to follow the path down to the tip of the vibrator to test her wetness for himself.

"Christ, you're creamy." He switched hands and put his fingers to his lips to taste her. "You taste good." He wanted his mouth on her pussy, her juice on his tongue. So many things he wanted from her.

But first he wanted her to come. "Is that the right spot?" He didn't care that he needed to ask.

"God, yes." She gasped, bucked once. "I mean, yes, Principal Hutton." Then her body began to move sinuously against him. She panted and huffed, murmured soft words, her head lolling against his shoulder. "Don't move, just hold it tight, right there, just like that." She moaned. "Yes, yes." First her legs began to shake, then her whole body quaked against his. He responded, riding her wave, thrusting into her bound hands.

"Tell me." His voice was a harsh rasp in his throat. The sight of her in the reflection, her body splayed before him, was as mesmerizing as the feel of her skin against his.

"Oh God, Principal Hutton. Yes, yes." She threw her head back and her orgasm rolled through her, rolled through him, shook him, took him, turned him into her servant.

He held her in place through the entire experience, relishing it, drinking in her sensations.

Finally, when her tremors abated, when it seemed her breath had come back, she whispered, "My, my, Principal Hutton, that was amazing. What would your students think if they knew what you're really capable of?" She tipped her head to the side, nipped his chest, the bite shooting sensation straight through to his cock. "Now I'm ready for my encore."

"And what would your students think if they saw you down on your knees, Miss Moore?" He was glad his voice didn't crack with need, but he was close.

Charlotte laughed. "They'd be horrified to know what a good little cocksucking slut I am, Principal Hutton."

"How good you are remains to be seen. I'm going to have to give you a little test run."

"Oh, Principal Hutton, it's not going to be little at all. Be prepared for mind-blowing."

He had a feeling she was right.

Shifting her, he set her to the side, adjusting the angle so he could watch her from above and still have a view of her head above the sofa in the window's reflection. His hands on her shoulders, he pushed her to her knees.

"Impress me, Miss Moore."

She looked up, fluttered her eyelashes at him. "You're going to have to undo for me."

"My pleasure." He unzipped without bothering to unbuckle his belt. He'd gone commando underneath.

"Oh my, Principal Hutton." She tipped her head back to gaze up at him. "I certainly don't think your students have any idea about that." She licked her lips.

"I do try to keep my private parts private."

"I'm honored you'd show this magnificent tool to me."

"As I said, Miss Moore, it's my pleasure. But I suggest you stop talking."

"I will if you fill my mouth with something."

He held her head by the hair, fisting his fingers in the silkiness of it, and wrapped his hand around his cock. His blood beat through him.

Charlotte opened her mouth. He watched in the reflection as he fed his cock to her. So many sensations he'd missed, as if he'd skimmed his sex life. Charlotte showed him how much more there could be. Then he couldn't miss another moment of the close-up as she engulfed him, sucked him deep, and blew his mind just the way she claimed she would.

HE WAS SALTY AND SWEET AT THE SAME TIME. THICK AND HARD between her lips, yet his skin was soft and resilient. A vein pulsed against her tongue. The principal was a hell of a man, something she'd never suspected. But then she'd never really looked. The age thing. But oh, what she'd been missing.

"Suck it, Miss Moore."

She relished the feel of his hand in her hair, guiding her, halfway to forcing her but in such a delicious way. Yes, there were a multitude of techniques she could suggest to her clients. Then Charlotte gave herself up to the taste and feel of him.

He filled her to the back of her throat, stopped just short of gagging her. With her hands secured behind her, she was at his mercy. His pre-come sluiced her tongue, the taste sweet enough to make her shiver and salty enough to excite her taste buds for more of him.

Above her, he let his head fall back, a low groan slipping from his lips. "Fuck."

Dirty talk was hot. She pulled away to whisper, "More. Talk to me. Call me names. Tell me what to do."

"Suck the tip hard, you dirty little bitch. I know you want it."

She did. Badly. Charlotte wasn't too old to learn new tricks. She swirled her tongue around the ridge, stabbed lightly at the slit, grazed his skin with her teeth, then sucked hard.

In turn, he gave her what she wanted: dirty words and his loss of control.

"Fuck, fuck, fuck, baby, yes, like that, shit." His breath puffed with every word. "Deep. Suck me deep, my pretty, perfect little whore."

She took him all the way. Where she'd muttered *Oh God*, he chanted, "Fuck, fuck, fuck," and she knew she had him. She was an A plus. She was his honor roll student.

His legs started to tremble, and he held her head with both hands, fucking her mouth, thrusting deep, a litany of swear words falling from his lips, words she was sure the principal practiced *not* saying. But then he never lost control.

Not until now. For her. Wrapping one big hand behind her head, he reached under and squeezed his balls, an act she was sure he would have made her do if her hands weren't bound. Then he filled her mouth, punctuated by dirty words even she'd never heard. Charlotte swallowed every drop, savored it all, drank him, feasted on him. Owned him.

She generally counseled sharing in ecstasy, but there was something so delicious in being restrained and unable to make herself come at the same time. Something so powerful. She sucked him dry. God, yes, she did. Savoring every quake of his body, every grunt and groan. Every word. Every sensation.

He opened his eyes to look at her. They were a stormy gray in the dim light.

She sucked hard and reveled in the jerk of his body.

"Well," he said, his voice harsh with aftermath, "you certainly took your punishment well."

She nodded, unwilling to let him loose. She flicked her tongue along his slit. He shivered. Oh yeah. She performed her detention well, very well. And that vibrator orgasm he'd given her was the icing on the cake.

He pulled out, tucked himself away inside his slacks. She wasn't ready to let him go. Charlotte wanted a lot more.

"Now what, Principal Hutton?" She smiled wickedly.

He was silent a long moment, glaring down at her from his position on high. "You look like the cat that ate the cream."

Charlotte licked her lips. "Oh yes, I did."

"Proud of yourself, aren't you."

She nodded. "Very."

"That deserves a little punishment, too."

He dragged an armchair across the carpet and pushed her face-first into it. She was still secured at the wrists, her hands at her back, and for a moment, she couldn't breathe. Then he spanked her hard. Charlotte turned her face to the side and shouted at him. "Bastard."

He leaned over the chair, bracing himself on the arm, slapping her ass again, hard, his fingers connecting with her pussy. Exactly the way that drove her insane. He smacked. She quivered. He swatted. She moaned. And gasped. And writhed. And finally came in an explosion of stars and an exquisite burning across the flesh of her butt.

7

IT WAS PERFECT. TOO PERFECT. CHARLOTTE COLLAPSED AGAINST
the chair cushion, her hands still secured at the small of her back
by the silk handcuffs.

She drew in a long, deep, satisfied breath. Yes, perfect, her body
humming, her clit buzzing . . . but there was one slight problem.
Anything this perfect could become addictive. Especially sex. Not
in the traditional "sex addict" sense, where someone had sex with
anyone, anytime, anywhere, like they were shooting a drug into
their veins. But sex was such an emotional time bomb. It was one
of the biggest battlegrounds for couples. Not *just* sex, but sex in all
its nuances: romance, physical well-being, emotional sustenance,
the need to feel loved, wanted, desired. She'd seen it all, talked her
clients down off the ledge, helped them shed the obsession.

Naughty, over-the-top sex could become addictive, and yes,
Charlotte could easily become obsessed with the way this man
made her feel. Being a therapist didn't preclude her from that. But
it did make her aware of the danger.

She waggled her fingers. "Principal Hutton, I think it's time to undo me. Now that I've received my punishment."

Even his scent was hypnotic as he insinuated his knees between hers, leaned over her, caressed the silk bonds, stroked her skin.

"We're not done, yet, Miss Moore."

What more could there be? He'd come in her mouth. She'd come multiple times.

He snugged up close behind her bottom, his cock hard, and she knew what more there could be.

"My oh my, I didn't think you'd be ready for that." So soon. Especially for a man his age. A quick recovery was another thing Charlotte liked about younger men. But Principal Hutton was turning all her misconceptions about older men upside down.

Yes, he was far too perfect.

And she wanted him inside her.

After a few rustles, his zipper, and the ripping of a condom packet, his warm fingers caressed the crotch of her thong. He pulled it aside, stroked her. Charlotte groaned.

"Christ, you're wet."

She waggled her fingers again, for a very different reason this time. "Please, please, Principal Hutton, won't you untie me? I'll do anything you want, if you just remove these cuffs."

"Anything, Miss Moore?"

"Absolutely anything." She'd think about obsession later. Or maybe later, she'd see the whole thing in perspective. That he was just a man. That this was just really good sex. And it probably only felt *this* good because she hadn't had sex in months.

Then her hands were free and Charlotte braced herself against the back cushion of the chair, pushing her bottom against him. Begging.

"Do you want me to fuck you, Miss Moore?" He rotated his hips, caressing her with his condom-clad cock.

She wanted it more than anything, to feel him inside her, hot, hard, filling her completely. "I had a fantasy about my high school principal." Her principal had been a woman. But if she'd been a he and he'd looked like Principal Hutton, well, she very well might have had a few fantasies. Before she decided younger men were better. Safer.

"What was your fantasy?"

"I imagined he took me right there in his office."

"Did he bend you over his desk?"

"No. Over his leather chair. Just like this." She pushed back, shimmied, teased.

"Did he lift your skirt?" He stroked her cheeks, held her hips, pressed hard against her center.

"Yes. Then he pulled aside my panties and slipped right inside."

"Like this?" He wedged a finger beneath the thin strap of her thong, slid it to the left, and teased her with the tip of his cock.

Charlotte moaned. Though he was kneeling between her legs, she spread her thighs wider for him. "He teased me like that for so long that suddenly I just had to make him do it." Her hands flat on the chair back, she pushed against him, forcing him to slip inside. But his hand was in the way, and for a moment all he did was short-stroke just inside her opening. It was enough, good God, more than enough, his cock caressing her G-spot.

Charlotte closed her eyes. Absolutely perfect.

"Then he fucked me," she whispered. "Hard, relentlessly. Until I was screaming."

Principal Hutton gave her everything she was begging for, hands on her hips, taking her hard, thrusting deep. She couldn't see. She could barely breathe. She for sure couldn't think. At the last moment, he pushed a hand between her legs, found her clitoris, rubbed her, circled her. And shot her off into outer space like a rocket.

Oh God, yes, this was addiction and oh so very good, the worst kind of habit to kick.

HE'D NEVER BEEN WITH A WOMAN HE SIMPLY COULDN'T GET enough of. She'd sucked him off. He'd come hard. But he'd needed more. Right away. No time necessary to recharge. The need was simply there, overpowering.

He lay like a blanket over her body, squashing her down in the chair. The distinctly feminine scent of arousal oozed from her pores. Turning his head, he licked the salt from her skin. He nibbled her shoulder, kissed her ear.

"That was better than my fantasy," she murmured.

"I'm so glad to hear it, Miss Moore. I've never fucked anyone in my office, but if you'd been my student, I most certainly would have taken you."

"Why thank you, Principal Hutton."

He contemplated meeting her at the school late in the night, when the halls were empty, all the lessons planned, and even the janitors had gone home.

He also contemplated taking her to his bed and having her over and over. She energized him. He was like a young buck again. "We need sustenance. Then we'll go to bed. I fancy having you in the middle of the night."

She was silent a moment. A very long moment. Then, "We wouldn't want to have too much of a good thing." She wriggled beneath him. "It just gets boring."

"I believe we have the capacity to add extra spice." After all, they'd only played this game twice. He certainly wasn't that easily bored. "And you're the slave. So we'll eat and I'll have you again. As many times as I like." Part of the game was being a dom.

She set both hands against the back of the chair and pushed.

Covering her as he was, his cock still buried inside her, she failed to dislodge him. "I'm ready to get up now, Principal Hutton. It's time for me to go home."

He nipped her neck, like a lion taming his mate. "I say when it's time for you to go."

He could almost hear her teeth gnashing. Then she spoke in an overly sweet tone. "It's getting hard to breathe down here. And I'm a little cold."

On one hand, it was an obvious ploy. On the other hand, he couldn't lay on her all night long just to keep her here. "I can put another log on the fire," he told her. "Don't get dressed." Then he pulled out and away, stuffing his cock back in his pants just until he could get rid of the condom.

Standing over her as she pushed herself upright on her knees, he added, "And don't leave while I'm gone."

Charlotte glared at him.

He narrowed his eyes. "I should spank you for looking at me like that."

"Don't push your luck, Lance," she said. No kowtowing to the principal in those words.

He would have stayed to deal with her if other needs weren't pressing. Though necessary, condoms sucked. He was back in less than five minutes. Charlotte was dressed, just the way he suspected she'd be, her hand on the front doorknob.

At least she hadn't left. "We're not done, Miss Moore."

"You punished me. You fucked me. That covers all the bases."

"You haven't learned to be submissive. You're supposed to do everything I tell you."

"I did. But I never said I was spending the night. This isn't a date, you know. It's sex. Fun and games. Nothing serious."

Well, that put him in his place. He was a fantasy, just like her long-ago principal. No spending the night allowed. No dating.

No attachment. Only fun and games. "And when you misbehave again?"

She cocked her head. "I might have turned over a new leaf," she said with a sugary smile.

He seriously doubted that. She'd need her punishment again. The next time, he wouldn't take off the handcuffs until he had her in his bed.

AT QUARTER TO TEN ON MONDAY MORNING, CHARLOTTE HAD another fifteen minutes before her first client arrived. So she curled her feet beneath her in the corner chair, sunlight forcing its way through the leaves and branches of the big oaks outside her office windows, and called Lola. Who, incidentally, had been MIA all weekend.

"We went wine tasting in Napa," Lola started out explaining.

"You don't need to justify to me, honey." Charlotte was exceptionally happy that Lola had found her perfect Coach.

"I meant to call you, but—"

Charlotte held up her hand as if Lola could see. "Say no more."

"All right, then just spill the beans."

"It was amazing," Charlotte said, her voice more musing than enthralled. "Like the first time you told me about Coach Barnett." Charlotte called him Coach because at the time that had been how Lola thought of him. Just as Charlotte liked to think of Lance as Principal Hutton, giving him that air of authority and a sense of illicitness. But it was also intimate to think of him as Lance. And that felt sexy, too. Maybe dangerously so.

"So of course you're seeing him again," Lola said.

"Of course. But here's the issue."

"Oh God." She could visualize Lola's eye roll. "You're not going to analyze yourself out of the whole thing, are you?"

Charlotte fully admitted she tended to overanalyze her relationships. She'd had five serious ones, but Martin was the closest she'd gotten to marriage. And therein lay the problem. Lance was a principal, a man of authority, and he definitely had the tendency to be autocratic. But she couldn't let him order her to spend the night. That was beyond the rules they'd established. Hmm, okay, they hadn't established any rules yet. Whatever. The bigger issue was that she'd *wanted* to stay, wanted him to take her in the deepest part of the night, one time, two, three, until dawn broke.

She cut her musings off right there. "Actually, it has nothing to do with Principal Hutton himself." Or her past relationship with a controlling father figure. "It's more that I'm totally obsessed with the sex."

"No," Lola said on a gasp, sarcastic wonder lacing her tone. "You? Obsessed with sex? It's impossible."

Charlotte tut-tutted like an old maid. Or the psychologist she was. "Just because I deal with sex on a daily basis doesn't mean I'm obsessed with it. In fact, I help people get over their obsessions and addictions. And that's why I know the signs."

Her sign? She wanted more of Principal Lance Hutton. Or rather, more of what he gave her, ordering her to do those dirty things, tying her up, forcing her. "Oh my God," she hissed.

"What?"

"You don't think I'm actually reverting to that pathetic young woman who needed a man to tell her what to do, how to act, someone who wanted all her decisions made for her by some older and wiser man?"

"Charlotte, you weren't like that." Lola had lived through those dark months when Charlotte felt like she was losing herself in the will of another. Martin had been subtle, even loving about it, but he'd been directing her life all the same. *Do you really think that's the right decision, Charlotte? Why don't you think about it this way instead, Charlotte? I'm sure when you think it through, Charlotte, you'll realize this is what you should do.* All those suggestions were supposed to help her. Instead they'd stifled her intuition. She'd begun to doubt herself. She couldn't make a decision without asking his opinion first. Which had always differed from her own. Until finally she'd managed to make a decision without consulting him first, the day she walked out to find herself again.

"You've only been with him a couple of times, Charlotte. Why are you overreacting?"

Why? "Because it was too good. I'm suspicious of anything that's too good." She was also cautious about allowing anyone too much control.

"It's too good with Gray, but you don't question that."

"That's you, not me. I have an obsessive personality."

Lola snorted. "You do not. It sounds more like you're trying to find an excuse to get rid of him. And you haven't even started yet. Not really anyway." Lola *hmmed*. "You know, you always begin overanalyzing when you're actually interested in a man."

"For God's sake, like you said, I've only been with him twice."

"Yes, but you've known him since he became principal three years ago. That's more than enough time."

"I was never interested in him. I never even looked at him. He's too old for me."

"That's exactly why you're overanalyzing," Lola insisted. "Because all of a sudden, your little *ooh-la-la* switch got flipped."

"*Ooh-la-la?*"

"Yeah. You know, when you suddenly *see* a man for the first time. Maybe it's the way he laughed. Or some little thing he said.

Or even a scent on him. And bam, you suddenly see him as a man instead of a boss or a coworker or a friend."

Charlotte didn't want to admit that Lola might actually have a point. For her, it had been the way Lance towered over her when she was down on the office carpet holding the apple. His amused expression. His arms folded over his chest. His suddenly impressive chest.

"So don't talk yourself out of this yet. At least give it more time."

Charlotte wasn't really planning to talk herself out of it. She just didn't want to let things get out of control. But when you were talking about addiction and obsession, the essence of the words meant losing control.

As usual, though, Lola had a point. Charlotte was over-analyzing. It was funny—funny odd—that she could be so level-headed with everyone else's problems but overreact with her own.

"All right," she agreed, "I'll stop analyzing." For now.

"Just enjoy. Go for it. Try everything you've ever wanted to try."

"Hey, who's the psychologist here?"

Lola laughed. "I know you better than you know yourself."

"Right," Charlotte said with a snap on the last letter. "And I know you. So stop analyzing and move in with Gray. You know you want to."

"I haven't said no yet." Defensiveness tinged Lola's voice.

"Then just say yes." Charlotte refrained from saying that it didn't have to be permanent. Anything could be changed, but Lola didn't need to hear that she could run away if things got tough. She needed to feel that taking the risk was worth it.

"I thought we were talking about you. You're trying to change the subject."

"Of course not. I love talking about myself. You know, you never ask for the dirty details the way I do."

"That's because I know you'll ask for mine if I ask for yours."

"Very true." The light on her phone began to flash. Jeanine Smith was out in the waiting room. "Well, you're lucky. I have to go."

"Ha, see, you don't really want to talk about the principal."

"I wouldn't have called you if I didn't." Maybe what she'd really wanted was for Lola to say exactly what she did: Go for it and enjoy. That's just what Charlotte intended to do.

8

CHARLOTTE OPENED THE DOOR FOR JEANINE. SHE DIDN'T HAVE A receptionist. The client simply pushed a button on a console out in the small waiting room, which set the light on Charlotte's office phone flashing. Her clients needn't meet each other either. There was an exit door that bypassed the waiting room, leading into the passageway with the restroom conveniently close by in case they needed to repair the damage an emotional session had on their makeup. Most of her clients were women.

Today Jeanine was impeccably dressed as usual, not a strand of blond hair out of place. Her blue knee-length skirt was neatly ironed, her white blouse buttoned to the neck. Charlotte had a feeling that the pressed and buttoned-up facade was something of a defense mechanism this time.

They took their usual seats in the corner by the window, Charlotte facing the clock and the desk. Perhaps it was her phone call with Lola, and Lola's words: *Go for it. Try everything you've ever wanted to try.* If Jeanine *went for it*, perhaps her problems would vanish. So instead of letting her client control the discussion—and deflecting any questions she didn't want to answer—Charlotte moved straight to the suggestion she'd made at the end of their last session.

"So, what were the results of the experiment we discussed last time?"

Jeanine arched one penciled brow. "What experiment?"

"You were going to indulge your husband's fantasy."

Jeanine pursed her mouth, tiny lines fanning out along her upper lip. "I'm not going to have sex with other men," she snapped.

Charlotte could see right through Jeanine's avoidance tactic. "I agree. But you were only going to fantasize. Discover what effect that had."

"You said I needed to get rid of the kids. I didn't get a chance. My youngest son had issues at school, and we spent most of the time dealing with that." Jeanine toyed with the strap of her purse.

She didn't want to address the sexual issues. When tasked with taking action, Jeanine evaded it. She wasn't ready to move beyond complaining. Her son's school issues were a way of not dealing with her husband's sexual issues, *her* sexual issues.

Charlotte chose a conversational rather than confrontational tone. "Would you like to discuss your son's issue during our time today?"

"I . . ." Jeanine hesitated. "I wouldn't exactly call it an issue"—though that was exactly the word she'd used—"just kid stuff. We'll get through it."

Which meant her son was merely an excuse not to carry through with Charlotte's suggestion. Of course, creating a fantasy with her husband about her being with another man *was* Charlotte's idea, not Jeanine's, and often a person had to come up with their own solution—or attempt a solution—for it to actually work.

Before Charlotte could speak or ask another question, Jeanine rushed on. "Look, okay, I was afraid."

Admitting fear was definitely progress. Instead of pushing, Charlotte let Jeanine continue at her own pace.

"You see, if I even suggest I might do it, he'd actually *want* me to do it. He wouldn't just fantasize. He'd keep pushing and pushing. He's just that way. So it could all backfire on me."

Charlotte knew how Jeanine felt. With Lance, Charlotte wanted it her way. She liked his orders, his authoritative attitude, his spankings, his willingness to play games, to experiment. But he'd pushed for more. And way too quickly to boot. She'd told Lola it was about obsession and addiction. But that wasn't truly the case. It was about losing control of the situation. Charlotte wanted to lose control on her own terms, not someone else's, especially not an authoritative older man who liked to dictate.

"So what you're saying is that you'd like to be in control of the situation."

"Well, yes," Jeanine agreed, her brow furrowed as if she hadn't truly considered that before. Feeling powerless was definitely one of Jeanine's issues.

"And if you even suggest you'd like to fantasize about being with another man, then he'll take over and force you to do it."

"Uh . . . yes."

"Then what's our solution?"

"*Our* solution?"

Charlotte meant it the way she'd said it, the solution to Jeanine's problem *and* hers. "Let's come up with a remedy together. Let's pretend we both have the same problem. Dealing with a man who wants his way." Though Charlotte had to admit she could be putting that onto Lance when really it was her own neurotic fears creating the problem. After all, they did say that many psychologists and psychiatrists entered the field out of a desire to fix their personal neuroses.

But for now, she would deal with Jeanine as if they indeed had a common problem.

"I just don't see that there's a remedy, Dr. Moore." Jeanine let an unpleasant whine enter her voice.

Charlotte wanted to squash it. "We're both feeling out of our depth, that we're losing control of the situation. How do we get that back? How do we stand up for ourselves?"

"By not playing their game?" With a slight rise at the end, Jeanine made it a question rather than a statement.

As women, they had to make it into *their* game. But first you had to figure out what the other party was after. "So what game are they playing?"

Jeanine rolled her lips between her teeth, not worrying about the smudges to her lipstick. Then she said slowly, thoughtfully, "David doesn't want to admit that he's got a sexual dysfunction . . . so he's trying to get me to do kinky things that he thinks will turn him on . . ." There she trailed off, frowning, obviously having no clue as to why her husband would choose this way to bring a spark back to their marriage bed. "Because he doesn't really want me?" She gave it that same rise in tone indicating a question.

"Let's give it a positive spin. He does want you, but he's having physical trouble, and he's falling back on the old teasing you used to do together. Bringing your past relationships into your sex play." It was a regurgitation of what they'd discussed last week, but Charlotte felt the wording was more palatable. Jeanine didn't answer, her gaze inward, so Charlotte prompted, "How does that feel? The idea that he's actively trying to find a way to bring sex back into your marriage?"

"But if he still desires me, why would he want to give me to other men?"

Charlotte held up a finger. "Let's not think negatively. He does desire you. But he's using unconventional methods."

"But isn't this all about what *he* wants, not what I want?"

Well, yes, it was, but Charlotte pressed on. "Let's assume for the moment that he's actually trying to bring back spark. How are you going to play along with him without compromising what *you* want?"

Jeanine stared at her lap. "I don't see how I can."

Charlotte suspected Jeanine still had a desire to wallow in her misery. "If it were me," she said, "and I had a man dictating what he wanted"—which she did—"I'd lay down a few rules first."

At this, Jeanine seemed to perk up, raising her gaze to meet Charlotte's. "Like what?"

"First I'd *tell* him this was only a game. Make sure he understands." The principal knew it was a game, one *she'd* actually started playing, not the other way around. "Once we're both clear that it's not reality, then we can say to each other that anything goes, that we can enjoy it without recrimination, and that either one of us can call a halt to it at any time."

"So you're saying I should insist I only want to fantasize and not actually do anything. And that's my rule. If he starts trying to push me to do things I don't want to, then the fantasizing ends."

Now she was getting it. "Yes. Exactly. Make a rule for him and stick to it. Give him a boundary. And a consequence if he crosses the boundary." Charlotte had made the rule. She'd told Lance that a whole night wasn't in the cards. But she hadn't given him a consequence. She didn't want to issue an ultimatum. Because she didn't want to stop. The sticky part was how badly she'd wanted to stay. Obsessed. Addicted. Her problem wasn't the same as Jeanine's at all.

But, luckily, they were analyzing Jeanine, not Charlotte.

"Do you feel comfortable with rules and consequences?"

Jeanine was staring at her lap again. "I'm not sure how good I'll be at following through."

"Just tell him what you want. And ask him what he wants."

Charlotte gave herself a wry inward smile. Those words were so easy to say, yet so hard to actually do. Asking Lance what he wanted could cause all sorts of problems she wasn't willing to deal with.

She just wanted to have fun without any pressure. Why had she suddenly made everything so complicated? Lola was absolutely right.

Note to self: Stop overanalyzing.

YESTERDAY'S SESSION HAD ENDED WITH JEANINE DECIDING TO tell her husband that she wanted to fantasize *only.* She wasn't committing to anything more. The appointment had also ended with Charlotte deciding that she definitely wanted more fun and games with Principal Hutton, and all she had to do if he started getting dictatorial was to put him in his place with an unequivocal *No, I'm not doing that.* Just the way she had on Friday night. Problem solved.

Melody Wright was scheduled for eleven o'clock. Last Thursday, Charlotte had discussed Melody's issues with her assistant principal, just to keep her up to speed. Then she'd had a five-minute conversation with Mr. Gunderson, Melody's science teacher. The only additional piece of the puzzle he could add was the boy's identity: Eric Collins. An older man in his early sixties, Mr. Gunderson was buried in his science. He hadn't paid attention to the intricacies of teenage relations until Melody dumped the sugar water on Eric's head. All he knew was that they were lab partners, nothing more. Was Lydia right? Had they been an item in middle school?

This morning, Lydia had searched out Charlotte to tell her there'd been another incident just before first period. After a brief, angry verbal exchange, Melody had grabbed Eric's backpack out of his hands and thrown it down on the concrete, spilling its contents. Nothing had appeared to be damaged, no teachers or monitors were present, and no students had ratted out Melody. Lydia didn't consider that telling Charlotte was "ratting out." Charlotte didn't consider it a major offense in and of itself. It was the pattern that worried her.

Okay. This gave her much to deal with in her session today. But first, she was obligated to tell Lance everything she'd learned. Charlotte knew it for the excuse it was. She'd been waiting all morning to see him, her nerves keyed up.

Mrs. Rivers pursed her lips but waved Charlotte right on in as if the principal had been expecting her.

The blinds closed over his window, presumably to cut down on the glare, Lance gazed intently at his computer screen, chin propped on his fisted hand. "Please close the door, Miss Moore," he said without looking up. "Sit," he added, with neither a *please* nor a *thank-you*, when the door was closed.

Charlotte wasn't about to let him start dictating to her. She didn't like being ignored either. "I prefer to stand."

"As you wish, Miss Moore." Finally he glanced up, and the slow burn in his eyes as he raked her with his gaze made her wet.

She realized he was anything but ignoring her. If she touched him, she knew she'd find him hard. If she moved to his side of the desk, he wouldn't be able to keep his hands off her. Oh yeah, she was the one in control here. He was just baiting her.

He lounged back in his big leather chair as he contemplated her. "What can I do for you?"

She'd intended to start with a discussion about Melody Wright and Eric Collins, pretending her visit was all business. But what she really wanted was to knock the polite conversation right out of him.

"We need to establish some limits."

His lips twitched. He might have been smiling, as if she'd said what he was hoping for, but Charlotte couldn't be sure. "I've been reading up on the subject," he said. "And you're right. A dom and his sub need to have limits and a safe word between them."

Too late, she realized that standing before him was a mistake. It made her submissive and subservient, as if she were a slave who wasn't allowed to sit or relax until her master granted her permission. In addition, establishing safe words and limits according to what *he* dictated wasn't what she'd meant at all.

He went on before she formulated an answer. "How about simply using the word *no* for anything you truly don't want to do?" He shifted, clasping his hands over his abdomen. This time there was no doubt about the smile, the curve of it exceedingly wicked when accompanied by the heat in his gaze. "If you don't use the word *no*, you're tacitly agreeing to do whatever I say, and that you'll let me do whatever I want."

She glared, but there were all sorts of physical reactions that gave her away, a flush creeping across her cheeks, her suddenly tight nipples, the rush of moisture between her legs. Sex scented the air, pheromones, arousal, *her* scent. But she needed rules. What were they supposed to be? Oh yes. "My limit is that I'm not spending the night with you."

"If your master commands it, why not?"

He was going too far. "Look, I never said we were dom and sub—"

"No, we're principal and student." He arched that devilish brow of his.

"It's just a game."

"Of course. But we need to make it fun."

"Then if I'm the student, there's no way I can spend the night with my principal."

He smiled indulgently. "Then I won't tie you to my bed for the entire night. Only part of the night. Shall we say midnight as your curfew?"

"I . . . well . . ." She wanted to fight, but he'd agreed to her rule: no spending the night. She could leave by midnight. She'd gotten what she asked for; she just wasn't sure she'd won the battle. And God, she wanted to be tied to his bed, completely at his sensual mercy.

"All you have to do is say no if you don't like it." He said the words with little more than the movement of his lips, just the form of them, hardly a sound.

No. No. No. He was taking control. But when she opened her mouth, what came out was a soft, breathy "Yes."

DONE. HE HAD HER.

He'd been waiting for her to come to him, the blinds closed, a budget spreadsheet on his monitor, the numbers failing to hold his attention. Now she stood before him, hands clasped behind her back as if she were begging him to bind her again. Her lips were plump and kissable, her natural perfume musky and sexual. Beneath the silky white blouse, her beaded nipples showed clearly, even through the covering of her bra. Her red skirt flared over her hips and was perhaps two inches too short to be circumspect, offering him a glance of creamy thigh that made his mouth water.

Friday night, he'd come harder than he had in more years than he could count, either with a woman or by his own hand. He'd liked having her bound. He'd enjoyed doing whatever he chose to do. He'd loved the heated feel of her red ass against his palm. But all of that had been nothing to the grip of her body around his cock, the way she'd milked him. She'd loved it all, too, despite the rule about not spending the night with him. She'd drawn him into the game in the portable that day after detention. She'd goaded him in his office. For some reason, Charlotte Moore liked turning over her control. It made her hot, got her off. The surprising thing was how much he'd liked it, too.

But to make sure . . . *"If,"* he stressed, "you don't want to be punished, all you have to do is behave."

"Yes, Principal Hutton." The green of her eyes was deeper than the brightest emerald.

"Was there anything else you wished to discuss, Miss Moore?" As nonchalant as he appeared, he was hard and aching beneath the desk, almost panting for her to do something, anything so he could touch her.

"Uh . . . well," she began, her eyes flitting around the office as if she couldn't recall her excuse for seeing him. "Oh yes, I wanted to tell you I'd updated Alice on the Melody Wright issue last Thursday."

Alice Sloan was one of his assistant principals and Charlotte's boss. Yet there wasn't a single reason Charlotte needed to trot down to his office to inform him.

"She's agreed I should have another session with Melody, which"—she glanced at her watch—"will be in half an hour. Sadly, there was another incident this morning. I'll see what I can get out of her."

"I'm sure you'll work a miracle." He smiled graciously.

"But there's something I need to show you, Principal Hutton."

"Of course."

She rounded his desk, stood beside him, her closeness doing things to him, setting his blood on fire. He could smell her sex.

Then she lifted her short, flared skirt.

Her pussy was naked, the plump, pink flesh beckoning. If he leaned in, he could taste her, lap her up with his tongue, drink her in. He was sure he'd lose his mind if he didn't at least touch her. He even put out a hand, stopped himself only in the last moment.

He glanced up. She was staring down at him, a seductive smile curving her lips. "Go ahead, Principal Hutton. I'm right here for the taking. No one will ever know. I promise."

She was the temptress he couldn't resist. Except in the interests of playing her game, upping the stakes, making what was between them hotter, sexier. "Miss Moore, I'm shocked at your lewd behavior."

She fluttered the skirt in front of her like the matador waving a red flag at a bull. "But you know you want it, Principal Hutton. I see the way you look at me."

He didn't look at her trimmed pussy, her enticing flesh. "Put that skirt back in place, Miss Moore. Lewd behavior at school is completely unacceptable."

The skirt fell into place with a small whoosh of air that wafted the scent of sex and sweet, delectable woman across his face. "I suppose that means you'll have to teach me a lesson, right, Principal Hutton?"

He could barely think of the appropriate answer. The woman beguiled him, surprised him, stole the very breath from his lungs. But the words came nonetheless. "You most certainly need another lesson. I will send you an email regarding your punishment." At the moment, he had no idea what it would be. All he could think about was the overwhelming desire to pull her down onto his lap and drive deep inside her. He pointed at the door. "Go. And put your panties back on, you dirty little slut."

He couldn't believe she'd taken them off. It was a bold move. Oh yes, Miss Moore liked ceding control to him, but she also loved turning the tables. One minute, he'd been the dom, the next, she'd topped him. Despite his words, he'd been only seconds and an ounce of willpower away from putting his hands on her.

Evidenced by that sashay of her sweet little ass as she made for the door, she knew it, too.

9

CHARLOTTE FELT UTTERLY DELICIOUS. SHE'D SHOCKED HIM. HE'D been *this* close to touching her. She knew that without a doubt. Removing her panties in the restroom just before she went to his office had been a stroke of genius. She'd gotten the upper hand. It was, however, totally inappropriate to go commando at school, so she'd visited the restroom again immediately after leaving him.

Of course, she hadn't said any of the stuff she'd gone to his office to tell him. In fact, after that sexy little conversation, most of it had flown right out of her head. He wasn't the only one affected by their hot little encounters. But she had her obsession under control; she hadn't gone too far. Only because he hadn't taken her up on the challenge? No, she wouldn't really have done anything. She just wanted the fun of it. Maybe, though, it hadn't been such a good idea to play her little game right before seeing Melody. As she returned to her office, Charlotte was still on an odd high, physical—because she was still wet—but her mind was foggy, too, like the aftereffects of too many margaritas the night before, not a hangover so much as a dreamy quality. Exactly as if she'd just had really good sex.

She gulped down two swallows of a fizzy juice drink she'd left on her desk, and the carbonation actually helped. She would have signed into her email to check for his message—she couldn't wait to find out what he planned—but Melody appeared in her doorway.

"Come in. Sit down." She gestured to the chair in front of the desk. Melody sat as Charlotte closed the door.

Instead of taking the seat behind the desk, she pulled one over from the little conference table just as she had in their first meeting. She crossed her legs and leaned one elbow on the arm, propping her chin on her hand, smiling, all very informal.

Melody stared at the carpet, her lips flat, neither an answering smile nor a frown. She wore the same brown hoodie and the ubiquitous frayed jeans, though whether they were the same pair or another Charlotte couldn't tell. Her hair hung limply, falling across her face. Perhaps the fact that her hair was oily added to her acne problem, but Charlotte knew better than to suggest that.

"So tell me how things are. Anything new?" Would Melody talk about her confrontation with Eric this morning? Or would Charlotte have to pry the information out of her?

"The same," she answered simply.

"How was your weekend?"

Melody cocked her head and eyed Charlotte briefly. As if she couldn't believe Charlotte had asked or was even interested. "Fine."

"Did you do anything special?"

Melody grimaced and shook her head slightly in bewilderment. "I watched a bunch of classic movies."

"Really? Which ones?" Charlotte was not a classic movie buff, but she'd seen the biggies like *Casablanca*, *Gone With the Wind*, and *Psycho*.

"It was a Joan Crawford marathon." Melody smiled, although it came off as more of a grimace, and added, "They topped it off with *Mommie Dearest*."

"Faye Dunaway was amazing," Charlotte said, wondering if the choice of movie to mention was significant. *Mommie Dearest*. Was it a metaphor for Melody's life?

"She was a sicko."

Charlotte had always wondered how much of that story was true, how much of it hype. It was so easy to pick on dead people, especially movie stars. "She was definitely a piece of work."

Melody opened her mouth, closed it, narrowing her eyes. "And no, my mother isn't Mommie Dearest. She doesn't go crazy about wire hangers or beat me."

"I'm glad to hear that." If that kind of thing had been going on, signs would most likely have cropped up before, not suddenly over the summer. "How has your morning been?"

Melody puffed out a breath. "Why don't you just ask me straight out?"

"About what?" Charlotte said oh-so-innocently.

"It's obvious that you know."

Charlotte decided to stop playing. "I heard that you accosted Eric Collins' backpack. You could get suspended if you keep up this kind of behavior."

The girl shrugged. "So fine. Suspend me."

"No, Melody, I don't want to see that happen. Right now, I'm more interested in why you did it. And why you poured the contents of your beaker over his head."

Melody was silent. Charlotte shifted, sitting straighter and leaning in to see Melody's face more clearly beneath the fall of her hair. "He used to be your boyfriend in middle school, didn't he?"

"No," she shot out. "He was never my boyfriend."

"Then what was he?"

"He's just a kid in the neighborhood. We used to play together and were in the same class in grade school. We were just friends. He was never my *boyfriend*," she claimed with a sarcastic intonation.

"Then why are you so angry with him, Melody? What happened?"

"Nothing *happened*. We just grew up. And he turned into a total dick."

Charlotte decided not to correct the language. She didn't want to stifle the girl now, not if she wanted to learn more. "What did he do that made him a total dick?"

"He's just like all the others."

"How is he like everyone else?"

Melody shoved her hair aside and glared at Charlotte. "He called me Mudly like they all do. So I poured the sugar water over his head." She smiled, an evil cast to it. "And I enjoyed it. Detention was worth the look on his face. I'd do it again just for that."

"And you dumped the contents of his backpack on the ground because . . . ?" She let the question hang.

"He called me a bitch."

"So you punished him."

"Yes." The word was almost a snarl.

Kids didn't go from being best friends to insulting each other without some inciting incident. Or maybe several. Though she couldn't rule out peer pressure either. Teenagers started high school among a whole new set of people, older kids they wanted to impress. When other people made fun of Melody, a weak boy might feel he had to follow suit.

"Melody, it only seems logical that something occurred before Eric called you Mudly and a bitch."

"Right. So it ends up being my fault." Melody sneered at her.

"I can't help you if I don't know the whole story." Charlotte paused.

"I never asked for your help," the girl snapped. "I don't need it."

"If you don't tell me, I'll have to ask Eric."

The girl's lips pinched. "Fine. Go ahead and ask him. I don't care what he says."

Charlotte waited, adding nothing.

The silence worked. "I don't want your pity," Melody burst out. "I'm flat-chested and I'm ugly, and I don't need you to feel sorry for me." She leaned forward, cupped her barely there breasts. "I'll grow a pair of these next year, and all the boys will be hot for me."

"It isn't about all the boys being hot for you."

"Then what is it about? High school is just one big popularity contest. You're either in or you're out. Bet you were in, weren't you, Miss Moore," Melody jibed.

"Actually I was a nerd. People made fun of me for studying too much. But I had a really good friend, and we always supported each other no matter what."

"Well, goodie for you. I don't have any friends."

"What about the kids you knew in middle school?"

"There was just—" She stopped.

"There was just . . . Eric? He was the only friend that mattered?" Charlotte asked softly.

Suddenly Melody's face crumpled. Two fat tears welled up, fell over the brim, and rolled down her blemished cheeks. She wiped one track away with the sleeve of her sweatshirt.

"It's okay, Melody. You can tell me."

More tears fell. She scrubbed them away. "I hate high school," she whispered.

"Most of us do." Charlotte's hadn't been unhappy, but honestly, she'd never want to be a teenager again either.

"Right, like you ever had big problems besides being called a nerd," Melody muttered.

Twenty years could certainly put it all in perspective, but Melody was too young to understand that now, and any words Charlotte said would be nothing more than trite.

"Why are you butting in anyway?" The girl's mistrust had resurfaced.

"I just want to talk, Melody. I'll listen to whatever you have to say."

"Yeah. Because it's your *job*." She emphasized the last word with disgust. "Well, I don't need to talk. And I gotta go. I'm going to be late." She grabbed her backpack off the floor and stomped to the door, flinging it open so hard it banged into the back of the chair she'd just vacated.

"I'd like you to come back on Thursday at the same time," Charlotte called as the girl stepped into the hall.

"I've got a dentist appointment," she tossed the words over her shoulder.

"Then let's make it next Tuesday."

"Fine. Whatever." Melody disappeared down the hall.

Grilling her hadn't gotten any answers. Empathy hadn't encouraged her to open up either. Charlotte's next move was risky. It could backfire and alienate Melody completely, despite the fact that the girl had given a grudging agreement. But there were always two sides to every story, and since Melody wasn't talking, Charlotte would have to get the other side from Eric Collins.

AT A FEW MINUTES BEFORE TEN IN THE EVENING, A BRISK WIND blew off the San Francisco Bay. Charlotte pulled her calf-length coat tighter around her, but goose bumps pebbled her bare legs. Her high heels clicked loudly on the concrete. A couple of cars still pockmarked the lot of Lookout Point, and she knew to whom the big black sedan belonged. Off to her right, headlights flashed along the San Mateo Bridge and on the other side of the bay, inky black at this time of night, the lights of Hayward and San Leandro twinkled. Overhead a jet roared its approach to the airport. Despite the noise, the county park with its paved walk was a haven for runners and dog walkers during daylight hours, but after dark, it was practically deserted. Which was exactly why Lance had chosen the location, she was sure.

His email had arrived in her in-box at two thirty. He'd told her when to meet him, where, and what to wear. After that, she couldn't concentrate on a single thing. Thank goodness she'd already had Mrs. Rivers send Eric Collins a note to come to Charlotte's office on Thursday morning. She'd wanted to meet with him today, but his class schedule was full.

She focused on the outline of a tall man standing at the rail. He was well outside the pool of light from lampposts on either side, and behind him, the waves of the bay crashed on the rocks.

She didn't pick up her pace. In fact, she slowed slightly, allowing a little more sway to her hips. As she closed in on him, she saw that he stood with arms folded over his chest and feet crossed at the ankles as he leaned nonchalantly against the railing.

"Miss Moore, I see you found a most appropriate coat. You follow instructions well."

It was long, flowing, and warm, exactly what she needed out here along the bay. "I thought you were going to make me come to your house, only to let me go at midnight." Like Cinderella.

"Perhaps next time," he said.

"Only if I'm bad."

He chuckled. "You can't help yourself." He held out a hand. "Come here."

She stopped when she was close enough for the wind to swirl aftershave and his musky male scent around her.

"Open the coat," he ordered.

They were alone. Whoever owned the other car in the lot was as invisible to her as she and Lance would be to them, lost in the darkness between the light posts.

She parted the lapels, the cool night air a shock to her flesh.

"Perfect," he murmured, his gaze on her nipples, his fingers only a touch away. "All that pretty, naked skin."

Those had been his instructions. The high heels, the coat, nothing else, not a stitch. Hands at her waist, he reeled her in until their bodies were separated by mere inches.

"I thought about this all afternoon." His breath was sweet with mint.

So had she. Wondering what he'd planned. She'd thought he would be waiting in his car for her. She imagined him laying her down on the back seat. Or pulling her onto his lap.

The pads of his fingers were slightly rough against her skin, and hot. Or maybe she was just cold.

"Now what, Principal Hutton? I'm not sure how this is going to be punishment."

He laughed softly again. "Everything doesn't have to be punishment. Sometimes it's just about obeying my whims."

"And what is your whim?"

"Hold your coat against my arms so the wind doesn't get inside."

She cocooned herself with him inside the jacket.

Leaning in, he whispered against her hair. "Spread your legs for me."

Right here? "But someone could come by. There was another car in the lot."

"All they'll see is a man and woman embracing."

She'd never had public sex, but its allure made her wet even as the risk pushed her heart to a faster beat. "You are a very bad man, Principal Hutton."

"And you're a very bad girl." He leaned back to reveal the spark in his dark eyes.

Then his hand was between her legs. Charlotte groaned, closed her eyes, shivered with the exquisite roughness of his fingers against her clitoris. He circled the nub, seduced her, drew forth another flood of moisture.

"You are so damn wet." He slid a digit inside her, found her G-spot, rubbed it gently, the slow stroke driving her almost to the brink. "This was what you wanted me to do this morning in my office, wasn't it, Miss Moore." There was no question in that statement.

"God, yes." She gasped as he added his thumb to the rhythm, doubling the sensation, taking her on the inside, the outside. She was so wet he glided easily over her flesh.

"Did you want me to make you come this morning, Miss Moore?"

"Yes, yes." She panted.

"Right there in my office?"

"You know I did." She sucked in a breath, let it out with a low moan, almost a growl.

"Such a risk-taker."

"Just like you, doing this to me out here." She squeezed her eyes tight as heat began to build deep inside her, spreading out, to her limbs, her skin. She was no longer cold. She burned for him.

"Are you afraid someone will see?"

In this moment, she didn't care. If they ended up in jail, so what? She gasped, shuddered, quivered, and rocked with him, adding her own motion to the heady mix.

"How sexy it would be to take you in front of an audience, Miss Moore. Or to watch you with another man."

Her legs trembled, her knees felt weak. She clutched the coat tightly around his arms. His words reminded her of something, someone. What? God, it didn't matter now.

"Don't scream, Miss Moore. Someone's coming. Don't make a sound."

She couldn't help herself. She opened her mouth, a cry welling up in her throat even as the climax began with a rumble, then a roar. Or maybe that was another jet overhead. His mouth covered hers, swallowed the sounds, swallowed her orgasm, possessed her, made her his slave.

SHE WAS AMAZING, GAME FOR ANYTHING, AND SHE TURNED HIM inside out when she opened her eyes to gaze up at him with sultry satisfaction.

"Such a dirty man. I'm shocked, Principal Hutton. Right out here in the open." She rubbed against his hard cock.

"You didn't want to spend the night. This assured the impossibility of that."

"Hold my coat in place." Heh, now she was issuing the orders.

When he tugged the collar closed, she drew her hands in and wriggled out of the arms.

"What are you doing, Miss Moore?"

She unzipped his slacks. "You don't think I'm going to let you have all the fun, do you?" She released him from the confines of his briefs.

"Jesus." He sucked in a breath. "Your hand is cold."

"Your cock is hot." She squeezed. "And extremely hard." She fluttered her eyelashes at him. "You've been thinking about me all day, Principal Hutton?"

He laughed hoarsely. "Fuck yes."

She stroked expertly. No woman had ever tempted him the way she did. How could he have waited three long years to take advantage of her?

She cupped his balls, and his world seemed to shrink down to just the feel of her hand on him, her seductive scent mesmerizing him, the ache building in his gut. A shadow ran by, man and dog, disappearing into the night, and Lance didn't care if they were seen.

"So who's the master here, Principal Hutton?" She swirled a drop of pre-come around the tip of his cock, used it to lubricate her strokes.

"You are, and you fucking know it." A deep groan rose from his belly, and his hands fisted tightly in the lapels of her coat. He'd never had anything like this, never touched a woman like her. It was more than a simple hand job. It was that she made a hand job the most important thing in the world, like a teenage boy touched by a girl for the first time, all new, all exciting, rushing him to the edge in a matter of seconds.

"Would you fuck me right here if I told you to?" she whispered.

"Christ. Yes. Please."

A great roar started in his head, made his body tremble. He put his head back, stared at the plane far above them, feeling the vibrations through his entire body.

"You'd do anything I say," she whispered. He shouldn't have been able to hear, but it was as if the words were inside his head.

He rocked to the rhythm of her hand. "Yes. Anything."

She teased and stroked, twisted and caressed. Sensation shot down to his balls, exploded out to his extremities, and he shouted. If not for the thunder of the plane, the world would have heard his climax.

He jetted, jerked, pulsed, throbbed, on and on, as if he were that same teenage boy, now totally out of control. Then finally he could breathe again, but all he could manage was a hoarse "Fuck."

She leaned back slightly. "Look at that, you dirty man. You made a mess all over me."

In the darkness of her voluminous coat, he couldn't see it, but the scent of come rose to his nostrils. Her hand moved, the back of it brushing his still semi-erect cock.

"I'll just have to rub it in," she said. "It's all slippery." Her hand circled and swirled around, rising to her breasts, rubbing his come there as well. Then she raised her fingers to her mouth and licked them, her gaze on his, her eyes beguiling him. "Yum," she mouthed, smiled, then went back to rubbing and stroking herself.

The act was sexy as hell, intimate in an elemental way. She wasn't afraid of his come, loved it, wanted it, massaged it into her skin. Even the taste didn't repel her. It was more than a woman swallowing a man's come during a blow job. His first wife had kept a box of mints on the side table. But Charlotte *loved* it. He'd never had a sexual partner like her, so sensual, so passionate, so in love with everything about the sex act, the tastes, the scents, the sensations. He was enthralled with her sensuality.

The words were on the tip of his tongue. *Come home with me. Stay with me.* But while she loved the act, she didn't want the intimacy. She wouldn't spend the night. Hell, she probably wouldn't even have dinner with him.

There was only one way to shut himself up. He cupped her cheek with one hand, holding the coat in place with the other, and lowered his lips to hers, took her mouth, tasted himself. It wasn't repellent. It was hot as Hades. She was his devil, tempting him.

Then she was tucking him back into his trousers, zipping up, patting him down. "I'm really going to need my beauty sleep tonight, Principal Hutton."

Come home with me.

"Well, at least you've had your beauty lotion," he said instead.

She laughed. Christ, even her laugh made his cock jerk with renewed desire. "I've heard it said that come is very good for the skin."

"And here I thought you simply wanted my scent on you when you woke up in the middle of the night."

She cocked her head slightly, batted her lashes, but didn't answer as she wriggled her arms back into her sleeves. Holding the coat tightly closed, she stepped back, putting cold air and space between them. "I think you're the one who's going to wake up in the middle of the night to taste me on your fingers."

He would. No doubt about it. He would think about her all tomorrow, too, then into the night again. He was on her skin, but she was definitely under his.

10

CHARLOTTE SLEPT NAKED. SHE HADN'T SHOWERED WHEN SHE arrived home after leaving Lance. She couldn't bear to wash him off. His come wasn't sticky; it was delicious. Once in bed, she pushed the covers aside so the scent of him filled the room, filled her head.

She was in control. Completely. Sure, at the moment of climax, she'd thought of herself as his slave, but then she'd switched everything around on him, turned him into *her* slave, forced him to admit he'd do anything for her.

Putting her hand between her legs, she caressed herself as his medley of aromas surrounded her.

This wasn't obsession, it was perfection. She ran a flourishing therapy practice, she helped kids as a guidance counselor, and now this. They were consenting adults, they didn't have sex at work—she didn't count that first time after detention, since she'd never even raised her skirt—and truly, no justification necessary, it would work wonders with her practice. In the heat of the moment, he'd suggested having an audience and even watching her with other men. A rush of moisture flooded her fingers, and she dug her heels into the mattress, arching into her touch.

On show for him. The thought made her hot and wet. It proved how powerful fantasy could be. It worked for her. It could work for Jeanine and her husband. Charlotte felt that truth deep in her core as her pussy contracted, her orgasm building. She imagined people watching as the principal filled her, thrusting deep. Doggy style. God. She tossed her head on the pillow, heat rushing through her body. Then she imagined Principal Hutton standing over the bed, pointing, directing. *Fuck her hard,* she heard him whisper. *Make her come.* Charlotte hit her climax, crying out, rolling and clamping her thighs tight around her hand, riding the wave of bliss.

When it was over, she spread out bonelessly on the bed. God. So good. It was one thing to tell Jeanine to experiment with fantasy. It was quite another to experience the wonders of fantasizing. Just add a little kink, not much, a little risky business, a shot of sexy role playing, and it worked miracles.

"WE NEED TO CONSIDER INSTITUTING SCHOOL UNIFORMS."

Lance barely suppressed an eye roll. There were a lot of things he'd rather be doing, the most delightful being a review of last night's spectacular adventure with Charlotte. Unfortunately, he had a lunch meeting.

Once a month David Smith, chairman of the district's school board, invited him to lunch for what Smith liked to call "a state of the union" discussion. They ate at the country club, the dues of which Lance suspected were charged off as a school-board expense.

Smith was in his early fifties with a thick head of silver hair and good looks that appealed to the ladies, though the growing inner tube around his midsection, revealed when he unbuttoned his suit jacket, indicated too many country club lunches with cream sauce.

Lance took a healthy swallow of his seltzer water before answering. He'd ordered a grilled chicken salad in deference to his last cholesterol test. His vision of his future did not include a heart attack, or an inner tube around his middle, for that matter.

With the water glass back on the immaculate white table-cloth, he said, "I see no need for it at this point. We don't have any gang colors infiltrating the student body, and requiring uniforms would put an undue burden on many of our parents."

Smith sipped his scotch and soda. "On the contrary, it actually saves money when parents don't have to put out for the latest fashion fad. Besides, it's not like we're an inner-city school district." The word *poor* being left out of the phrase.

Lance's district comprised an affluent area of the San Francisco Peninsula, and the schools were highly regarded. Indeed, many parents moved here just for the educational system. Smith's own children attended the district's public schools—it wouldn't do for the chairman to send his kids to private school—a stepson in high school and two younger children in the middle and elementary grades. Lance's school had no gang troubles, no severe drug problems, no real disciplinary issues other than the usual minor infractions of the sort Charlotte encountered in detention hall the previous week. He saw no need for instituting uniforms. The suggestion was simply a ploy to show that Smith was trying to stay in touch with the community's needs. The man would be better off spending less on monthly lunches and using the money for improving the classrooms. Not that Lance felt his students lacked anything. He monitored the budget with close scrutiny and questioned any superfluous spending.

"The school board believes that uniforms improve the appearance of the entire student body. No more midriff-baring T-shirts or short-shorts." Smith dabbed at a bit of Alfredo sauce on his chin.

"We don't have bare midriffs or butt cheeks." Lance enforced a dress code. No bare stomachs or exposed cheeks, or cracks, for that matter. "I'm not taking action against a nonissue."

Smith harrumphed. "Well, the board might consider it for the next school year."

Lance would make sure the board didn't. The uniforms were probably a bug up only one ass—David Smith's—and the remainder of the board would be glad to dispense with the issue.

Smith slapped the table as if closing that discussion. "Now what do you think of Alexander's proposal for a bond measure to build a new library?"

In an unfortunate accident, fire had gutted the elementary school library during the summer. Principal Alexander had designs for an entirely new library building that would include a computer lab. In theory, not a terrible idea. In practice, totally unnecessary. "The insurance payout covers a complete overhaul and the restocking of every damaged book. There's no need to go to the voters for a bond."

"But we need a computer lab."

"Then don't try to fool the taxpayers into believing the existing building isn't usable or that the insurance won't cover the costs of repairs and restocking." The details were in the fine print of the bond proposal, but what the voters would hear was a sob story about the poor students who were without any books or resources. What hadn't been publicized was that grade school students had been granted access to both the high school and middle school libraries for any research needs they might have in the interim. The arrangement had actually increased traffic through the libraries. All three schools were in basically the same complex, the elementary school on the other side of the football field and the middle school across the street.

"We're not *fooling* anyone," Smith stressed. "We're simply seeking to upgrade our facilities."

"There is no money."

"Which is why we need a bond." If approved, the measure would show up on the June ballot.

"But interest needs to be paid on a bond." Did Smith need an economics lesson? Floating a bond wasn't free. You got the money now, but you had to pay later.

"You're standing in the way of progress, Hutton."

He was standing in the way of bankrupting the school district, the county, and the state of California. "I'm not backing it," he said unequivocally. "We don't need it."

Smith opened his mouth, closed it, rolled his lips between his teeth, then puffed them back out. He resembled a fish. "Let's move on for now." He smiled his politician's smile. "Have you considered our last discussion?"

"Which part of it?" Lance knew which part.

"The school board needs a good man like you. It's the next step. It would give you the chance to influence all these decisions. You'd have my full support in the election."

Despite his battles with the board over issues like school uniforms and a gratuitous new library, Lance did not view becoming a member of the school board as an advancement. Being the principal, he protected his students from bad decisions. He was in the trenches with them daily. It was where he wanted to be, not out playing politician. And he was very good at influencing school-board resolutions right from the principal's office.

"Thanks, but no thanks." Which was the same answer he'd given last month. And the month before that. He figured the only reason Smith wanted him on the board was because the man believed Lance would then be under his thumb. No way. He would never be anyone's toady, and certainly not Smith's.

The waiter arrived, cleared their plates, offered the dessert menu. Lance waved him away. "I need to return to school," he told Smith. The lunch had gone on long enough, and the school was where he belonged. Of course, he'd need to make a few calls to the other board members, do a little backslapping and influencing of his own.

"THANK YOU FOR COMING TO SEE ME, ERIC." CHARLOTTE SMILED encouragingly.

"You're welcome."

Hmm. A polite boy, handsome, too, with blue eyes and blond hair cut relatively short. The only strike against him in the teenage world was his height. He couldn't have been more than five-three. Being only a freshman, he would probably still have a growth spurt, but for now, he looked like he should be in middle school. He was dressed neatly in a blue shirt and jeans that fit, were free of holes, and hadn't been washed so many times they were threadbare. Of course, kids could buy them that way right off the rack.

"Have a seat." Charlotte closed the door and sat next to him.

"I know why I'm here," he said. Charlotte's office was warm and he removed his jacket, folding it on his lap. "Melody told me you'd be calling me in."

Now that was unexpected. So they were actually talking.

"What did she say?"

"She said I could tell you whatever I wanted to, it didn't matter to her. But I suppose you're interested in why she poured the water on my head."

He was direct, she'd give him that. "She said you called her Mudly."

He laughed without a trace of humor. "I did."

She knew there was far more to the story. "And?"

"My mom says you should turn the other cheek. But my dad says you can't let people walk all over you"—he glanced at her and added—"my real dad, not my stepdad"—as if that made a difference. "I don't know how you're supposed to do both."

It was a thoughtful statement that deserved a thoughtful answer. "To me, it's a matter of using the politest possible terms to tell people when they do something wrong or hurtful."

He smiled softly, and Charlotte liked him. He was a good kid, she knew it instinctively.

"I guess I wasn't polite enough," he said, looking through Charlotte's half-closed blinds. "But she can be so mean, just picking and snapping and making a guy feel like an idiot. So I asked her why she was treating me like dirt." He gave an eloquent teenage shrug. "Then I told her that maybe she really was Mudly just like everyone says."

Despite the shrug, he wasn't your typical teenage boy. She'd found the majority of students were closer to Melody on the communication spectrum, unwilling to talk candidly with an adult, unless it was about college or football. Which worked for her, since she normally counseled pupils on career choices and suitable universities. But it was as if Eric Collins had needed to talk and no one was willing to listen until now. She barely had to prompt him.

"I just wanted to talk to her this morning. Tell her I was sorry. I asked her if we could have lunch sometime." He shook his head, as if the world of teenage girls totally baffled him. "And she got all uppity. She said she didn't need my pity." He looked at Charlotte.

"That wasn't why I asked her. But then she made me mad, and I said it was hard to pity someone who was a total bitch." His lips twisted in a wry smile. "So she grabbed my backpack."

Melody hadn't lied about what happened. She'd merely said as little as possible. Maybe to her it was the truth. Eric had called her Mudly, and she'd dumped a beaker on him. He'd called her a total bitch, and she'd thrown his backpack on the ground.

"She never used to be like this. We were friends. She was nice. We've lived in the same neighborhood and been in the same class since my mom and stepdad got married. I . . . she . . . we . . ." He clamped his lips shut.

Charlotte leaned in. "You like her a lot," she said softly.

"Used to," he said with equal softness.

"Not anymore?"

"She makes it too hard."

"You know, she might not even hear how bad it sounds when she's snapping at you or making you feel like an idiot."

He curled his lip slightly. "How could she not know?"

"Sometimes we're in pain and that's all we understand. We take everything that anyone else says the wrong way. We don't see how bad our own behavior is."

"I never said anything about her face. Not once. I didn't even look at it. I pretended it didn't exist. But that was never good enough for her. It was like she *wanted* me to say something." He shook his head slowly. "Probably so she'd have a reason to slam me down."

"Maybe she thought you didn't know *she* existed anymore."

He huffed out a great breath. "Well, a guy can only take so much, then he's gotta stand up for himself."

Jeanine Smith could take lessons from this kid. "Don't give up on her yet."

Eric looked at her, his eyes the deep blue of a cloudless sky. "I didn't give up. She did."

CHARLOTTE SAT AT HER DESK A LONG TIME AFTER ERIC LEFT. SHE didn't have another student meeting for half an hour.

When she was ten, she'd had a huge fight with her best friend, Sharon. They'd borrowed each other's clothes, played dolls, swam in Sharon's parents' pool every day in the summer. They were inseparable at school, eating lunch together, sharing the same seat on the bus. Then one day, Charlotte had marched over to Sharon's house and stuffed the shorts she'd borrowed into the mailbox. They didn't speak for over a year despite the fact that they'd lived only half a block from each other and rode the same school bus every day. For the life of her, Charlotte couldn't remember what the argument had been about. She simply remembered the birthday party they'd both attended one year later. Sharon had walked up to her, said hello, and suddenly they were best friends again, until Sharon's family moved to Chicago.

When you were young, small things, an unkind word, a snarky remark, a thoughtless action, could seem so important. Charlotte snorted aloud. Hell, that happened even when you were old and should know better. The thing she remembered most was that she'd regretted the year she'd lost with Sharon. She'd missed all the games and the secrets and the laughter.

She didn't want Melody and Eric to have that same regret.

"Are you daydreaming on duty, Miss Moore?"

Lance filled her doorway. The sight of him, big, solid, handsome, sexy, made her realize she didn't want to regret missing a moment with him. It would come to an end soon enough—they were too different, incompatible, he was too old for her, et cetera, et cetera—but until then, she was going to savor each encounter.

"Fuck you, Principal Hutton," she said softly enough to contain the word within the confines of her office.

He closed the door, just the way she'd hoped he would, and stood towering over her on the other side of the desk. She really did love his height. "On Tuesday it was lewd behavior in my office," he began.

"Not to mention all that lewd behavior at Lookout Point." She was feeling giddy with his scent permeating the small office.

He parted his jacket to jam his hands on his hips. "Lewd behavior, provocative attire, inappropriate language, Miss Moore, it's beyond the pale."

She wondered where the old expression had come from. "It most certainly is. I'm at your disposal for punishment tonight. What time shall I come to your house?"

"I'll come to yours. At seven o'clock."

Her stomach sank. "But—" Her house was teeny-tiny and hopelessly out of date compared to his.

"That way you can throw me out when we're done."

"What if you refuse to go?"

He smiled, a spark in his dark eyes. "That was one of your limits. I can't very well ignore a limit since I told you to set them."

What had she just been thinking? She didn't want any regrets. She didn't want to miss a moment. She didn't want to look back on this short period and say *I wish I'd done this or that.*

"Fine." She leaned forward, grabbed a notepad. "Here's my address. But don't forget that at midnight you turn into a pumpkin and roll out of my house."

She felt his laughter deep inside her chest long after he'd left.

11

LANCE HAD NEVER MET A WOMAN WHOSE COME-ON LINES WERE *fuck you* and *cocksucker*. But when Charlotte wanted sex—or punishment—she had a mouth her mother would have surely washed out with soap when she was a child.

Her home was in a tidy little neighborhood built in the late forties. The streets were laid out in a grid pattern and named after trees. Neat houses with clipped lawns and manicured hedges lined the sidewalks, and those that hadn't been remodeled came from a time of one-car garages. An economy model he recognized as hers sat in the driveway. Her home was fronted by a stoop edged with flower pots and a bay window covered by lace curtains behind which she'd closed the blinds. He couldn't see a thing inside.

She opened the front door before he rang the bell. His breath caught in his throat. Her sweet little rump was covered in the tightest pair of short-shorts imaginable, and the top bared her midriff almost to her bountiful breasts. Smith would have gone apoplectic and demanded school uniforms even for the staff.

Hand on the door, she fluttered her eyelashes at him. "You accused me of provocative attire, but since I don't recall wearing anything provocative, I thought I'd better make up for it."

"Slut," he muttered, infusing the word with heat that had nothing to do with anger or disgust.

"Why thank you, Principal Hutton." She stepped back to let him in, then closed the door.

"What would you call your attire the other night if not provocative?" he said. "Nothing more than a coat and shoes, completely naked underneath."

"You ordered me to wear it." Her makeup was heavy, dark liner, penciled eyebrows, deep crimson lips. She was too sexy for words.

"You could have said no."

"Then you'd have had to punish me even more."

He advanced on her, backing her into the room. "Oh, Miss Moore," he said softly, "I don't need any extra excuses to punish you."

She raised one brow and put a finger to his chest, holding him off. "This is my house, Principal. And my rules."

The touch of her finger was like a brand. Though he towered over her, she held all the power. And he was sure she loved it. "I don't recall that being part of the bargain."

She smiled with those kissable crimson lips. "I must have forgotten to mention that. But I've got a plan for tonight."

He realized then that candles flickered on the mantel. The fire was lit, probably in deference to the brevity of her outfit. She must have rearranged the furniture slightly because a chair didn't face the TV, but was instead turned toward the sofa beneath the bay window. On a small table beside the chair, she'd set out a glass of wine, and next to that, a vibrator standing on its base.

His heart started to hammer in his chest.

"Sit," she directed. "I hope you like white wine because it was all I had."

"White is fine." Neither of them mentioned the vibrator. Sitting, he gave himself up to her plan. She wasn't a submissive. She liked to call the shots. She only let him play at being the dom when it suited her. Lance didn't care. He wanted whatever she had planned for him.

She reached for a wineglass on the coffee table, then curled into the corner of the couch. The shirt was cut low as well as short, and she was more skin than clothing. He felt a rise in his jeans.

"So, the other night you mentioned having me in front of an audience"—her lipstick glistened with wine—"and also watching me with other men."

The thought had popped out in the moment. He might have led a vanilla life, but he was a red-blooded male and he'd wondered what a threesome would be like. Not that he would actually give her to other men the way that woman in the sex shop had suggested. No way. But he sure as hell could fantasize about it. He could imagine anything where Charlotte was concerned. "I believe I mentioned something like that."

"Then I think I should tell you the things I used to do with one of my boyfriends."

"If you feel it's necessary." He felt a little kick, a tightening in his groin. He'd never questioned his wives or girlfriends about their pasts. It was a don't-ask-don't-tell society. But as always, she was nothing like other women.

She licked her lips, shifted her legs, drawing his attention to the creamy smoothness of her thighs. "Well, since you're dying to know—"

Yes, he was dying to know. What had this extraordinary woman done?

"—he used to send me out to have sex with other men." She smiled, sipped, let him digest, then she added, "Sometimes he liked me to call him right in the middle of the act."

"Jesus" was all he could say. It was like phone sex. Only better.

"We'd go to hotel bars and pick out a man together. Then he'd stay there having a drink while I went upstairs. Sometimes I'd call him. Sometimes I'd make him wait until I came back down." She smiled a sultry smile. "Then I'd tell him detail by detail. And he'd kiss me, taste the other man on me." She dropped her voice to a whisper. "A couple of times he came up to the room after the man had left and licked me clean." She emphasized with a sweep of her tongue across her luscious lips.

He swallowed with difficulty.

"Have some wine," she urged.

He drank thirstily. He imagined her on a bed, her legs spread, her boyfriend between them. He didn't know why it turned him on. It was the fantasy. The ultimate cuckold. The kinkiness.

"Take off your top," he demanded.

She drew it over her head, tossed it aside, her hair cascading down like a cloud around her face and shoulders. The bra was see-through lace, her nipples dark and tight beneath. He wanted to suck them.

"What else did you do?" He was embarrassed to hear that his voice cracked.

"He made me take pictures to show him."

Christ, did she still have them? "Get rid of the shorts."

She unsnapped the waist and wriggled them down her legs,

rolling her panties off as well. She was naked but for the sexy see-through bra. He tossed her the vibrator. She caught it deftly.

"Now spread your legs, use it on yourself, and tell me the kinkiest thing he made you do."

She propped a pillow behind her head so she could still see him, put one bare foot flat on the carpet, and opened her luscious pink center to him. Christ, the woman drove him crazy, and her voice sent him into orbit.

"We picked out a man together. But we already had the room. While I was coming on to our quarry, he went up and hid in the closet, leaving the door slightly ajar so he could see everything."

She held the vibrator straight on her clit and groaned for him. "He'd told me exactly where I was supposed to lay on the bed so he could see the guy enter me. He wanted to see his cock filling me."

He couldn't imagine any man devising such a plan, but his cock was harder than the marble of her fireplace mantel.

She arched into the vibrator, twirling it slowly, expertly around the turgid button of her clit. She was pink, plump, so aroused that moisture coated her thighs.

"I let the man fuck me. He was huge. He did me doggy because it was easier to take all of him." She gasped, panted, moaned, then reached down to shove the vibrator deep inside.

His ears roared. He needed her bad. But he wanted her story first.

"My boyfriend took a video of the whole thing. Every second." She made a keening sound as if she were on the edge of orgasm. Her pussy seemed to pulse. "When the guy was about to come, I made him pull out, rip off the condom, and come all over my ass. Oh God." She cried out, unintelligible words.

Christ, she couldn't stop now. He lunged for the couch. "More."

"I—I—" She panted, tossed her head on the pillow, worked the vibrator in, out, back up to her clit, around.

He tore the condom packet he'd had in his pocket, ripped at the buttons of his jeans. "Tell me," he demanded, his voice harsh with need.

She opened her eyes. "I made him leave. And my boyfriend came out." Her body jerked.

Lance was ready, the condom in place. He tore the vibrator from her hand and plunged deep.

Charlotte cried out, clutched his shoulders as he took her relentlessly.

"More," he insisted.

The rest of the story came out between her pants. "My boyfriend hooked the camera up to the TV. He played the video while he licked all the come off."

Holy hell. Lance felt himself losing his mind, losing himself in her. She was crazy. Kinky. He couldn't get enough.

"Then he entered me right when the guy was coming all over me on-screen. He fucked me until we passed out."

Her body contracted around him, dragged him deep, pulled him under, and Lance shouted his release. The woman made him lose his mind. And he didn't give a damn.

Though he was crushing her, he couldn't move for long moments afterward. He wanted to stay inside her forever. He was hooked on her.

"You are the dirtiest girl I have ever met, Miss Moore."

Her chest quivered with silent laughter. "I most certainly am," she said, only a slight strain in her voice from his weight on her.

He moved, pulled out, asked, "Bathroom?"

She pointed down the hall. Opposite the living room through an archway was a small dining room with a table and four chairs and a door into the kitchen. He caught a glimpse of black-and-

white tile. The bathroom was the first door on the left, while farther down lay another opening to the kitchen.

The bathroom was tiled completely in pink and gray, the
floor, countertops, the walls above the bath. It was probably the
original scheme, but had been kept in immaculate shape. He got
rid of the condom, washed his hands. And looked at himself in
the mirror.

He'd be fifty in less than a year and a half. She was still a
couple of years shy of forty. He bore years of lines on his face. She
was still smooth and supple. He didn't let his thoughts drift to the
inevitable conclusion. She was amazing, unlike any woman he'd
had, probably unlike anyone he would ever have in his bed. She
was changing his view, opening him up. God, she was even teach-
ing him things. It didn't matter how much older he was.

He found her sprawled on the sofa exactly the way he'd left
her. Only Charlotte could have lain there so unself-consciously.
Her skin was creamy and smooth, her dark makeup sexy, her
breasts mouthwatering, and the trimmed thatch of red hair
between her legs beckoned him.

She smiled when she saw him. "Did you like my story?"

"Fuck yes." He liked the ability to use dirty words with her.

"It made you hot, didn't it?"

"Were you in doubt?"

"No." She shook her head, her hair flowing across the cushion. "What if it was just a fantasy? Would you still have liked it?"

He grabbed the wineglass off the table and sat on the end of
the couch, his hand on her leg. "Were you lying, Miss Moore?"

He drank the wine. He should have known. Even Charlotte
would probably draw the line at that level of kink.

She widened her eyes. "I didn't lie. I made up a story. And it
got you incredibly hot."

He wasn't sure if he preferred that it were true. The thought of this wild woman picking out other men with her boyfriend, yes, God, it had made him hard. But he was already recharging simply with the thought of the other things her mind conjured. She was one surprise after another.

Yet she had lied.

"Lying is a punishable offense."

She pushed herself up on her elbows. "Fantasy, not lying."

In a quick move, he grabbed her ankles and flipped her. "Lying requires a spanking."

He wanted to spank her. Badly. He wanted to feel her body tremble when he followed a swat with a delicious foray into her wet heat.

She cried out with the first smack on her pert ass. He pulled her to the edge of the sofa until her knees were on the floor and her pussy exposed, her ass high, tempting. Then he began the spanking in earnest.

CHARLOTTE CURLED HER FINGERS INTO THE COUCH CUSHIONS and moaned loudly.

"You never learn, Miss Moore."

Oh, she learned all right. She knew exactly how to goad him. "It's not my fault, Principal Hutton." It was all her fault. She loved the slap of his hand, the ripple of it all along her flesh, the sting, the bite. And the scent of his sex all over her.

"This hurts me more than it does you, my dear."

The tremble started in her legs, rising up. He swatted her, then slid down to play with her pussy, manipulating her. She closed her eyes, buried her face against the pillow and muffled her cries. He smacked once more and she came, whimpering, crying, spasming, until she seemed to hang off the edge of the sofa, just flesh, just bones, and utterly satisfied.

Her butt tingled. Sitting on the couch beside her, he stroked the hot flesh. His touch seemed to burn.

"So," he said. "Where were we? Oh yes, you were about to tell me how on earth you came up with that kinky fantasy."

Ah, the fantasy. It had come to her in a moment of genius. She'd told Jeanine to fantasize with her husband and see if that could work for them both. It certainly generated spectacular results with Lance. But she couldn't move yet. "I haven't recovered enough to talk," she mumbled into the pillow.

He slapped her butt. A delicious tingle rippled through her, like an orgasmic aftershock.

"Sit up and answer my questions, wench," he demanded.

She rolled over to find him seated in the corner of the sofa drinking the wine. He was fully dressed. Charlotte bent down for her panties and shorts. Lance put his foot on them.

"Don't put them on. I want you just like that, only the bra." Instead of a demand, it was almost a plea.

"All right." But there was a sense of vulnerability in it, all her flaws revealed while all of his were covered up. Not that she'd noticed any flaws about the man. Unless it was his autocratic attitude. Of course, that worked perfectly for her when she wanted to be punished.

Picking up her wine, she pushed back into the opposite corner of the couch. She couldn't help tucking her legs beneath her and holding a pillow to cover her stomach.

"Tell all, dirty girl."

His words eased the slight tension. "A client told me about it." She would not reveal Jeanine's name or her situation, and Charlotte didn't consider it breaking a confidence to say she'd heard of this kind of thing in her practice. "Her husband wanted her to be with other men. It turned him on."

"What was wrong with him?"

"I don't know if anything was wrong with him."

He raised a brow. "So she did it?"

"She didn't want to. My suggestion was that she create a fantasy and see if it satisfied her husband."

"You're a sly one," he said, a half smile of admiration creasing his lips. "Did that work?"

She evaded an actual lie. "You tell me. Did it work on you?"

He laughed. "Hell, yes. It was fucking amazing, Miss Moore, but part of the high was that it came out of your imagination, not something a client told you."

Charlotte began enjoying the conversation. "She didn't give me any details. Those were all mine." She tapped her temple. "Right out of here." Now she had to somehow convey to Jeanine how well it could work.

"Would you ever want to actually do it?" He was eyeing her with a darker gaze.

"I'm not sure. In a way, it's very sexy, the idea of having your husband watch you."

"What if he turned the tables and had sex with another woman in front of you?"

That had been Jeanine's fear, that her husband was suggesting it only so he could have the same freedom. "Now you see the problem. What about you? Could you let your wife be with another man?" She raised a brow. "After all, you did suggest it."

"Weren't you giving me a hand job at the time?"

Charlotte laughed. "I have no idea. I can't remember how it came up in conversation."

"It was a fantasy. Something you say in the middle of a heated moment, to make it better, hotter, sexier. But I'm too territorial to let another man touch my woman."

The words sent a thrill through her. As if she were the woman he was territorial about. It had nothing to do with wanting a relationship, of course. It was that elemental desire to feel like you were owned, body, heart, and soul. She decided against saying any of that.

"But you like the role playing, fantasizing. A lot of men don't." Here was another of Jeanine's fears. That her husband wouldn't be satisfied with pretending. But if he was willing, fantasy was amazingly potent. She'd just proven it.

Lance leaned forward, setting his now empty wineglass on the table. "My dear Miss Moore, we've been role playing all along. I'm your principal. You're my student."

She twisted her lips, shooting him a cheeky look. "It's pretty kinky."

"You don't advocate kinkiness to your clients?"

"I don't tell them *not* to be kinky. Kinky is good if it works for both parties. I say embrace your kinkiness as long as it doesn't hurt anyone. The problem is that many times one partner is coerced into playing the other partner's kinky games, and in the end, that can only spell disaster."

She thought he'd ask if that's what happened with her client, but instead he directed his question at her. "Am I coercing you?"

She leaned forward, hugging the pillow tight to her. "Am I coercing you?" she countered. "Because if I recall correctly"— and of course she did—"I was the one who told you I needed to be punished."

His mouth moved. She thought it was an answering smile. "And as I recall," he murmured, "you keep using inappropriate language and exhibiting lewd behavior so that I'm forced to punish you."

"I could stop if you want me to."

He moved in fast and grabbed the pillow, tugging it away to leave her naked from the waist down. "One of the things I like best about you is your filthy mouth, Miss Moore. Don't stop using it on me. In every way, shape, and form."

He took the wineglass from her hand and set it on the table, then hovered over her, a hot blaze in the depths of his gaze. "All this sex talk has gotten me worked up again."

He put her hand on his jeans. Good God, the man was already hard. At his age. Amazing.

"Before the clock strikes midnight and I turn into a pumpkin that has to roll out of here, I have a feeling you'll say something for which I'm going to have to teach you another lesson. Right, Miss Moore?"

God. She wanted to giggle. He actually remembered her stupid metaphor. And hell, yes, he was right. She would do something that would earn her one of his delicious lessons. "Cocksucker. Is that inappropriate enough, Principal Hutton?" She fluttered her eyelashes.

"Actually, it's the most appropriate thing you could say."

That was exactly the lesson he taught her. Not that Charlotte had a whole lot to learn in that particular area, if she did say so herself.

12

LANCE COULDN'T GET ENOUGH OF HER. IT WAS CRAZY. BUT HE adored her unconventionality. She always did something that managed to surprise him. He needed more of Miss Moore, no pun intended.

It was a Friday afternoon, the November day outside his office window blustery, the last of the students rushing to their cars or the buses or waiting for their parents to pick them up. Though it was the end of the school day, it was not the end of his day. He had work to do, but his mind kept returning to Charlotte, to last night in her house, on her couch.

In addition to his growing obsession—and not because of it—he had to admire her as well. She didn't automatically condemn her clients. He'd always thought of sex therapy as the psychologist helping the client overcome kinky tendencies, becoming *normal*. From what she said, he surmised that she was more into helping her clients accept their kinkiness as long as it hurt neither them nor their partners. The attitude was refreshing. If more people believed that, could more marriages be saved? He thought of his two failures. They had not died because of sex or a lack thereof. They had died because of an inability to talk about needs.

Charlotte allowed him freedom to explore. She loved games. Nothing was out of bounds for her. He wanted her to fulfill his fantasy. He needed it. He'd never fantasized about any student in his office. The thought had never occurred to him and never would. But he fantasized about Charlotte. He wanted the scent of her in this room. He wanted olfactory reminders of her. He wanted to sit in his chair with the door closed and remember.

He gave in to the urge he'd been holding off all day. Sending her an email, he typed out a brief list of instructions. He gave her a time and a place.

Then he buzzed Mrs. Rivers—she was always Mrs. Rivers, never first names, he wasn't even sure she had a first name—and asked her to phone in a sandwich order for him because he'd be working late.

CHARLOTTE PARKED IN THE FAR LOT OVERLOOKING THE football field. At this late hour, the school was deserted. She made her way through the dark, empty halls to his open office door. The blinds were closed, only his desk lamp was on for illumination. In the light of it, his swarthy face was as dark as the devil. The shadows gave his brow the cast of a satyr.

"You're insane," she said.

"But you're here, Miss Moore, so you must share my insanity."

She did. In the email he'd told her that the security service drove by every hour. She'd seen the small truck leave before pulling in. The clandestine nature of their meeting excited her. So did the risk.

This was not a fantasy she would advocate for clients, and she wouldn't tell Lola about it. But as soon as she'd read his email, she wanted it.

"Close the door," he ordered.

She wasn't sure exactly what he had planned. Would he spank her? He'd told her to wear a skirt, blouse, high heels, but no underwear.

Once the door was closed, he stood, rounded the desk, and moved a chair out of the way. "Pull up your skirt."

Her blood seemed to rush in her veins as she bared herself to him.

"Bend over my desk, chest flat against it, arms straight ahead."

A spanking. Like that day in detention hall.

She assumed the position, eyes closed, and steeled herself for the first blow. But the caress that came was incredibly gentle.

"You have the most beautiful ass I have ever seen, Miss Moore." He stroked her, cupped her, squeezed.

She tensed for the moment he would swat her. It was coming, she knew it. She wanted it. But she couldn't help tensing for it.

"Your pussy is so incredibly sweet." He went down on his knees behind her. She heard him breathe deeply. "Such an erotic scent." He trailed a finger down her outer lips, slipped inside, stroked, then he parted her and put his tongue against her clit.

Charlotte gasped and curled her fingers around the edge of the desk. "Oh God."

"Principal Hutton to you," he said and blew a warm breath on her. Then he licked her. He worried her clit, suckled, lapped at her opening.

Charlotte's legs began to shake. It wasn't what she'd expected at all, this sweetness, the gentle touches. He filled her with his fingers, pumped inside, stroked her G-spot. Now she was panting.

"How badly do you want it, Miss Moore?"

"Oh God, please, so bad. I need it."

Then his fingers were gone, and his tongue. She was still quivering on the edge. Until she heard the rasp of a condom wrapper.

She was so wet, he slid deep. Instead of thrusting, he leaned over her body, covering her even as he filled her.

"I want to sit in this office and see you lying on my desk." He nibbled her ear. "I want to close my eyes and smell you all over it." He tongued the shell and she shivered. "When you come in here to talk business, I want to look at you and know you're remembering that I had you right here on this desk."

"Yes," she whispered. "Please."

He moved, slowly at first, caressing that nub inside, making her tremble.

"I'm going to fuck you here like never before." He held her down with his body, positioned her with his hands, and thrust deeper, harder, faster.

Charlotte braced herself on the desk, pushing back on him. He dropped one hand from her hip, insinuated it beneath her, and found the hard bud of her clitoris, rubbing, circling. His touch, inside and out, had her right up on the edge again in a matter of seconds.

"Yes, yes, yes," Charlotte panted for him.

"Remember this when you're standing in my office."

"Oh God, yes, I will." She would touch the wood and remember the feel of it against her body, the heat of him inside her.

The quakes started in her calves, worked their way up, then everything exploded out from the point at which she was joined with him. Her body jerked, and she squeezed her eyes shut tightly enough to see stars. When the sensations would have faded, she felt him throb inside and he thrust harder. Then he buried his face in her hair and held her tight against him as his cock pulsed in climax.

They were both breathing hard. His tremors died away. So did hers. Then finally he moved, stood straight, pulled out. Against her backside, she felt him remove the condom, then he leaned over her to grab a tissue from a box. She wondered idly if he kept the tissues there for students who broke down, the way she had a tissue box on the corner of her desk.

Or had he put it there for this very purpose?

"Stand up, Miss Moore."

As she did, rather unsteadily, he smoothed her skirt down over her rump.

"You have to go now."

She didn't want to leave. She wanted to curl up in his arms. In his chair. On his lap. And stay.

But of course she couldn't. They couldn't.

"Yes, Principal Hutton," she murmured.

"You performed well, Miss Moore."

She left his office, her legs a bit wobbly. She didn't see a janitor. She didn't see a security truck. When she started her car engine, it was only twenty past the hour. The whole thing, from the moment she'd watched the security guy drive away to fucking Lance to returning to her car had taken twenty minutes.

It was surely the best twenty minutes of her life.

"FUCK," LANCE WHISPERED ALOUD TO THE EMPTY OFFICE ON Monday. He'd had a morning of calls, and now, the last of them made, he stared at the desk. He could still see Charlotte lying there. He could smell her sex. He could taste her on his tongue. He'd thought of nothing else the entire weekend. Of course, he could have called her, ordered her to his house, gone to hers, but he'd wanted this, to arrive at his office with the last memory of her being on that desk.

He'd never done such a thing in his life. He would probably never do anything like it again. He'd planned, mitigated the risk by choosing a late hour for the rendezvous, but he'd taken what he wanted.

She'd done everything he told her to. Dressed the way he'd insisted. Lifted her skirt when he demanded it. Let him fuck her.

He'd had sex in his office. He'd embraced his kinkiness. He started planning the other things he'd get Charlotte to do for him.

He was well and truly obsessed. And never more satisfied in his life.

His phone buzzed, interrupting his reverie. "Yes, Mrs. Rivers."

"We've got a problem out here, Principal Hutton." For the unflappable Mrs. Rivers, the thread of tension in her voice was unusual.

"What's going on?"

"Could you come out here, Principal?" Again, highly unusual.

He punched off the intercom button and opened his door to find his assistant principal and two teenagers, one girl, one boy. He recognized the kid immediately. Eric Collins, David Smith's stepson.

Shit. This was something he didn't need.

"What's the problem, Mrs. Sloan?" In her midthirties, Alice was short and stocky, something akin to the stereotypical image of a prison matron, but she was fair. She'd been one of his assistant principals since the beginning of the school year, and she usually took care of disciplinary issues on her own initiative unless they were particularly egregious.

"Fight in the quad, Principal Hutton," Alice said in a clipped military style.

He stared at Eric. "You were fighting with a girl?" He didn't care how sexist the statement sounded, in his world, you never hit a female.

"Eric didn't hit Melody," Alice informed him. "She knocked a soda can out of his hand."

"Melody Wright?"

The girl nodded, head down and eyes on the floor so that her lackluster brown hair obscured most of her face. Yet enough was visible to make out the ravages of acne.

Damn it to hell. The boy she'd been harassing was the stepson of the school board's chairman. Why the hell hadn't Charlotte told him? Then again, being here only two days a week, she was uninvolved in school politics and most likely didn't have a clue.

Pointing, he said, "The both of you, in my office." Once they were inside, along with the assistant principal, he moved behind his desk. He chose not to sit, nor to allow them to.

"Fighting can be cause for expulsion," he said harshly.

"It wasn't a fight, sir," Eric interrupted. "She slapped the soda can instead of slapping my face, then it was over." His shirt was neatly tucked in, his jeans sharp, marred only by the dark stain of the soda along one pant leg, and he met Lance's gaze boldly. In contrast, Melody was unkempt, her expression sullen, and her shoulders rolled into a slump so extreme it actually looked painful.

"Any kind of violence is unacceptable." He looked at Melody. "Why did you do it?"

"It was my fault, sir," Eric jumped in. "I called her a bitch." The boy was actually defending her.

For the first time, Melody raised her eyes from the floor and glanced at Eric beside her.

"Why would you use that kind of language about a young lady, Eric?"

"It was totally uncalled for, sir." He was exceptionally polite and deferential. He was also chivalrous, taking all the blame.

Melody was staring at him wide-eyed. Her face was a landscape of red pustules and small scabs where previous pimples had burst. The teenage years were bad enough, but being a teenager with acne to this extent? A great sympathy burned in his gut, yet the behavior couldn't be tolerated.

"Melody?" he queried softly.

She looked at him, then just as quickly dropped her gaze again. "I," she started.

Without the benefit of reading her lips at the same time, Lance leaned forward to hear her better.

"I was maybe a little mean," she admitted.

"I'd like specifics, Melody."

She shifted from one foot to the other. He glanced at Alice Sloan, who shook her head slightly to indicate she didn't know.

Then Melody's words rushed out. "I sorta said he was a creep and I hated his guts and if he dropped dead, I wouldn't care."

Eric pressed his lips together and said nothing.

"Was there a reason you said that to him, Melody?"

She shrugged. "I wanted to know what he said to Miss Moore when she called him into her office last week. He told me it was none of my business."

"So you got mad," Lance concluded for her.

She nodded. "I didn't want him bad-mouthing me to Miss Moore."

"But Miss Moore didn't tell me anything Melody said, so I didn't see why she should know what I said." Though Eric was willing to take the blame, he also seemed to want his side heard.

"Then you both resorted to name-calling, and, Melody, you slapped the can out of Eric's hand. Have I got all that correct?"

"Yes, sir," Eric said.

Melody gave her characteristic nod.

Lance turned to his assistant principal. "Mrs. Sloan, under the circumstances, what is your recommendation?"

"One-day suspension for both of them," she said immediately.

Suspending Smith's stepson could be a political fiasco, but the boy had admitted to provoking Melody. Though she'd provoked him, too. Lance wasn't about to show favoritism to Eric simply because of whose son he was.

"And a parent conference," Alice added.

The parent conference might indeed be more frightening to the two teenagers than the threat of suspension. "I concur." He looked at the two combatants. "Your parents will be contacted to arrange for your pickup as soon as possible. This is not a holiday. You will be required to complete all homework assignments from your teachers. Mrs. Sloan will make the arrangements to have your parents meet with us. You will not be included in that discussion. Do you understand?"

"Yes, sir," Eric answered.

Melody didn't move for a moment, didn't acknowledge the punishment in any way. Until he was about to dismiss them. "Eric didn't touch me. I was the only who did anything physical. He shouldn't get the suspension."

"If Mrs. Sloan hadn't shown up, I would have slapped Melody. Or worse," Eric said.

Jesus, they were both defending each other. Lance didn't believe for a moment that Eric would hit a girl. He'd figured that out in the first five minutes of the interview. But the mutual support was a good sign. Perhaps the problem was already halfway to being solved.

He considered them a moment. "I will delay your suspension until tomorrow. We'll have both your parents in here, discuss the situation, and I'll make the final decision then. You're dismissed."

When Alice would have followed them, he signaled for her to close the door and stay while he punched the intercom button. "Mrs. Rivers, please call the parents and set up a conference for tomorrow." In the office outside, Melody and Eric would be able to overhear Mrs. Rivers making the phone calls. A little fear went a long way.

He turned back to Alice. "Charlotte told me you'd discussed the situation last week."

"Yes. We agreed it wasn't an easy fix. But we both believed that at least if there was a dialogue going on between Melody and Charlotte, it wouldn't come to this."

"You should have let me know it was Eric."

She tipped her head. "Because of who he is?"

"Yes."

"You think there'll be a stink?" Her mouth pinched in a worried line.

With Smith, yes, there could be a stink, but Lance would deal with it. "I simply like to be informed."

"Sorry. It didn't really occur to me." She tapped her lip. "I'd like Charlotte to be there tomorrow, since she's talked to both students."

"Good idea."

"If you could have Mrs. Rivers call me when she's got a time set up, I'll let Charlotte know."

It was on the tip of his tongue to say he'd call Charlotte himself—a good excuse to hear her voice—but it was totally inappropriate. "You can tell Mrs. Rivers on the way out. Thank you for bringing the issue to my attention as quickly as you did."

She nodded her head in salute and made a half turn as if she intended to leave before slowly reversing back to him. "Eric's a good kid."

"I feel the same way." Despite his stepfather, he'd turned out well.

She was not a pretty woman, but something softened on her face as she said, "And I think Melody's actually a sweet girl. She just needs help."

"I realize that, too." The question was how best to provide it.

13

THE CALL TOOK LONGER TO COME IN THAN LANCE HAD FIGURED it would. Smith didn't get on the horn until almost three in the afternoon.

"What the hell is going on, Hutton? My son, involved in a fight? Impossible."

Last Wednesday, he'd been Lance. Now he was merely Hutton. "He's admitted it. That's why I've scheduled a parent conference tomorrow."

"It's out of the question," Smith barked. "Don't you know how busy I am?"

As chairman of the school board, Smith was an excellent delegator. He spent most of his time drumming up support for pet projects and attending so-called business lunches at the country club.

"If you don't feel it's important enough for your attention, I'm sure your wife's attendance will be more than adequate," Lance delivered the slam.

Smith fell for it. "Of course I'll be there. Give me the details."

"The details have been explained to your wife. I suggest you discuss it with both her and your son tonight."

"Goddammit, Hutton."

He knew Smith's intention, to insert himself into Lance's game plan, to direct what happened in tomorrow's meeting. "We'll cover it with you and Melody's parents as scheduled." With Smith involved, they needed Lance's mediation; otherwise the man could become combative.

"If you suspend him, Hutton, you better have a damn good reason."

"I'll be fair and impartial. But we *will* work this out with the girl's parents in attendance as well. You don't want it to appear that I'm showing your stepson favoritism."

Smith grumbled unintelligibly. Appearance was of utmost importance to the man. "I'll be watching your every move, Hutton."

"I have no doubt." Lance wouldn't let it sway his judgment over what was best for his students. Never had, never would.

He'd already concluded that he would not suspend Eric. The boy hadn't hit back, he'd defended Melody, and taken blame for his own actions. At most, Lance might send him to detention.

It was Melody he hadn't decided what to do with. She'd been in detention more than once. It hadn't helped. By strict definition, what she'd done was considered violence, punishable by suspension. She was, however, a girl in crisis, and he was less concerned with following stringent rules and more concerned with doing what would best help the student. A year ago, she'd been bright, energetic, good grades, glowing reports from her teachers. He doubted any of them would recognize the girl who'd been in his office today.

He was more inclined to sentence her to two days a week with Charlotte.

It was a sentence he wouldn't mind serving himself. An hour in her office, the door closed, the blinds pulled, anything could happen. And he would make sure everything did.

Of course, it was a fantasy. Reality was dealing with Eric and Melody. And their parents.

"HELL," CHARLOTTE SAID. "I TOLD MELODY I WAS GOING TO TALK to Eric, and she said it was fine, that I could discuss anything I wanted, as if she didn't give a damn whatsoever." She'd been afraid it would backfire, and it had.

Lance's voice came as a delicious rumble against her ear. "Obviously she gave a very big damn."

Curled up on her sofa, a blanket over her knees, she wished she could see Lance's face, but all he'd deigned to give her was a call this evening.

Alice had phoned in the afternoon to let Charlotte know about the latest altercation and the parent conference at two o'clock tomorrow. Good God, the situation was escalating rapidly. Charlotte saw it as Melody hitting out in frustration, but it was a troubling trend.

Because he couldn't see her, she put a hand to her forehead. It hadn't been a good day. First, Jeanine had made absolutely no progress since her last session. She was no longer willing to concede that fantasy might work, no matter how Charlotte tried to extol its virtues, from personal experience, no less. And now this.

"I'm not blaming you, Charlotte."

She wasn't Miss Moore now. She was his employee. "I didn't realize who Eric's stepdad was either."

"I know that, too, and I said I'm not blaming you."

But she was blaming herself. She didn't pay attention to school politics. It was one of the reasons she'd never considered being a full-time guidance counselor, so she didn't have to bother with who was grumbling about what.

"I'd like you at the parent conference to discuss your thoughts on what's happening between Melody and Eric. You've talked to them both. You have good insight."

Blame gave way to her natural instinct to analyze. She was also pleased with his praise. "What did you think of Eric?"

"He's exceptionally polite."

"Yes. But what about his attitude toward Melody?"

"He defended her. That was surprising under the circumstances."

"I think he's in love with her."

"In love?" He said it as if he couldn't fathom that a teenager would even know what love was.

"They've been best friends since they were in grade school. He's terribly upset that she won't talk to him anymore. I think her problem is her acne. She can't imagine he would love a girl with a face like hers."

"That seems rather simplistic. The issues have got to be far more complicated."

Her explanation was exactly the kind of teenage angst that made sense to Charlotte. "You were never a teenage girl."

"I was a teenage boy."

"It's completely different. You were probably captain of your high school football team with an adoring cheerleading squad at your feet."

He laughed. "I played basketball, but I wasn't the captain and the girls didn't fall at my feet. I was average."

"You could never have been merely average, Principal Hutton." He would always have stood out.

"We're all average except in our own minds. Everyone but you, Miss Moore."

The compliment made her glow, even if he was pandering to her ego. "Well, I hope the parents can shed some light on the situation."

He sighed. "Don't look for anything from Eric's stepfather. He's more likely to be an obstructionist and possibly combative."

"Damn."

"You don't know the half of it. The only good thing is that the meeting will be in my office."

"Isn't your office too small?"

"It'll be a tight roundtable, but it'll work. While I'm confronting Smith, I'll be able to imagine you spread over my desk the way you were on Friday night. With my cock deep inside you."

She gasped. "Principal Hutton." Heat rushed through her. "It's the worst thing to think about in the situation."

"On the contrary, it's very powerful. Why do you think I ordered you to come to my office?"

"Because you're kinky."

"True, but I wanted images, Miss Moore, memories stored up. Tactile. Olfactory."

"Now that you've brought it up, I don't think I'll be able to concentrate on the meeting."

"It'll make everything sharper. I'm hard. I want you right now."

Her heart began to beat in a fast staccato rhythm.

"What are you wearing?"

"My robe." She'd just finished a long soak in the tub when he called.

"Panties?"

"No."

"Touch yourself. I want to hear you come, Miss Moore. Where's your vibrator?"

"In the bedroom."

"Go lay down on your bed. I want to hear the hum of your vibrator."

She didn't know how he could switch so quickly, one moment engrossed in the issues of a troubled student, then consuming her with sexual desire in the next second. But she let him drag her along.

He created dirty word pictures as she traversed the hall, telling her all the things he'd do to her if he were there. She was damn near ready to come by the time she'd retrieved her vibrator from the bedside drawer.

"Fuck yourself, Miss Moore. I want you on your knees, the vibrator between your legs, and you riding it."

"I've never done it like that."

"Do you have a mirror by the bed?"

A full-length one covered the closet door. "Yes." She knelt on the side of the bed right across from it.

"Look at yourself and describe it all to me. Every detail."

She'd recommended phone sex to her clients, not the paid kind, but the sexy calls between partners. It was another venue in which to add spice. Lance took it to a new level for her, making it visual as well as verbal.

Her robe was old and flannel, green with multicolored dots all over it. So not sexy. "My silky pink robe is hanging open."

"Can you see your nipples in the mirror? Are they hard?"

She pinched herself, moaned. "They're tight and hard."

"Tell me how wet you are."

"I'm creamy, Principal Hutton, practically dripping."

"Taste it for me."

"You're so naughty." Charlotte put her hand between her legs, rubbed her clitoris, then licked her fingers. "Sweet," she whispered. "Slightly spicy and salty, too."

"Christ, yes, that's just how you taste, sweet and spicy. Turn the vibrator on and tell me how it feels when you ease down onto it. Like you were riding my cock."

Charlotte tucked the phone between her shoulder and ear so she could part her folds. Then, watching herself in the mirror, she described exactly what she saw. "My legs are spread wide, and it's disappearing deep inside me. Ooh. Yes." She closed her eyes and expressed just the feel of it. "It vibrates all the way up into my stomach. And ooh, God, tipping forward, it's right on my G-spot." Her body quaked. Moisture coated her hand where she held the vibrator. "It's so good."

"Fuck it for me, Miss Moore."

She looked at herself again, and instead of pulling the toy in and out, she tensed her thighs and rode, just as if she were riding a man. "Oh my God, that's so hot. It's almost like watching that movie I made up in my fantasy, the one of me fucking another man for you."

"I would never have hidden in a closet taking videos. I'd have stood in front of you while he fucked you doggy style and forced my cock down your throat." His voice was guttural, strained. He was as turned on as she was.

She loved his visceral description, the dirtiness of his words. He'd come so far for her in such a short time. He hadn't even used the word *fuck* until the first time she'd taken his cock in her mouth. But listen to him now, coming up with a naughty scenario that topped hers.

"You want to do everything I say, don't you, Miss Moore?"

"I'm dying for your commands, Principal Hutton." Then she

couldn't manage anything more than moans, groans, pants, and "Oh God, oh God."

Her breasts bounced, and the vibrator thrust and retreated. Her thighs ached with the position, and her body began to tremble. All the while, the principal's voice rumbled in her ear. "Fuck it, Miss Moore. Take it deep. Pretend it's me. Take me. Fuck me."

When she climaxed with a rush that dropped her down on the bed, she was sure she heard his answering cry, his simultaneous orgasm. His surrender.

IT WAS IMPOSSIBLE NOT TO REMEMBER HOW HE'D TAKEN HER ON that desk just a few nights ago. Or his voice on the phone last night as she rode her vibrator in front of a mirror for him. Charlotte squirmed in her chair, the phantom feel of him inside her, her bottom tingling as if he'd just spanked her. She could smell him in the office, a spicy aftershave and the equal potent scent of man and sex.

"I'm not going to suspend them," Principal Hutton said.

Alice and Charlotte had arrived ten minutes early for a strategy meeting before the Smiths and the Wrights appeared. Lance sat behind his desk, and she and Alice took chairs to the side in a wing formation. The four conference-table chairs—which were to be occupied by the parents—had been arranged in a semicircle facing them.

"Eric will receive one detention hall for inappropriate language"—Lance looked at Charlotte when he said it—"and Melody will take detention with you twice a week for six weeks during which she will receive counseling."

Okay, it wasn't a strategy meeting. He was dictating. He hadn't even asked her opinion. Charlotte couldn't be sure whether that glance was a reminder about *her* inappropriate language or whether it had been simply because he was assigning counseling duty to her. Putting aside her irritation over not being consulted, his plan wasn't all bad.

But . . . "Don't you think Eric needs counseling, too?" Charlotte queried.

"Quite frankly, no. That boy's got his head screwed on straight."

She was aghast, as if he'd intimated that there was some sort of stigma attached to counseling.

"I agree with the principal," Alice said. "He's a good kid. One detention hall is all that's necessary."

"But I'd like to talk to him. It could really help Melody."

Lance held her gaze steadily. "We can't sentence one student to punishment simply for another student's benefit."

Sentence? Punishment? "I don't see it as either of those things. He could benefit from it. He really got some stuff off his chest when I spoke with him last week."

"If he chooses to make an appointment with you, Charlotte, he's perfectly free to do so. But I'm not making it a requirement."

She was offended. He wasn't listening to her advice. He was simply dictating. She opened her mouth to object.

Alice beat her to it. "We can talk with him about it later, Charlotte. Let's deal with the incident at hand."

She felt ganged up on. She wanted to protest. But the intercom buzzed, and Mrs. Rivers announced the Wrights arrival. The imperious Principal Hutton waved a hand at Alice, indicating she should open the door.

With Alice's back to them, Charlotte glared at Lance. Instead of discussing his intentions with her last night, he'd turned the call into phone sex. Now he merely regarded her without expression. What happened to the whole thing about imagining her over his desk while they were in this conference? It was as if

Friday night had never happened. As if nothing had happened between them at all. As if—

Charlotte caught herself, horrified. Good Lord, she was mixing business and pleasure. She was expecting him to treat her differently because they were playing sex games. She might not like his dictatorial attitude, but then she'd known he was a dictator—benevolent as he may be—before anything sexual had begun.

She had to ask herself, would she have been angry with him now if nothing had occurred between them during the last two weeks? Or would she simply have accepted his high-handedness?

She didn't have adequate time to figure it out as Melody's parents entered the office and everyone stood.

The girl's mother led with her breasts. There was no other description for it. Model-thin, her chest bordered on abnormal in comparison. Charlotte feared the weight of them might topple her, especially with the five-inch stilts she wore. Without the heels, the woman might actually be shorter than Charlotte. Not a single line or wrinkle marred her features, though Charlotte thought she could use a little more adipose tissue in her face. She'd styled her hair a la Farrah Fawcett in the *Charlie's Angels* era and frosted it with varying shades of blond and red. Her features were nothing short of gorgeous, but like a beautiful actress on the big screen, she seemed untouchable.

She went immediately to the only other man in the room besides her husband. "You must be Principal Hutton. I'm Kathryn Wright. We're completely devastated by this incident involving Melody. I assure you we'll get it all straightened out."

For his part, Lance didn't seem to notice her breasts—God only knew how, perhaps with superhuman effort—and shook her hand. "Thank you for your cooperation." Then he turned to the man who must be Melody's father. "Mr. Wright, good of you to come."

"Please, call me Steven." While his wife made a big impression, Steven Wright made only one: average. Average height, average weight, brown hair, brown eyes, unremarkable features. Perhaps that was just in comparison to his wife's shadow.

Lance completed the introductions. "This is our assistant principal, Alice Sloan, and our guidance counselor, Charlotte Moore." He waited a beat for the handshaking. "The Smiths should be here any moment. I assume you know them well since your children used to be such close friends."

Kathryn Wright attempted a frown that didn't reach her forehead. "Yes, well, we don't run in the same circles, you understand." That could mean anything from casual indifference to hating one another on sight.

The door hadn't closed, but the intercom buzzed again, though Mrs. Rivers didn't make any announcement.

This time the father entered first, obviously David Smith. A handsome man despite his silvered hair, he was exactly what she would expect in a politician, slightly louder than normal, a big smile, handshakes all around as if he were at a campaign rally. "Wright. Mrs. Wright. Hutton." He shook Alice's hand as Lance introduced her, then Charlotte's as her name was said.

Then he flourished a hand in the air. "My wife, Jeanine."

Good God, it wasn't a false name at all. Barely managing to keep her jaw from a dead drop, Charlotte gaped at her client, Jeanine Smith.

Then she stared at David Smith, the husband who wanted his wife to have sex with other men.

14

THE ATMOSPHERE WAS ONLY SLIGHTLY CRAMPED, JUST ENOUGH
to keep the occupants of his office from getting too comfortable.
Since Lance was behind the desk, he had the most room and
therefore the upper hand.

He did not, however, have Jeanine Smith's full attention. If
anything, aside from her facial features, she had more in common
with Melody than she did the reasonable young man standing up
in his office yesterday to defend a girl who'd essentially been
harassing him. Mrs. Smith stared at her hands, fiddled with her
handbag, crossed and recrossed her ankles, and continuously
shifted in her chair. He'd met her before at various school-board
functions and events, and he didn't recall this same level of ner-
vousness. Maybe she just needed to use the ladies' room.

Whatever her problem, the most he could do at this point was
ignore it.

"That's the situation as it stands, and those are my plans for
disciplinary action," he said after a summary of events and the

consequences he would mete out. He spoke dispassionately and without blame.

It was, of course, Smith who answered first. "It's obvious that my son did nothing wrong at all. I'm not sure why my wife and I are even here."

"He called my baby a bitch," Kathryn Wright jumped in.

He wouldn't allow the meeting to degenerate into a fight between the parents. "It's not about who did what to whom. It's about events over the summer that ended their friendship and what we, as the adults in charge, are going to do to resolve the situation."

"Nothing happened," Smith blustered.

"It's just teenage angst," Kathryn said.

"Inappropriate language and physical altercations can't be ignored," Alice interjected. "It sets a bad example for other students."

"We need to get to the root cause," Charlotte added.

"But first, we'll deal with the immediate problem," Lance said.

Jeanine Smith suddenly clapped her hands over her ears. Her handbag, the handle of which was still clutched in her fingers, banged solidly against her cheek. "Would you all just stop arguing? I can't stand it. Eric's got detention, fine. There's nothing left to say." Her eyes were squeezed tightly shut.

"Je—" Charlotte started, her hand out. "Mrs. Smith, are you all right?"

The woman's eyes popped open, and she jumped to her feet. Then she looked at Charlotte with something closely resembling fear. Though that was ridiculous. By this time, Lance had risen, too. "Mrs. Smith, please, let's be calm."

She opened her mouth, closed it, and finally managed to get her words out. "I'm leaving. My husband can handle this."

Her exit was so startling that no one said anything for an

interminable five seconds. Then Smith stood, pointed his finger to the room at large and Lance in particular. "Look how you've upset my wife. And over what? A silly fight. Eric called her a bitch. Fine, give him detention"—he turned on Kathryn Wright—"but if your daughter comes near my stepson again, I'm getting a restraining order."

The door slammed behind him. The office walls shook, and the blinds rattled in the windows.

Lance stared at the closed door. "That went well," he said, a sense of shock robbing him of anything intelligent to say.

"Oh my," Kathryn Wright said, her face expressionless since her Botox injections—oh yeah, he'd take that bet—allowed for little physical response.

"I have no idea what that was about," Steven Wright said.

Neither did Lance, but he needed to get the meeting back on track, even if it was missing half its contingent. "I'm sorry about that unfortunate interruption. I would have liked to discuss the problems more with both sets of parents present, but since that's not possible, I'd like your impressions on what's happened between your daughter and the Smiths' son."

Kathryn Wright put a hand to her more than ample bosom. "I'm certain I have no idea."

"None at all," Steven Wright agreed.

"We've never tried to stop their friendship." Kathryn gave him a wide-eyed, innocent look as if she were an ingénue instead of the mother of a fifteen-year-old. "Even if David Smith is a total PA," she added.

"Pompous ass," Steven clarified.

She pursed her lips. "I've never liked that man."

"So we've tried to have as little as possible to do with the parents." Steven shook his head sadly.

"We've always thought Eric was a good boy." She glanced at her husband.

He nodded. "But we have no idea what happened between them."

It was like one person speaking, Steven Wright finishing his wife's thoughts. They were getting nowhere. Time to move to phase two, although at this point, he doubted Melody's parents would have much more to add.

"I'll turn the discussion over to Miss Moore. She's spoken with both Melody and Eric, and I believe she can shed some light."

He took his seat once more and gave the floor to Charlotte.

For the first time since the meeting had begun, he thought about Charlotte and his desk and Friday night. Even that, though, couldn't erase the fiasco of the last five minutes.

CHARLOTTE COULDN'T MAKE HER LIPS MOVE FOR ONE SECOND, then two, three. And counting.

The others had been in a state of shock at the Smiths' abrupt exit, but she knew exactly what happened to Jeanine. The woman had sat in terror for the entire ten minutes during which Lance had reviewed the details. Charlotte's first reaction had been to run after Jeanine. But that wasn't possible. She could not reveal their connection, especially not in front of her husband.

Imagine. The chairman of the school board wanted to hear the dirty details of his wife enjoying sex with another man.

It was like seeing the president of the United States in his underwear, far more than you really wanted to know. All right, she was in *more* shock than everyone else. She never would have made the connection; Smith was too common a name. Charlotte wouldn't have connected Jeanine to Eric Collins either, though she recalled Jeanine saying that her ex refused to allow her second husband to adopt her son or change his last name. That had been a sore spot in the first years of her marriage to David.

What to do with the information and how to handle Jeanine now that her secret was out, at least with Charlotte, was going to take some consideration. But the meeting was moving forward without her.

Melody's mother pursed her mouth, tiny lines fanning out from her upper lip. The rest of her face, however, didn't react. "I feel we're being singled out and ganged up on." She glared at the three educators in the room. "It certainly isn't *our* fault." She allowed herself an elongated O on the word.

Her husband immediately jumped to a defensive posture as well, leaning forward in his seat, chin jutting. "We've done everything we can to help Melody, spent a fortune."

Lance handled their indignation with aplomb. "We're not casting blame. We're thinking only of the children and what we can do to help them." He eyed them each in turn. "I'm sure you want the same thing."

"Of course we do," Kathryn Wright snapped.

"We've thought of nothing else," her husband insisted.

"Then I'm sure you'll agree that there needs to be a discussion, no matter how sensitive the issues are, so that we can do what's best for Melody." Lance held the woman's gaze. "We desperately need your help, Mrs. Wright."

Wow. He was good. *He* should run for the school board. There was no way the Wrights could back out now.

Charlotte had a compromise in mind that might put them more at ease. She looked at her principal. "May I suggest that Melody's parents and I shift over to my office for a more private discussion. I'm sure they'll have no problem with my providing you and Mrs. Sloan with a report."

"Good idea, Miss Moore."

God, she loved it when he said her name that way, slightly

imperious but loaded with meaning. And no one else would suspect.

He turned to the Wrights. "Is that acceptable?"

"Well . . ." Mrs. Wright dithered.

"Hmm . . ." Steven dithered with her.

"Yes, I suppose so," she concluded.

"I agree," Steven followed up.

She wondered what he did for a living and if his career required any original thought.

"That's settled." Lance wouldn't want to sit through a long counseling session, and that's certainly what Charlotte intended. When a child was having trouble, the parents needed as much counseling as the student did.

The Wrights shook hands with both Lance and Alice, then followed Charlotte down the hall. "Would you like some coffee?" she offered.

"Oh no. Coffee stains the teeth." Mrs. Wright pulled a bottle of zero-calorie vitaminwater from her bag. Mr. Wright asked for nothing.

Charlotte indicated the chairs around her small conference table. "Now, Mrs. Wright," she began once they were all seated.

"Please, call us Kathryn and Steven. We don't need formality."

"All right. I'm Charlotte. First I'd like to establish that I don't want to keep anything said here a secret from Melody. If I feel the need to bring up a point in my sessions with her, I'd like your permission to do so. Does that work for you?"

"Certainly," Kathryn said. "We'll do anything we can to help."

"No secrets here," her husband confirmed.

"I won't mince words." Charlotte smiled to take the bite out of it. "I believe the root cause of the problem is Melody's acne."

"Well, duh," Kathryn said just like a teenager.

Steven Wright snorted in support.

Charlotte didn't allow their response to stop her from delivering her prepared speech. She didn't believe they understood the full impact.

"Severe acne like Melody's can cause social withdrawal"—oh yes, Melody certainly exhibited that symptom—"low self-esteem, a loss of self-confidence, and poor body image." She paused to give impact to the list. "All of this leads to anger with the world, depression, and even aggression. Which is exactly what we're seeing with Melody."

"We know all this, Charlotte." Kathryn gave the *T* a hard edge.

"We've seen it every day," Steven emphasized. "We've taken her to every doctor."

"I'm sure you have. Melody told me she's taking medication, but it doesn't seem to be helping." Obviously. She cocked her head. "How's her diet? Kids often eat too much junk food, fast food, processed foods."

Kathryn pursed her lips. "I've been very diligent about her diet long before the acne. I didn't want to turn her into a fat child who could never lose the weight when she was older. It's horrific what some parents do to their children by sheer neglect of watching what their kids put in their mouths."

"My wife has always declared she would never raise a fat child."

"I would never let a child of mine be made fun of because she's fat."

"Providing a healthy diet is admirable," Charlotte agreed, but she feared their diligence was more about appearance than health, especially with repeated use of the word *fat*. That wasn't good for Melody either. It bred intolerance, both for herself and other kids. "Let's talk about positive reinforcement. What strategies are you employing right now?"

"Positive reinforcement? How can you positively reinforce acne?" Kathryn scoffed.

Charlotte smiled tightly. It was better than swearing. "You can help her see beyond the acne."

Kathryn reared back, on the edge of indignation. "We tell her she'll grow out of it."

"We've got her on the strongest meds money can buy." Steven seemed to be all about the fortune he spent on his daughter.

Hadn't Melody's doctors discussed her emotional well-being with the Wrights? "I'm talking about affirming how beautiful she is *as* she is. You could encourage her to look at herself in the mirror and help her see beyond the acne to the beautiful girl inside."

This time Kathryn snorted. "You're joking, right? I can't in all good conscience let her stand in front of a mirror and look at those horrible—" She shuddered, as if the mental picture was too much to bear.

Good Lord, with reactions like that from her parents, how was Melody supposed to deal with the cruelty of high school kids?

Kathryn sat up straight, shoulders squared. "We've done everything we can to help her self-esteem. When she came home last year crying because her breasts weren't developing and one of those mean bitches called her flat-chested, I offered to get her breast implants. I've planned low-fat, low-carb menus so no one could ever accuse her of having a muffin top. I said we could start her on Botox injections so she wouldn't get those horrible frown lines on her brow." She ran her fingers over her perfectly smooth forehead. "I told her she could have any surgery she needed to make her feel good about herself."

Charlotte was horrified. "You offered breast implants and Botox to a fifteen-year-old?"

Kathryn sat even straighter, back rigid, though her face showed not an ounce of emotion. She couldn't move her features enough to form an expression, Charlotte thought maliciously.

"So you're telling me," Kathryn said between tight lips, "that it's okay to take Melody to a dermatologist who gives her enough drugs to turn an elephant's hide into silk, but it's not okay to fix her flat chest?"

Steven reinforced. "We're getting mixed messages here, Miss Moore. We're willing to spend whatever it takes to fix her."

That was Melody's problem. Her parents wanted to fix the outer shell as if that would suddenly show Melody how beautiful she was on the inside. The more her mother suggested surgery for that issue or a cosmetic injection for that problem, the lower Melody's self-esteem slipped and the more breakouts she would have from stress.

"We love her and we're doing everything possible," Kathryn said, her voice as stiff as her body.

She probably wasn't a bad woman. Steven Wright probably wasn't a bad man. But they were bad parents. Charlotte had to learn how to fix them before she could even begin to help their daughter.

"OH MY GOD, THEY WERE HORRIBLE." CHARLOTTE ROLLED HER eyes expressively.

She and Alice were sitting out in the quad with steaming mochas from the deli next to the high school. The sun had dried up the concrete, and the day had turned quite warm as long as you were wearing a jacket and basking in the sun, though that would be dipping below the horizon in half an hour or so.

Charlotte had needed some air after the grueling session with the Wrights. She would have liked to discuss it with Lance, but Alice was her assistant principal and her boss. Besides, Alice had always proved a good sounding board.

"They're just clueless," Alice said. Having entered the army for the educational opportunities, Alice still maintained that military bearing, whether intentional or not, but she was quite soft-hearted and always tried to see the best in people.

"*Clueless* is the most diplomatic word you could apply," Charlotte said with a sarcastic note.

She'd spent another half hour with the Wrights. Melody had trouble during the school year with some of the kids making fun of her lacking in the breast department. Then, just at the end of the year, the acne started.

"They don't even know what happened with Eric and Melody, yet the kids were supposedly best friends. How could her parents not know?"

"You're being too hard on them," Alice countered.

"I thought I wasn't being hard enough. Is it possible to charge parents with child abuse if they give their girls breast implants and Botox injections for their sixteenth birthday?"

She was being facetious but Alice was a very literal person. "There's a parental faction who believe surgery is the ultimate answer to their children's esteem issues." She shook her head at Charlotte. "Don't you watch the afternoon talk shows?"

"Like I have time?" She arched a brow. "When do *you* have time?"

"I record them. I love Dr. Phil." Alice's face softened with awe. "I never miss an episode. Not that Dr. Phil advocates that kind of thing at all."

Charlotte had seen Dr. Phil, and he was quite reasonable for a talk show host. "Honestly, the whole thing is just plain crazy.

Any parent pushing surgery to solve an esteem issue doesn't deserve to have kids." She was overstating, but all she could think about was the harm this kind of thing had done to Melody.

"You're not usually so judgmental."

"There's something about that woman that gets to me," Charlotte said in defense. "I think they're ashamed of Melody. Maybe they're afraid her face will be pockmarked." She grimaced. "God forbid."

"The more emotional *you* get, the less you'll be able to help Melody."

Alice was right. A counselor had to step back to maintain impartiality. She couldn't do that if she let herself be emotional. The key word was *empathy*.

"So tell me what they *think* happened." Alice steered them back to discussion rather than judgment. "Was Eric part of this hazing Melody received?"

"Not as far as they're aware. There was no big fight. They used to text constantly, then she started ignoring his messages, and they weren't disappointed because they'd never liked Eric's stepfather. They thought it was all for the better." Charlotte pursed her lips. "I'd like to have the Wrights start some family counseling. What do you think?"

Alice shook her head. "It's a touchy issue. We have no authority for ordering them to do it. But they've agreed to Melody's seeing you twice a week. Let's start with that."

In many ways, the school's hands were tied these days, and there'd been a lawsuit four or five years ago, before Lance's time, in which the school had been sued for "usurping parental rights." They'd lost. Charlotte didn't agree with negating parents' rights, but on the other hand, educators had become terrified of making decisions that might result in even a whiff of the word *lawsuit*, despite what was in a child's best interests. "What about talking with Eric again?"

"That wasn't part of the agreement in Principal Hutton's meeting. You don't have permission."

Damn. How was she supposed to help Melody under these conditions?

Alice patted her hand. "You've got your session with Melody on Thursday. Stop trying to fix her and just let her talk."

Alice had a good point. Everyone was trying to fix Melody. What Charlotte needed to do was get Melody to open up. The problem was how to encourage her to do that. Charlotte had two days to figure it out.

15

CHARLOTTE STAYED LATE AT SCHOOL TO MAKE NOTES IN Melody's file regarding both the meeting with the Wrights and her subsequent discussion with Alice. It was best to document everything when it was all fresh. After that was done, she closed her door and dialed Jeanine's cell phone. It rang an extraordinarily long time.

"Hello?" Jeanine's voice was soft, hesitant, almost as if she were afraid.

"Jeanine, it's Charlotte Moore."

"Oh God, I was afraid it was you. Don't call me here." Her voice rose, panicky.

"Where?"

"I'm hiding in the laundry room."

"I called your cell, as we agreed." Charlotte had never gotten her home phone number.

Jeanine lowered her voice. "I can't see you anymore."

If someone was listening in on the conversation, it would

sound more like Jeanine was talking to a lover instead of her therapist.

"Let's talk about that, Jeanine. I realize you don't want your husband to know. But nothing has changed. We aren't required to tell him if you don't want to."

"You don't understand."

"I'm sure it was hard for you to come to me in the first place, and it's your business whether you tell him or not, though I would recommend you do so. But regardless, I still believe it's in your best interest to continue your therapy."

"But he knows about us," she hissed softly.

Again, there was that vague sense of tryst rather than therapy. "How?"

"He just kept asking why I'd acted so oddly in the meeting. Finally I just told him. I had to. Now he's mad as a hornet."

First things first. "Are you afraid he'll act violently toward you?"

Jeanine snorted. "Nothing like that. It's just that he can be so"—Charlotte could almost see the woman gesturing in the air as she searched for the right way to put it—"so difficult to live with when he doesn't get his way. He's worried about what I might have told you. It's just not worth it."

This was the problem with only one spouse receiving the counseling. You needed buy-in, and Jeanine didn't have it. But things wouldn't get better for the Smiths if she simply gave in to her husband.

"Before we break it off completely, may I suggest one session with both of you in attendance. I can assure your husband that whatever we've discussed is confidential and—"

"No," Jeanine said sharply. "It's not going to work. I want you to know it wasn't my fault. Now I have to go."

Charlotte was left talking to dead air. What wasn't Jeanine's fault? The words sounded almost ominous.

"Gee, that went well." The sentiment echoed Lance after the disastrous parent conference.

Which reminded her, the principal was exactly the person she needed to talk to. For a lot of reasons, half of which had nothing to do with Melody, Jeanine, her husband, or the Wrights.

But Lance's office was locked up tight, the lights off. Damn. He was gone.

IT WAS LONG PAST DARK WHEN HER CAR PULLED OUT OF THE school parking lot. Lance followed.

When he'd left, her office door was closed but a light glowed from beneath the door. He'd pulled his car out onto the street, no particular plan in mind. Even as he waited for her—over a quarter of an hour—his mind was a jumble of sexual images but nothing specific.

He should have been thinking about this afternoon's parent conference. He should have discussed what she'd learned in her session with the Wrights. But it was after school hours and the only thing on his mind right now was getting up Charlotte Moore's skirt.

From two car lengths behind her, he called her cell phone on his Bluetooth.

"Pull over," he said after her clipped *Hello*.

"What on earth—"

"Pull into that parking lot on the right," he ordered.

"Where are you?"

He flashed his lights. "Right behind you."

"You're crazy." But she tapped her brakes and pulled into the mini-mall lot.

The spaces fronting the stores were full, but next to the road, the row was empty. He rolled into the spot on the passenger side of the one she'd chosen. Looking at her, he said, "You were extremely insolent in our preplanning meeting today."

She gaped at him. "I most definitely was not. I showed great restraint."

The combination of watching her lips move from afar yet hearing her voice intimately in his ear got him hard. "Don't argue with me. Get out of your car and into mine to receive your punishment." All he could think about was having her.

"Don't you even want to talk about my meeting with the Wrights?" Even at this distance, he could read the consternation on her face.

The parent conference had been rougher than most, but nevertheless manageable. Alice Sloan had dropped by before leaving for the day and briefed him on Charlotte's observations during her one-on-one—or two-on-one—with Melody's parents. He hadn't expected one meeting to solve the girl's problems. Kathryn Wright was a superficial woman, and her husband played the part of her trained lapdog. It would take several sessions with Charlotte for Melody to make any headway, and Lance wasn't above asking the parents to enter family counseling in short order if the girl's attitude and behavior didn't improve. As for Eric, it was a nonissue. He'd attend his one detention hall and that would be that. The rest was up to Melody. But he had faith in Charlotte. She would do everything in her power to help the girl, and he believed she could work miracles, she was that dedicated.

"That's work, which we'll discuss tomorrow," he said. "Right now it's about *your* discipline. So get out of your car and into mine without further argument." He stared hard through the car window. "Or it will go worse for you."

She harrumphed over the phone and narrowed her eyes at him.

Oh yeah, he was getting hard, his blood pumping faster.

"Where are we going?"

She was stalling just to be ornery. "I'm counting, one, two, three," he said slowly.

"All right already." She shut off her engine and the Bluetooth cut out. Pulling the key out of the ignition and gathering her purse from the seat beside her, she climbed out and rounded the back of the cars. In his rearview mirror, he saw just her torso as she passed, then his passenger door opened and she slid in.

"In my estimation," he said, "your submissiveness has severely declined."

"I have to be in the mood," she answered flippantly. Though her face was in shadow, he thought he detected a slight curve to her lips.

"I don't recall that was an option." He backed out of the space and maneuvered onto the road again, then stopped for a red light. "It's my mood that counts."

She glared at him. "You are becoming terribly dictatorial."

He raised a brow and looked askance. "I thought that's what you liked about me."

"It's what I *didn't* like," she groused.

He laughed, rolling through the intersection when the light changed. "But you love the spankings and the kink, so you're willing to put up with my authoritarian attitude," he supplied for her.

"Well"—she shrugged—"the orgasms are pretty spectacular. But don't let that go to your head."

"Which one?"

She looked pointedly at his lap. "Either one."

"Too bad. It's already gone to both." He took her hand, forcing her to lean over, and molded it to his cock.

"And I'm supposed to take care of that?" she asked mildly.

He glanced in the rearview mirror, then to the side. No one nearby. "Yes. Work it."

She huffed. "Whatever my master wants," she said with far too much sugary sweetness. Dipping her fingers down between his legs, she caressed his balls, then stroked back up the length of his cock. "Like that, Principal Hutton?"

"You learn quickly, Miss Moore." They were now on a long stretch of darkened road that led up to the freeway.

"I've become accustomed to what you like." Even through his slacks, she hit every spot designed to make him squirm.

And squirm he did, sucking in a breath when a particular touch shot a jolt of electricity straight up the center of his body, jump-starting his heart rate. "Fuck yes."

"Gotcha," she whispered.

He couldn't disagree.

Passing under the freeway, he pulled into a Park and Ride nestled in the trees. A damn good thing because soon he would have been incapable of controlling the wheel. With the commute over, the lot was only half full. Charlotte was forced to remove her hand as he backed into a spot beneath an overhang of trees.

"Get in the back seat," he ordered.

"Make me," she said.

He leaned over like a shot, wrapping his hand around her throat, pushing her head back against the seat. "You're trying my patience, Miss Moore."

"I'm trying very hard." The branches swayed in the wind outside and a stream of light flashed across her face, revealing the emerald sparkle of her eyes.

"Get. In. The. Back." Each word a sentence on its own. Each said between gritted teeth. He wanted her now. He could have taken her right there in the front seat, hauled her over his lap, spread her legs, impaled her.

"Yes, Principal Hutton," she whispered, and surprisingly, when he backed off, she crawled through the two seats. "Now what?" She tapped her fingers together.

Without a word, he climbed out, opened the back door, and slid in beside her. "Now what," he mused softly. His heart beat loudly as her scent called to him. "Do you deserve a spanking, Miss Moore?" He was going to give her exactly what she wanted.

"Oh yes, Principal Hutton, I definitely deserve a spanking." She raised her skirt.

He couldn't wait to get his hands on her.

CHARLOTTE'S CHEEKS WERE FLUSHED, AND HER SKIN STILL tingled with the feel of his cock against her palm. She'd been pissed that he'd completely ignored this afternoon's events. All he'd done was dictate when she wanted him to ask her opinion, her impressions, her plan of attack, get his buy-in, his approval . . .

Damn. She most certainly did not need his approval.

But she did need his hands on her. Here in his back seat, no matter who was master, she was in charge.

"Shall I remove my panties, Principal Hutton?" she said with a sweetly innocent affectation.

"Definitely." The harshness of his tone pleased her. He'd been stone hard beneath her palm and putty in her hand.

Thank goodness she hadn't worn pantyhose. The effect would have been lost. His eyes tracked every movement as she lifted her bottom, tucked her fingers beneath the elastic of her thong, and slowly slid the delicate confection down her legs. Lifting one foot only, she let the thong dangle around her ankle, just above the high-heeled shoe.

There was no one around. They were invisible from the freeway. If anyone pulled into the lot, they were hidden by the darkness of the trees above. A cop could have patrolled the area, so there was a risk, sure. That only served to heighten her excitement.

He moved to the center of the seat. "Lie over my lap."

Charlotte kicked off her high heels, then twisted until she lay prone on him, lengthwise across the seat, butt in the air, knees bent, toes tapping the window. The thong slid down her calf. Against her belly, she could feel the pulse of blood through his cock.

He desired her, needed her, regardless of who was doing the spanking and who was being spanked. This was power.

"I'm ready, Principal Hutton. Do your worst." She crossed her arms on the seat beside him and laid her head on her forearms.

Putting one foot onto the middle hump on the floor, he raised her bottom higher, and spanked her hard. The smack rippled through her whole body, and she was suddenly wet and hot and gasping.

He smacked her again. Then again. "I love how red your ass gets, Miss Moore." His voice was hoarse.

Charlotte breathed hard, biting her lip to keep the moans low in her throat so he wouldn't hear. All the other times, she'd been standing, her legs spread, and his fingers roamed freely down to her pussy, her clit, caressing, enhancing the pleasure. She'd thought that's what it was all about. But now his touch didn't reach beyond the lips of her vagina, yet the pleasure and pain were as potent as always. She clenched her fists beneath her cheekbone.

He squeezed each globe, then swatted her again, over and over, his hand against her ass until her flesh burned, until her body quivered, until she moaned, and finally cried out.

"Enough, my little slut?" His harsh whisper filled the car.

Charlotte gave in to the need. "More. More. Please." She gasped between each word. What was that about power? She had it all? Until now, when she gave it all back. "Don't stop. Please." She stretched her arms out, leveraged herself on the door and pushed back, raising her butt higher until his smacks reverberated straight up into her pussy. The orgasm began as a single kernel of heat deep inside, building, growing, bursting. She heard herself wail, couldn't stop it, climaxing in wave after wave.

Then he was hauling her up, spreading her legs over his lap.

"Inside you, now." His voice was guttural, the words slightly slurred as if he were drugged. Or high on her.

He wasn't too far gone, though, to pull a condom from his suit pocket.

"Dirty man, you were planning this." Her voice didn't sound like her own either, soft, seductive, breathless.

"Of course."

They worked together, taking care of his belt, his zipper. She held his cock in her palm; he placed and rolled the condom.

Then he took her by the hips—"Fuck me"—and impaled her.

Her hair brushed the roof as she put her head back, taking him all the way in. Then she rested, flexed around him, tipped her chin back down, and put her hands on his shoulders. His eyes were hot with desire, his muscles rigid beneath her touch.

"Slowly," she whispered. She moved on him, just enough to stroke her G-spot. "Yes, just like that." Ultrasensitive from her orgasm, she was on edge almost immediately. Yet she watched his face, the shifting and tensing of muscles, the flare of his nostrils. She recognized the moment when he could no longer hold out.

"Faster," he muttered.

She let him guide her hips, clenched her fingers in his jacket, her nails biting all the way through to his shoulders.

"Ride me. Fucking ride me hard."

When her head bounced against the roof, she didn't care. She was too far gone, their bodies pounding. All she could think was that there was too much material between them, too little skin on skin.

Then she couldn't think at all, falling down into climax, dragging him with her.

Until his voice rumbled against her ear. "Come home with me. We're not done. I want more."

Ugh. The man was a buzzkill.

He was still deep inside her, but their cries had faded into the night. Her arms locked around his neck, Charlotte's face was buried against his shoulder, his hair against her face, the sharp seductive scent of his skin tantalizing her. She couldn't move, didn't want to.

But she could say no. "I'm not spending the night. Plus, I need clothes for tomorrow."

She felt him tip a hand to read his watch. "It's not midnight yet."

"If you wanted me to come home with you," she murmured against his neck, "you shouldn't have fucked me here."

"I wanted you here. And I want you there, too."

"No." It was their safe word. She didn't want to sleep beside him, cuddle him, let him wrap his body around her. She didn't want to wake up beside him in the morning where he could reach out, touch her, take her. And maybe even steal her will. It was too intimate. "I like it the way it is."

He pushed her away and tilted her head up with his thumbs beneath her chin, his fingers bracketing her throat. "You'll like it better when you're tied to my bed all night long."

Well, maybe. If she could be sure that's all they'd do. But eventually he'd untie her, and, God forbid, he might try to snuggle.

She rotated her hips on top of him. "*This* is better. Hard and fast. Cataclysmic. Sexy. Risky."

He pulsed inside her.

"This is how I like it," she whispered.

Still holding her firmly by the neck, he kissed her openmouthed. He took her all over again with that kiss, turning her mindless, until there was just his lips, his tongue, his scent, and his breath filling her.

He kissed like a bad boy. Or an angel. Sweet yet hot. Dangerous kisses, bone-melting, will-stealing.

"I have to go." It would have been easier if she had her own car here, but she had to make him drive her back to the strip mall's parking lot.

"Afraid to spend the night, Charlotte?" he queried softly. His face was too close to read an expression. "Afraid you'll like it too much?"

"Yeah, right." She gave the saying her best derisive tone. But yes, she might like it too much. She didn't want a relationship with him. This afternoon in his office had proven his dictatorial nature. It was one thing—one very good thing—when he was spanking her, quite another when it was about her counseling. Plus, they worked together. Plus, he was too old. Plus, plus, plus.

But dear God, when he pulsed inside her, when he kissed her, when he spanked her, she wanted to give in on every point.

That was why she couldn't spend the night.

"No," she whispered. "Isn't that my safe word?"

16

DAMMIT, SHE'D HAD HIM THERE. HOW COULD THE WOMAN KEEP saying no? But Charlotte had last night, and he'd been forced to drive her back to her car.

He was too old to ache for a woman. Yet he ached for *her*. And liked it, too. He reveled in the crazy things he did to her, relished the risk of fucking in a parked car. He loved the feel of her ass, hot and sweet against his palm.

But she'd said no. Again.

She was driving him mad.

Christ, he even liked that.

"You've got a visitor," Mrs. Rivers mouthed in exaggerated lip movements, pointing to his office.

He glanced at his watch, confirming that he was starting his workday fifteen minutes early. Who would arrive early without having a scheduled appointment? He raised his brow, but Mrs. Rivers' extravagant hand gestures, pointing, and head bobbing didn't elucidate.

David Smith was seated at Lance's conference table, his fingers drumming the wood top. "We need to talk."

His face was florid, his pupils dilated, his breathing fast. Lance worried about all the cream sauce on his country club lunches and the potential risk for hypertension. He hoped the man wasn't about to have a heart attack in his office.

Closing the door, Lance said, "I'm at your disposal." He took the chair opposite.

"Do you realize that woman is a sex surrogate?" Smith's complexion deepened.

Lance had an inkling, but he asked anyway, "What are you talking about?"

"That counselor."

"Miss Moore?"

"Yes. That one. She's a sex surrogate three days a week, and she spends two days here at the high school counseling kids. My God, do you have any idea how she could be influencing impressionable young minds?"

Lance didn't let out the bark of laughter surging up from his gut. He didn't even smile. He maintained his composure and his diplomacy. "Miss Moore is a part-time guidance counselor with an outside therapy practice. She is most certainly *not* a sex surrogate." Did the man even know what a sex surrogate was?

Smith pounded the table. "How can you allow this in your school, Hutton? What if she's sexually harassing students who come to see her, making advances? What if she actually touches them?"

"David," he said harshly, "stop right there. I assure you that none of our counselors ever touch the students. They do not sexually harass them. They do not make advances."

But Smith wasn't listening. "My son was alone in her office

with her." He was almost snorting with indignation now, and Eric had become his son, not just his stepson. "*Completely* alone. No supervision whatsoever."

Lance narrowed his eyes on Smith. "Did Eric say Miss Moore was inappropriate in some way?"

"No, but—"

"Then what's gotten you so worked up, David?" He used the man's name gently, hoping to calm him down before he burst a blood vessel. He was sure Eric wouldn't have lied about such a thing. Just as he was sure Charlotte would never say or do anything improper.

Smith spluttered a moment, then managed to say, "I've heard things about her."

"What exactly? We need to deal in specifics here if you're going to comment on her practice." He didn't want to use the word *accuse* yet. It was too strong.

"She tells her patients to commit deviant acts."

He also didn't want to use the word *ridiculous*. Smith might go apoplectic at that. Just the same, the man was definitely ridiculous. "You've misinterpreted whatever you were told, David. Miss Moore is a therapist. She helps people work through their feelings about what's happened in their lives, past and present. What you've heard is gossip, nothing more."

"It's not gossip, dammit." Hand raised, Smith looked ready to pound the table. "I *know*."

"You can't know unless you're in her office when she's talking to a client."

Smith glared at him. "I know because my wife is her patient." Then he spoke through gritted teeth, "And that woman has been giving her unspeakable advice."

Shit. Suddenly everything made sense.

* * *

LANCE HAD MANAGED TO CALM SMITH DOWN, BUT NOT WITHOUT one last parting shot. "Keep her away from my son, Hutton."

The man had ended there, just short of making a threat, which had surprised Lance. He'd expected it, but for some reason Smith hadn't taken that last step. Perhaps he'd been afraid of repercussions. Who knew?

What pissed Lance off was that Charlotte hadn't forewarned him about the wife being her client. He didn't like being blindsided. If he'd known, he'd have prepared a response.

He pushed her button on his cell phone. She was now one of his speed dial numbers. In his memory. Indelible.

She didn't answer. He was forced to leave a message. "This is your principal, Miss Moore. Call me right away."

So what could she have said to Smith's wife that would make the man foam at the mouth? He thought about the client whose husband wanted her to have sex with other men. Instead of denouncing the desire, Charlotte's suggestion had been to fantasize about it. She was certainly unorthodox, but he wouldn't call her deviant. Not for creating a fantasy for him that damn near blew his brain circuitry. Good God, if she would be considered deviant, what was he after all the things he'd made her do? Sex in his back seat. Anyone could have returned to the Park and Ride to pick up their car. What about that night at Lookout Point? Risky, public sex. But he still wouldn't call anything they'd done deviant. People thought about having sex in public all the time. It was probably a universal fantasy, at least for men.

She returned his call half an hour later. Glancing at the time, it was close to the top of the hour and he realized she must have been with a client.

"I'm at your service, Principal Hutton."

Just her voice made him smile. Her words made him hard. "We need a meeting."

"Tonight."

"Today." It was a delicate situation and a phone call wouldn't suffice. Or maybe he was just searching for an excuse to see her.

"Well, um . . ." She did a little hemming and hawing. "I have back-to-back appointments with only half an hour at lunch. I can't get to the school and back and have any time to . . . talk."

"I'll come to you. Where are you?"

She gave him brief directions to her office.

It wasn't far. "What time do you finish your last appointment before lunch?"

"A little before noon."

"Thirty minutes. That should be enough time. I'll be there at noon."

He wouldn't touch her. He wouldn't spank her. All they had time for was the discussion about David Smith and his wife.

A NOONER. CHARLOTTE DIDN'T HAVE TIME, BUT SHE COULDN'T say no either. Not because he was her master or any such thing, but because she wanted it. That sexy little episode last night in his car had only whet her appetite for more. And so what? What was wrong with getting dirty during lunch? If a married couple had come to her and said they'd made time for a little noontime nookie, she'd have cheered. People needed to make time for intimacy, do something wild and crazy, add pizzazz to their lives.

But if a woman had said she was having nooner sex with her boss?

This was different. Lance wasn't her boss, at least not directly. She sounded like she was making excuses.

Her client left ten minutes before noon. Charlotte rushed to the ladies' room, freshened up. And removed her panties.

Okay, she was definitely crazy.

She had physical signs, too, like the way her heart raced when he sauntered through her door and her nose twitched for the scent of him. How she watched him for signs of approval over the décor and her degrees and certificates on the wall.

She remained seated at her desk, controlling her physical urges while he strolled from door to window.

"Very nice," he said. "The comfortable corner group by the window with a view of the trees." He glanced out. "You can't even see the parking lot or the other buildings. Almost like you're in the woods." He adjusted the tissue box. "Everything right at hand."

She could have beamed with pleasure, but caught herself before she fell all over him with gratitude. Instead she folded her arms across her chest and crossed her legs. "May I ask what was so important, Principal Hutton?"

He pulled a chair closer to the desk and sat in front of her. "I had a visit from David Smith this morning. It seems his wife is your client."

Her stomach dropped sickeningly. She'd been thinking sex, sex, sex, but he was here for something altogether different. "I'm afraid I can't discuss that."

There were near imperceptible changes in his face, a slight flare of his nostrils, a flatness to his lips. Then he said, "You should have at least warned me after the meeting yesterday."

"I couldn't. I can't reveal anything a client tells me or even that they are a client."

"Fine." His voice was clipped. "Now it's out in the open. Let's discuss it."

She pursed her lips. His attitude was starting to rile her. "I don't have her permission to discuss anything."

"Well, her husband is claiming that you suggested she commit deviant acts."

Deviant acts? David Smith had proposed the deviant act to his wife, for God's sake. But she couldn't say that. "Like what?"

"He wasn't specific."

"So how do you know if my suggestions were really deviant?"

"I don't."

"Then how can you come here and accuse me of—"

He cut her off. "I'm not accusing you. I'm telling you what he said. This is a warning."

She was so angry, her back teeth started to chatter. "Warning me about what? That you're going to fire me?"

"Calm down."

"Don't tell me to calm down. You're threatening me."

"No, I'm not. I'm only warning you that he's upset."

"Well, it sounds like *you're* accusing me, like you believe him."

He raised a brow. "I have to admit I was reminded of that little scenario with your boyfriend taking a video of you and another man."

"That was a fantasy," she snapped. "I didn't suggest my client actually do it, only that she fantasize about it with her husband." That bastard. Smith was telling lies. He was the one who wanted to loan his wife out to other men. What had she told Lance? She hadn't said it was a current client. She'd made it sound like it was someone in the past.

He held up a hand. "Don't get upset, Miss Moore. I'm not questioning you."

The *Miss Moore* pissed her off. This wasn't one of their sex games. "Then what exactly are you doing? Besides warning me."

"Smith is uncomfortable with the idea of a sex therapist counseling students."

"Oh my God." She gaped. "He wants you to fire me?"

"He simply said that he didn't want you to talk to his son one-on-one."

She made a sound in her throat, indicating her disgust. "What the hell does he think I'm going to do to Eric?"

"You just need to be prepared. Steer clear of Eric and deal with Melody only. It's what we'd already decided to do anyway. I calmed Smith down, but he's got a bug up his ass. I'll stand by you."

"Well, thank you very much," she said, not even trying to hide the sarcasm.

"Charlotte. It'll be fine." He cocked his head. "Would you rather I hadn't told you?"

"No." She would have preferred that he'd told her a different way instead of making it sound like an accusation. "I've done nothing wrong. I didn't say anything after I realized she was my client, because our sessions are confidential, as is the fact that she sees me."

"Then perhaps you should ask her what she told him."

She stood, paced. He stayed in his chair, and her skirt brushed his arm in the cramped space as she passed. Her office was meant for sitting, not pacing. "She's ended her sessions with me." Charlotte had, however, planned to make a follow-up call in a couple of days, just to check that everything was all right.

She stopped mid-pace. "You don't think—" She cut herself off. She'd been about to wonder aloud if David Smith had done something worse than harp on Jeanine until she told him why she'd run out of the meeting. Coupled with Jeanine's ominous words about *it* not being her fault. But anything Charlotte said about the Smiths came dangerously close to breaking confidentiality.

Lance wrapped a hand around her forearm. "Don't worry. I'll take care of this."

She looked down at his fingers gripping her. "I don't need you to take care of anything."

"Don't you?"

The atmosphere heated. His hand branded her flesh through the thin, silky blouse. His gaze was dark, penetrating. Suddenly this wasn't about the Smiths at all. Her breath caught in her throat. Her nipples tightened, aching.

She wasn't even wearing panties.

Lance let go of her arm. His fingers touched her calf lightly. Slid up, stroking the back of her knee. Then higher, slipping around to caress her inner thigh.

This was absolutely crazy. Because she actually wanted it. Even after he'd marched into her office and accused her of malfeasance. "No."

"Yes," he whispered, sliding up, high enough to graze her pussy with his index finger.

She swallowed. Her throat was dry. Everything else was wet. "*No* is my safe word." But her voice didn't sound assured. It was almost a question.

He held her gaze, mesmerized her like a hypnotist or a magician. "Are you sure you want to say no? You aren't wearing panties. That indicates intention, my dear Miss Moore."

His finger barely moved, but it was enough. Simply with the heat of his skin, he made her body clench with need. Her lips formed the word *No* but the sound didn't come out.

He shot her that devilish grin of his. "Which means you're not sure you want to say no." Delving deeper into her sex, he let out a low groan. "Oh, Miss Moore, you are so very wet."

Charlotte's breath came faster as he stroked her clitoris, light, teasing swirls around it. Her legs shifted of their own volition, giving him better access.

Then both his hands were up her skirt. She grabbed his shoulder to steady herself.

"You want it, Miss Moore. You can't help yourself. You need it badly. Because you're such a dirty girl." He talked and stroked, drove her up on the ledge, her legs beginning to quiver. "You love sex. You love to come. You need a man inside you every day. You need my tongue on you, my cock in you. Don't you, Miss Moore." No question about it.

"Yes. God, yes." She sank her fingernails into his shoulder, the climax building, exploding, carrying her away. Red lights flashed before her eyes, bright spots of color, on, off, on, off.

Lord. The light on her phone was flashing. How had they used up half an hour? Her next client was here. And she was letting the principal make her come right here in her office as if nothing else mattered.

She'd lost her mind.

17

"JEANINE, WE SHOULD REALLY TALK." IT WAS AFTER FIVE o'clock, and Charlotte was thankful Jeanine had at least answered her phone.

"I told you I can't see you anymore, Dr. Moore."

"That is your choice. But we need to discuss your husband's mistaken impressions." Charlotte couldn't go to David Smith and tell him exactly what she'd told Jeanine, but she could ask Jeanine to do it. "He believes I encouraged you to"—she put her finger to her lips as if Jeanine could see—"hmm, I think the words were 'to commit deviant acts.'" Yes, her sarcasm was showing. She should have curbed it, acted professionally. But even therapists got angry. "Why would he think that, Jeanine?"

Jeanine stuttered before she finally got her words out. "I don't know, Dr. Moore. I didn't tell him what you said, honestly."

Charlotte wanted to beat her head against the desk. She hadn't been able to call Jeanine until after her last appointment of the day. But that created a problem, too, because she couldn't properly concentrate on her other clients between wondering what David Smith knew, what he planned to do, and the way Lance had made her come against her will. Okay, it wasn't totally against her will, but she'd started out saying no. She just hadn't stuck to it, dammit. The man could talk her into anything.

Note to self: You are losing control of the entire situation. Fix it.

The least she could do now was concentrate on Jeanine. "I'm sure it was a very difficult session with your husband after you two left the meeting. You might have said things you didn't mean because he flustered you." It was better than saying that Jeanine had lied. "So I suggest one last session where we can get all that off your chest. Or we could schedule something with you and your husband, clear the air and work toward straightening things out between you."

Jeanine gave a strangled sound. *"Nooo."*

All right, she simply had to be blunt. "What did you tell your husband about our discussions?"

Jeanine stuttered again before finding her voice. "Just that I discussed his—I mean *our* sexual problems, and that you suggested fantasizing."

There had to be more than that. "He seemed angrier than I'd expect if that's all you said. He went to my principal."

Jeanine sniffed. "I know. I'm so sorry. He just got all wound up about Eric and you being a sex surrogate and—"

"What?" She almost shrieked.

"A sex surrogate," Jeanine said softly, a note of terror in her tone.

"I'm a sex *therapist*, not a *surrogate*. I do not have sex with my clients."

"Oh, oh, yes, I mean sex *therapist*."

"You need to make the distinction with your husband. I would like to talk to you both to work this out."

"He won't come," Jeanine said bluntly. "He wouldn't consider it before. Now he's angry because I didn't tell him and I went behind his back. So he's not going to do any sort of counseling."

Then how the hell was Charlotte supposed to fix this?

"Please, Dr. Moore. I'll take care of it. I'll talk to him. Please."

I'll take care of it. That's what Lance had said. She didn't like it any better when Jeanine said it. "If I could talk to him—"

Jeanine cut her off with an even more forceful plea. *"Please,* Dr. Moore. I'll do it."

Her hands were tied, and not in a good way. She couldn't talk to David Smith without Jeanine's permission.

"All right, Jeanine. But I must insist you come in for one last session on Friday."

"I can't make it Friday."

Charlotte flared her nostrils and narrowed her eyes. If looks could kill . . . But Jeanine couldn't see her. That was a good thing. She was the psychologist after all and needed to maintain some decorum. "Then I'll put you in at your regular time on Monday."

She was pushing, sure, but if she let Jeanine go now, she'd be worse off than when she'd first come to Charlotte. And so would Charlotte.

How had she let things get so out of control?

ON THURSDAY MORNING, MELODY HAD SHUFFLED INTO CHAR-lotte's office wearing the same shapeless brown hoodie, head down, hair lanky and hanging over her face. She'd flopped into the chair opposite and had immediately begun beating her fingernails on the armrests.

Charlotte had been patient. When she thanked Melody for coming in, the reply had been something surly about how she'd been forced. When Charlotte told her they had permission to discuss what happened in the one-on-one session with Melody's parents on Tuesday, she got an eye roll.

Charlotte had trotted out the trite phrase *They only want to help you*, feeling it was necessary. She didn't want to turn them into the villains in Melody's eyes, especially since she intended to disagree with some of the things they'd done.

Yet nothing had much effect on Melody. Charlotte simply couldn't engage her. After fifteen minutes, she'd gotten nowhere. Since it didn't appear she had anything to lose—Melody was already alienated from everything and everyone—Charlotte went to the issue that bothered her the most.

"Your mother said she offered to pay for your surgery to have breast implants. How do you feel about that, Melody? Is it something you want to do?"

Melody's lips pursed and Charlotte sensed she was gritting her teeth. Finally she said, "No," her voice clipped, angry.

"Why not?"

Melody turned the question back on her. "Do you think I should do it?"

It was the first time Charlotte felt she'd truly engaged the girl. She wasn't going to cop out by asking another question. "No."

"Why not?"

"I don't think breast implants solve the fundamental issue."

"How would you know?" Melody pointed at Charlotte's chest. "Obviously you've never had to worry about it. You never had kids make fun of you."

True, her breasts had never been an issue for her. But funnily enough, they weren't something Lance had gone gaga over. He was all about spanking her. And other things. At her age, breasts didn't really matter anymore, except to worry about sagging.

"You're right. That wasn't one of my problems. But there's always something you don't like about yourself. If you have breast enlargements, that solves that. But then you'll worry about your acne. And when your acne is gone—"

"What if it's never gone?"

Charlotte gave her an earnest look. "It will go away. It just doesn't feel like that now."

"Easy for you to say."

"Yes, it is. But the issue is that we're worried about the outside, not the inside. If all we ever like about ourselves is what we look like on the outside instead of who we are on the inside, then we're never satisfied."

Melody shook her head. "That's for sure."

The fact that the girl sounded neither sullen nor combative gave Charlotte hope. "Women will always find something they don't like about themselves. They look in the mirror and they hate this or they despise that." She rolled her eyes. "And don't even get me started about how we react when we start to age." She tried to smooth out the wrinkles across her forehead. "No one told me not to frown when I was a kid."

"Maybe you should try Botox." Something glinted in Melody's eyes, and Charlotte realized the teenager was looking at her, not hiding behind her hair. And that perhaps the girl had made a joke.

Charlotte smiled slightly. "No, I don't think so."

"Why not? My mom gets it."

Yes, and Kathryn Wright wanted her daughter to get injections, too. But Charlotte gave Melody her most honest answer. "For a lot of reasons. First, it's botulism, and I just have a problem with injecting deadly stuff into my forehead. Second, I'm the type of person that when I fix one thing, I'll start wanting to fix something else. I'm not sure where it would stop. And what if I didn't like the results?" She pointed at Melody. "But you're young enough to remember not to wrinkle your forehead."

"My mother tells me not to all the time. But that's the least of my worries right now." Melody put her hand to her forehead, stopped short of actually touching her skin which was marred by several pimples. "I don't want to be like my mom," she said softly.

"Then how would you describe your mom with that idea in mind, of not being like her?" Charlotte asked with equal softness.

"She's all about food and counting every calorie and never gaining an ounce." She pulled her sweatshirt away from her body. "That's why I always wear baggy stuff, or she'll start nagging me to have liposuction. She always tries the latest fad, every new wrinkle cream or whatever. Like that stuff that grows your eyelashes. I don't know why she needs it all. I think she looks great for her age."

For her age. "She's afraid of growing old, like we all are when we're past thirty-five."

"I *wanna* be old," Melody said emphatically. "Then you don't have to care what people think of you anymore."

Right. When you become invisible. Charlotte didn't say that. "That's the thing, though. If you're all about appearance, you'll always care what people think of you. You'll never be able to stand in front of the mirror and look at yourself without wanting to change it all." She didn't know if this was the right time to say it. Maybe it was too soon and she'd drive Melody away. But Charlotte took a chance. "You have to like yourself, flat chest, pimples, and all. Or you'll end up like your mom."

"But how do I like *me* when I'm like this?" Melody whispered, tears suddenly brimming in her eyes.

Charlotte tipped her head, considering. "Tell me something you like about yourself."

"Nothing."

"Well, for one thing, you're pretty smart."

"I guess so."

"I saw your middle school transcripts. Almost all A's. Especially in math and science."

"Yeah."

"Give me another thing that's good."

"I don't know." She shrugged.

Charlotte took another chance. "Tell me something that Eric likes about you."

Melody's head snapped up. "Eric? He hates me."

"No, he doesn't. You two used to be best friends."

"We're not best friends anymore." Charlotte detected a note of sadness in the girl's voice.

"All right. Then tell me why he *used* to like you."

Melody didn't say anything. Charlotte let the silence hang between them, waiting her out.

"He used to say I was funny. That I made him laugh."

"Did you make other people laugh, too? They probably liked you for it."

Melody nodded her head.

"Maybe you used to be able to laugh at yourself. Like when you did something silly. And you and Eric laughed about it."

"Yeah. There was this time we were flying kites, and I was running and running. And I ran right into him, knocked us both down, and lost my kite. My dad was really mad because the kite cost a lot of money, but Eric and I just laughed and laughed 'cause I was so stupid." A smile curved her lips, and Charlotte noted how it changed her face. She was pretty despite the acne.

She let Melody sit with the memory a moment, then asked, "Do you feel stupid about it now?"

Melody shook her head. "No, it was just funny."

"I bet if we asked Eric, there'd be other things he likes about you besides being funny."

Melody shrugged, suddenly shy.

"Our time's almost up. But I've got some homework for you. I want you to think of some other things that you like about yourself. Because I know there's more."

"Yeah, sure, whatever," Melody said, her tone once again sullen, as if she was suddenly aware that she'd given away too much of her inner self in the meeting and needed to hold it close again.

They had so much to work on, but Melody had opened up for a very short time. Charlotte decided to count that as progress.

LANCE HADN'T CALLED HER LAST NIGHT, NOT TO CHECK UP ON her session with Melody, not for phone sex. Nothing. Charlotte told herself not to be disappointed.

Besides, she had clients today. Friday was usually a busy day until midafternoon, then her appointments trailed off. With the weekend coming up, people didn't want to get into a bunch of messy emotions. She'd been told this by a couple of clients. So with some free time, she was updating file notes.

Hearing a noise out in the waiting room, she glanced up. She'd left the connecting door open since she was alone.

"Hello?" she called, pausing with her fingers on the keyboard.

"Miss Moore?" Eric Collins stopped in the office doorway.

She gaped. "Eric, what on earth are you doing here?"

"I looked you up on the Internet. It has your address and phone number and everything." He was neat, as usual, wearing jeans and a leather bomber jacket. She hadn't realized they'd come back in style, at least not for teenagers.

"Well, I'm glad my website comes up in the search engines," she said noncommittally.

He took one tentative step inside, though she hadn't invited him. "My mom and stepdad were looking at it last night."

Her stomach sank. That couldn't be good. "That's interesting. Was there a specific reason they were doing that?"

"Something about wanting to know exactly what you did. They shut it down, though, as soon as they saw me." He shifted from foot to foot.

Definitely not good. But worse was Eric showing up at her office. "You shouldn't be here without your parents' permission."

"I know, but please, I need to talk to you." He was such an earnest kid. All he wanted to do was help Melody.

Charlotte knew she was on thin ice, but she desperately wanted to help them both. Though it might prove to be the wrong decision, she relented. She had to do whatever she could for these kids. "Sit down." She indicated a chair. "Pull it over here."

He sat facing her. Charlotte saved her file, pushed the keyboard aside, and leaned her elbows on the desk. "Is that why you came? Because your parents looked at my website?"

"They're both acting like total freaks. Always whispering, arguing really, then shutting up the moment one of us walks into the room." She assumed he was including his half brother and sister.

"You realize your dad wouldn't like you being here," she felt obligated to say.

"He's not my dad. He's only my stepfather." His voice held no inflection indicating how he felt about his stepfather. Perhaps it meant that they didn't get along well.

"Regardless," she said, "he's expressly told the principal that you and I shouldn't be talking. I'm sure he told you that, too."

Eric tilted his chin defiantly. "I don't see why. I'm fifteen and if I'm going to follow some prime directive from him, then I deserve to know why. Since he won't tell me, I decided to ask you."

A near irresistible urge to slump her shoulders threatened. It all seemed too complicated to explain. Yet she gave Eric as much of the truth as she could because he was correct, he deserved it. "Your stepfather doesn't approve of my outside practice."

"That's because it's sex therapy," he said softly, looking at the top of her desk as if suddenly embarrassed.

She wanted to explain how what she did wasn't about *sex* in the dirty way David Smith meant it, but that was entering dangerous territory. "I help couples. I help individuals. With a variety of issues. I deal in relationships. But your stepfather has a right to decide whether or not he wants me to be your guidance counselor. And he's decided not to."

Eric flared his nostrils mutinously. "But I'm not coming to you for guidance. I wanted to talk to you about Melody. I only want to help her. If I can't talk to you, how am I supposed to do that?"

Her heart melted for the boy. He was sweet and caring. At his age, so many kids could be inner-directed, making everything about themselves. Even Melody. But all he cared about was helping her. Yet Charlotte was caught between his parents and the school system of which she was a part. She couldn't go against a parent's wishes without a damn good reason.

"I don't see what the big deal is anyway?" Eric went on. "Why's he so angry? Why's he upsetting my mom about what you do outside of school? It's not a crime or anything."

A thread of tension tickled her belly. Eric made it sound like David Smith was suddenly on the warpath. And Lance had told her to stay away from the boy. Could the man actually be after her job? He *was* chairman of the school board. He could make her life very difficult. She loved working with kids. She didn't want to give that up.

"Here's my suggestion," she said calmly. "Talk to Melody on your own."

He made a disgusted sound in his throat. "I've tried that."

"I have a feeling she might be a little more conducive to listening after all that's gone on in the last couple of weeks." She'd sensed a softening in Melody yesterday.

"But what do I say to her?"

"Just tell her how you feel. Tell her things you like about her. That you want to be her friend again. Because that's what you want, isn't it?"

He nodded. "What if she rejects me?"

Nobody liked to put themselves out there only to have their heart stomped. "I can't guarantee she won't. But you could remind her about the good times you had, the fun things you did together. You could say nothing has changed for you." Charlotte shrugged. "Maybe she'll tell you why things changed for her, and that's at least a starting point."

He sat silent for a long moment. He was a thoughtful boy— no, not a boy, a young man—and she had high hopes for him. And for Melody. He could be good for her.

Then he brightened. "All right, Miss Moore, I'll give it one more try."

"Good." She hoped Melody would listen to him. Eric would actually do more good for Melody than Charlotte herself could accomplish.

As he rose to leave, she thought about suggesting that he keep their meeting secret. But she couldn't do that. She could not, in all good conscience, involve a student in a lie.

If he told David Smith, so be it. She'd deal with the fallout.

18

LANCE STOOD ON HER DOORSTEP, ARMS AKIMBO, HANDS ON HIS hips. "Didn't I tell you not to talk to Eric Collins?"

That got Charlotte's back up. "Well, hello to you, too."

He hadn't contacted her all day. He hadn't even called to say he was coming over. He'd simply shown up uninvited. How did he even know Eric had been to see her this afternoon? It was eight o'clock on Friday night. What could have happened in the four hours since she'd seen Eric?

"Answer the question," he snapped.

Okay, that was going too far. She crossed her arms and glared at him. "Eric came to my office. What did you expect me to do, throw him out?"

"Politely escorting him from the premises would have sufficed. Besides, how did he even know where your office is?"

She narrowed her eyes. "Are you accusing me of something?"

"No. I'm asking a question for which the answer confounds me. I was hoping you could clear it up."

"If you stop yelling at me, maybe I could."

"I'm not yelling," he insisted.

It was dark, it was cold, and he wore a thick jacket and dark jeans. She was dressed only in an oversize sweater, black leggings, and silly fuzzy slippers, while the door was standing wide and letting out all her hard-earned heating. Yet she wasn't sure she wanted to invite him in. "You're being autocratic and a bit of an asshole. I'm only inviting you in because it's cold out there and you're wasting my heat."

"Thank you." Once inside, he closed the door behind him, then stood too close, towering over her.

She'd always liked his height, but now she wanted to step back. That, though, seemed like it would be giving him the advantage. "There, now, if you'll remain calm, I'll tell you that Eric overheard his parents talking and he saw them looking at my website. My office address is right there for all to see."

"That's a reasonable explanation."

"Well, thank you very much," she said sarcastically.

"I'm not angry with you," he said flatly.

"Then why are you standing all tall and mighty and glowering at me?" She glowered right back, though with her height, it didn't have the same effect.

"I'm simply pissed at Smith's interference. This is my school, and it will be run my way. I am there every day, and I know what's best for my students."

That was pretty autocratic, and know-it-all, too. On the other hand, when the school board started getting into the minutiae of day-to-day procedure, it undermined a principal's authority in the eyes of the student body and the parents.

"Look," she said, "Eric came to me. I told him that his stepfather disapproved and that he had to leave."

Lance raised one brow.

Good God, this was ridiculous. She sighed. "I felt compelled to explain about my practice, but we did *not* talk about any sexual aspect of what I do. I told him that the best he could do for Melody was to talk to her." She tipped her head. "So what did Smith say?"

"He said you were counseling Eric in an offsite private office with no supervision whatsoever. After he'd expressly stated that you were not to talk with the boy."

"It was five minutes," she said, her tone edged with disgust. "It was definitely not counseling." She hadn't told Eric to keep it a secret. But why had he told his stepfather? He must have known it would cause trouble.

"Why can't you just follow orders, Miss Moore? I told you not to talk to him. I'm taking care of things."

He was tall, she was short, so she couldn't very well get right up in his face, but she stood her ground before him, meeting him glare for glare. "Excuse me, but I'm the one coming under fire with Smith, not you. And it's my job we're talking about. You will not take care of things for me. I'll do it myself." But up to this point, everything she'd tried to do had only made the situation worse.

Lance clenched his back teeth as he spoke. "You need to be taught another lesson, Miss Moore, because you simply didn't learn the first time." He pointed. "Get in the bedroom. Right now."

He was still glaring at her, yet the words completely threw her. They were the things he said to her when they assumed their roles. They were sexual. And they were hot.

"Now," he whispered, catching her with the gleaming light of his gaze as he reached into his coat pocket for something.

Then she saw what he held: the silk handcuffs. And a coil of rope.

She was suddenly and inexplicably wet.

* * *

CHRIST, SHE MADE HIM HARD WHEN SHE GOT ALL FEISTY.

"Don't test my patience, Miss Moore," he said with a hard edge that promised retribution if she didn't obey.

Her features softened, her eyes going wide, and a little pucker of a frown creased her forehead. "But we were talking about Eric." Her tone hinted at bewilderment.

"We're done talking about Eric. Move. Now." His voice was dangerous enough to make her back up.

"But—"

"Your punishment will be worse with every second you delay."

Finally realizing there was no alternative, she turned her back on him and flounced down the hall. He enjoyed the incongruous effect of the sexy, skin-tight leggings outlining her thighs versus the fuzzy blue slippers. What were they? The Cookie Monster? Or was it Barney? No, Barney was purple, the Cookie Monster was blue.

Removing his jacket, he tossed it over the back of a chair. Smith had called him over an hour ago. Eric had arrived home extremely late from school, late even for dinner, and when questioned— Lance imagined Smith strong-arming him with gestapo tactics— he'd admitted that he'd been to see Charlotte. Smith had been damn near frothing over the phone.

"I won't have that woman corrupting my son, Hutton." He'd gone on to say he'd even bring in the Wrights to help "shut that woman down."

The man had stopped short of demanding Lance fire Charlotte. Which Lance had no intention of doing. She'd done nothing wrong, and he wouldn't be bullied by Smith. He would stand by her, protect her. She was his. But that didn't mean he wouldn't use the incident as an excuse for a little punishment session.

Damn, he was really getting into the role of master. He followed her into the bedroom.

She stood at the end of the bed, which was covered in a thick flowered comforter. Brass rails stood at the head and the foot. Good thing because he had plans for those rails. The room was done in shades of lavender, with white furniture, the drawers painted a contrasting pale lavender. The lampshade matched. The room was small, as they usually were in these old houses. The closet had only one door with a full-length mirror secured to it.

Her mouth was set in a mutinous line now. She'd obviously gotten over her shock at his abrupt switch from work to sex.

"Pull back the covers and get on the bed," he directed.

"Make me." She scowled. His jeans got tighter over the growing bulge of his cock.

Marching to the head of the bed, he laid the rope and silk cuffs on the side table. Then he grabbed the edge of the comforter, making sure to take the top sheet and blanket with it, and pulled the whole assembly down, bunching it at the bottom of the bed. Stomping back to her, he hauled her up and around, then tossed her into the center of the mattress. Landing on her back, she squealed. Before she could scurry away, Lance secured her wrist in his hand and dragged her to the edge of the bed closest to the side table.

She tried to wriggle free. "You bastard."

He held tight. "You, Miss Moore, are incorrigible. You can't follow directions. You don't obey orders. The only choice is to tie you up and make you take whatever I dish out."

Of course, he had a problem now. If he let go of her wrist, she'd roll away and run. But without releasing her, he couldn't get the damn cuffs on.

She looked from him to the bedside table, reading his mind, and smiled wickedly. "Gotcha."

"No such luck, Miss Moore." He flopped down on top of her, surprising an *oomph* from her. "You have to remember that I always win." The silk cuffs were in reach and within a few seconds he had her wrists secured.

She glared at him, her lips set in a grave line, and tried to buck him off.

"Oh baby, that only makes things so much better," he whispered.

When she opened her mouth, presumably to hurl a few more insults or to scream, maybe even to bite him, he sealed his lips on hers. He drugged her with the kiss, taking her deep with his tongue until she fell still except for the slight rise of her head to meet his mouth. A moan vibrated in her throat.

He backed off. "You are so easy, Miss Moore."

"Actually, I've got you right where I want you, Principal Hutton." She gave him a haughty little smile. "You've stopped castigating me about Eric and now you're going to make me come. Gee"—she flashed him toothy grin—"looks like I'm the one in charge."

Hell, yes. She was. He was completely smitten. He'd do anything she wanted. If she said she wanted to tie him to the bed, he'd have handed her the rope and loved everything she did to him. Of course, he wasn't going to tell her that.

He flicked the neck of her sweater. "Is this an expensive outfit you can't live without?"

She laughed. "It's so old, half the nap has worn off. Since you failed to let me know you were coming, I didn't have a chance to dress up for you."

"Good." He reached for the rope he'd brought with him. Already cut in lengths, he wound one of the pieces through the center of the silk cuffs between her wrists and secured it to the brass rail above her head.

"Does it hurt?" he asked.

"Will you untie me if I say yes?"

"Only if I think you're telling the truth."

"You're not going to have any idea."

He eyed her. She would never be any man's submissive. She would always give her master hell. That's why she was so perfect. He didn't want a doormat. "In that case, I presume everything feels fine."

He left her there, her wrists bound and tied to the headboard.

"Where are you going?" she called.

He padded into the kitchen, opened and closed drawers until he found what he wanted. Then he returned, laying a pair of scissors on the side table.

She narrowed her eyes at him. "What are those for?"

"If you stay very still, this won't hurt a bit."

He tucked his fingers in the waistband of her leggings and yanked them down over her hips, pulling her panties right along with them. Her pretty little bush was a lighter shade of red than her hair, almost a strawberry blond. He couldn't resist putting his lips to her trimmed mound. Then he couldn't resist flicking his tongue between her lips. She was spicy and hot, potent on his tongue. And very, very wet.

Charlotte groaned.

"Why, Miss Moore, for all your talk, it appears you're actually enjoying this." He blew a breath on her and was rewarded with a shudder. Her legs moved restlessly.

Lance tugged the leggings and panties all the way down. "Love the slippers, Miss Moore." Then he tossed everything aside.

She lifted her head to look at him. "I hate it when I'm naked and you're fully dressed."

He trailed a hand up her shin, over her knee, along her thigh. Then he toed off his shoes and climbed onto the bed to straddle her. "All in good time, baby."

Retrieving the scissors from the table, he slit the sweater up the front.

Charlotte shrieked. "Oh my God."

He brandished the scissors. "Settle down, Miss Moore. Or I'll have to gag you." After cutting the shoulder, he sliced the sweater down her arm. Charlotte didn't struggle. Repeating the procedure on the opposite side, he yanked the ruined material away to reveal her gorgeous breasts in a black lace bra. His mouth watered with the need to taste her.

"You could have just taken it off me before you tied me up," she said dryly.

"You were struggling." He flashed a wide grin. "Then I forgot until it was too late. At least I remembered to take off your pants before I tied your legs."

"Oh no, please. Don't tie my legs. I won't struggle anymore, I promise." She was such a good actress that tears brimmed in her eyes.

"I don't trust you not to kick me."

"I promise I won't."

He shook his head slowly. "No. This is what I've dreamed of and this is what I'll have."

Climbing off, he surveyed her ankles, her legs tight together. The possibility of rope burns existed. "Stay right there."

"It's not like I can go anywhere," her voice followed him down the hall.

He found two washcloths, one pink, one gray, in the pink-and-gray bathroom. They'd work perfectly. Back in the bedroom, he was struck anew by the sight of her. The glow of the lamp through its colored shade bathed her limbs in lavender tones. The sweet triangle of hair at her apex beckoned. Her lush breasts spilled over her bra cups.

His gaze traveled up to the hollow of her throat, then to the frowning, narrow-eyed glare focused on him.

"Someday, you will pay, Principal Hutton."

"I look forward to it." He swathed her ankle in a cloth, knotted a length of rope and twined it around, then ended by tying it off on a foot rail. "This is going to be so good," he mused as he rounded the bottom of the bed. He spread her legs, tied her down.

Fishing in his pocket for the condoms he'd brought, he laid them on the side table within easy reach. He'd need them eventually, but first, he was going to play. "Now, what to do with a naked woman all spread out for me like a feast?"

"Eat me?" she suggested.

"Good idea." He leaned over and sucked her big toe.

She giggled.

He licked his way up her shin, over her knee cap, along her inner thigh, following the path he'd taken earlier with his hand. Dew drops glistened on her neatly trimmed curls, the bud of her clit pink and plump. Instead of his tongue, he used his nose to nudge her, breathing in her spicy scent. He felt the slightest of tremors travel through her body.

Then he looked up. She'd lifted her head to watch him, her eyes an exotic, primitive jungle green, her hair a sexy, rumpled mess.

"I'll make you scream with pleasure, Miss Moore. Then I'm going to fuck the hell out of you." He slipped a hand into the cup of her bra and pinched her nipple, startling a gasp from her as her body arched into his touch. "But first I'm going to feast on these perfect breasts."

* * *

CHARLOTTE COULD BARELY BREATHE. THE PINCH HAD BEEN LIKE a live wire attached directly to her clitoris. Her body was on fire, her pussy dripping with need, her nipples aching for more.

Then he took off his clothes, standing gloriously naked before her.

She'd never met a man who could make her lose all sense the way he did. One minute he was berating her, the next he was spreading her out on her bed. And she let him. She wanted everything he did to her.

She was completely under his spell.

He grabbed one of the pillows he'd thrown on the carpet earlier and tucked it beneath her head. Better. Now she could see everything he did without getting a crick in her neck.

"Don't you dare cut this bra," she said hotly as he straddled her, his leg hair soft against her skin, the underside of his balls caressing her, his cock hard and pulsing. The words were supposed to give her a modicum of control, but she was totally in his power. Not because she was tied down and at his mercy, but because she wanted this.

"It's too pretty to destroy." He undid the front clasp, pushed the cups aside, and let out a long, slow breath of appreciation. "Your breasts are so fucking gorgeous."

She wanted to preen beneath his gaze. She wanted to hold them out for his touch and his taste. Instead, he gathered both nipples between thumbs and forefingers and tweaked hard.

Charlotte cried out as sensation zinged straight down to her clitoris.

There were things they needed to discuss. Eric. His father. Her job. Melody.

But in a split second, Lance had turned off all those switches and flipped on the one that was all about sex, about touch and taste and sensation.

"These are mine," he whispered, bending low over her, plumping one breast in his big hand, and devouring her nipple. He licked and laved and sucked hard until she was on the edge of pain. It made the pleasure all that much greater. She tried to form words, but there were only sounds, a groan, a sigh, a moan. He switched his attention to her other breast, gave it the same treatment, and just when she was sure it was pain and not pleasure, he pinched the opposite nipple. Charlotte cried out. She almost came. She quivered, felt a rush of moisture inside, close, so close, yet she squeezed her muscles, holding it off. Not yet. It wouldn't be good enough. She needed his fingers on her clit, his tongue in her pussy, his cock filling her.

Just when she thought she might not be able to fight the climax, he lifted his head to gaze up at her. "Perfect," he whispered as he insinuated a hand between their bodies and dipped his fingers in all her moisture, stroked her. Her body started to hum again. She thrust her head back into the pillow, arched into him.

"This isn't punishment," she said on a gasp.

"It is. Because you're going to beg me to stop at some point. And I'll just keep going until you scream for me."

She couldn't hold out. The climax roared through, blinded her. Until he was no longer straddling her, but lying beside her, knees bent by her ear, his shoulder next to her thigh.

"Now I'm going to lick you, baby. You're going to come again for me." He spread her folds, put his tongue to her. Charlotte's body jerked. She was still sensitive.

"No flinching. Or I'll hold you down."

"I can't help it." She gasped and jerked as he sucked on her. Too much, too much.

He climbed over her in a classic sixty-nine position, gathered her buttocks in his big hands, and went at her. Trapped beneath him, she strained and bucked. His cock bobbed close, and Charlotte opened her mouth, capturing him between her lips, drawing him in. She couldn't come when she was sucking his cock. She'd ride the edge, but Charlotte had never been able to do two things at once, at least not those two things.

Yet somehow it was worse—or much, much better—where her body felt ready to tumble, almost there, quivering, rolling, needing, wanting, but just a second away from implosion. His taste in her mouth, his scent swirling around her, thick, hard, hips pumping slightly, fucking her mouth. There were only the guttural sounds of sex, its mesmerizing aroma.

Then he put two fingers inside her, and Charlotte opened her mouth to scream, lost him, felt only the warmth of his flesh against her cheek as she shattered yet again.

He barely let her catch her breath. Once again, he was lying beside her, his lips and chin glistening with her juices. "Where's your vibrator?"

"In the drawer." She pointed with her chin.

He rolled over her body, found the toy, flopped back down beside her, and switched it on. She felt the buzz of it deep in her body before he even pressed it to her.

"You like it right here, don't you?" He glanced up as he circled her clitoris with it.

"Oh God, oh God." The sensations were almost too intense to bear after having already come twice.

He circled lightly, didn't press too hard, didn't enter her, just swirled round and round until she was mindless. When she was alone, she could come, then rest, start again, build again, come, rest.

But Lance never stopped. He just kept on and on at her. With his fingers, the vibrator, his mouth, his tongue. She rode from peak to peak, or maybe it was all one long orgasm that never ended. She begged but he didn't stop.

When she couldn't have said her name or his name or even her safe word, Charlotte gave him what he demanded. She screamed.

19

CHARLOTTE COULDN'T OPEN HER EYES. HE WAS ADDICTIVE. SHE was supposed to be angry with him about something, but he had the ability to make her completely forget everything else.

He leaned over her, his skin brushing the length of hers, his cock hard against her belly, his breath sweet in her hair. "We're not done yet, Miss Moore."

She groaned. She simply couldn't take another orgasm. But he was off the bed, padding around it. Charlotte couldn't find the strength to open her eyes to see what he was doing. Then he was touching her, lifting her, shoving a pillow beneath her bottom. If her ankles weren't tied, it would have been quite comfortable.

His hairy legs nestled between her thighs. He teased, petted, stroked, and her body responded despite the fact that she was drifting in another plane of existence.

Then he caressed her folds with the blunt tip of his cock. Her body began to tingle the way her mouth did after a breath strip or a potent mint. He eased inside her, just the head, pumped slowly, filling her with barely more than an inch or two. The tingle became heat, then fire, but somehow icy at the same time.

Finally Charlotte opened her eyes. "Oh my God. What are you doing?"

"Special condom," he said, his body arching, withdrawing, hands on her thighs.

Of course she knew about them. She'd recommended such items, even used them, but in that slow, shallow rhythm, he caressed her G-spot with heat and frost that had the potential to drive her mad.

Yet this time she needed to watch. With his swarthy features and his hair more dark than gray, he was like a wicked satyr plundering her. She wanted to reach out to stroke the light dusting of silver-and-black hair on his chest, but her hands were tied. She wanted to curl her legs around his hips, pull him in, but she could do nothing more than strain at the ropes binding her ankles.

"Untie my legs," she begged. "Please."

He smiled his devil smile, knowing he had her, that she'd given in to all his temptations. He leaned right, then left, the knots releasing easily, and Charlotte wrapped her legs around him, drawing him deep inside her. "God," she whispered, shoving her head back into the pillow and arching.

"Jesus, that's hot."

She looked up again to find him watching the slow glide of his cock in and out, thick and hard, possessing her. Wrapping her fingers around the bedrail he'd tied her to, she braced herself, bearing down on him.

"Fuck." His whisper was harsh and guttural. His eyes on her were smoky hot.

She'd always told her clients to let themselves go, try new things, experiment. She'd claimed that with the right partner, anything could happen. But in this moment, she knew she'd never achieved what she'd recommended for her clients. She hadn't even come close. Until now, with him, her principal.

Then he reached for something on the bed beside her, the vibrator. Its heavy buzzing filled the air as he parted her, pressing the edge to her clit and the tip against his cock. Her body started to tremble, her breath puffing. Everywhere they touched was hot and icy, and the vibrator simply intensified it all.

"Put your legs up here." He patted his shoulders.

She lifted her limbs, laid her calves on his chest, her feet up close to his ears. He held one ankle. "Squeeze your legs tight."

As she did, the sensations magnified tenfold, the vibrator on her clit, his cock stroking her with the tingly, icy heat of the condom. Her body contracted around him, her legs quaked, and she felt herself riding the edge of an endless orgasm.

SHE WAS BEAUTIFUL IN HER BLISS, HER EYES SQUEEZED TIGHTLY shut, lashes fanning her cheeks, red lips pressed together, fingers white with tension around the bedrail above her. Her body's contractions urged him on to a faster pace, pulled him in, but he kept up that slow, inexorable thrust. He'd found her G-spot and he rode it relentlessly. Her legs trembled and shook against him, but he imprisoned her ankle in one hand so she couldn't wriggle away or dislodge the vibrator. She bucked and heaved against him, her hair flying across the pillow, strands catching in the lipstick that remained on her mouth. She was no longer aware of him, he was just a body, a cock, hard flesh. He'd never felt anything like it, the tight squeeze of her muscles along with the zing of the condom. He'd felt it the moment her body had begun to heat the latex, setting sensation loose. It was enough to drive a younger man to fucking her hard and fast and deep, taking his pleasure, needing it. Yet Lance didn't give in, not yet.

He had never done to a woman what he'd done to her, never made a woman scream, never made her lose herself the way Charlotte was lost in this moment. Now that he'd had it, he'd never give it up, never give *her* up.

She wailed with her release, her body bowing. If her hands had been free, she would have curled into him. Fixing him with a suddenly fervent gaze, she chanted, "Now, now, now."

It was time. He tossed the vibrator, parted her legs and fell on her, taking her, plunging deep, pounding her with his body, her cries in his ear. She took him with the same ferocity, muscles clenching, milking, working, until he was as lost in her as she was in him. Until the orgasm that tore through him was both pleasure and pain, infinite ecstasy.

For long moments, minutes, or hours, he was aware of nothing but the heat of her skin against his and the lush feel of her pussy surrounding his cock. He didn't know how long he'd lain flush atop her with his full weight, but he became aware of her laughter, soft, a little crazed.

"Oh my God," she muttered. "So that's what they mean by having died and gone to heaven."

"I'd say it was just going to heaven," he murmured into her fragrant hair. "We're still alive to do it again." And they would, over and over. This was just the beginning.

"I'll definitely have to recommend those condoms." She sighed. "And the position. And the vibrator. My God, I felt like I didn't stop coming for about five minutes, but then there was a major explosion. God."

He nuzzled her. "You moved me to greater heights." He'd planned only to tie her to the bed and have his way with her. The rest had been inspiration, including the condoms which he'd seen at the drugstore. He hadn't realized the effect they'd have. He didn't know shit about kinky sex, but he sure was learning. That was an educator's motto: You're never too old to learn.

"But my arms are starting to feel like they'll pull out of my sockets."

Hell. "Sorry. I just didn't want to pull out yet." He reached high, fiddled with the knots—they'd come apart so much more easily in the throes of passion—then pulled her arms down to rub her wrists. He needed to get rid of the condom, too, yet he hated to leave her.

"Don't move," he said. She was still crashed on the bed when he returned, a pillow beneath her sexy ass, another under her head. She'd ditched the bra, though, and was now gloriously naked.

Standing in the doorway, he realized he could stay in that bed with her forever.

She turned and rolled to the edge of the bed, moving slowly, as if her muscles were sore.

"I'll give you a back rub," he said.

She nodded. "I have to use the bathroom." She rubbed her face in his chest hair as she passed. It was surprisingly intimate, and his gut tightened with more than desire.

She didn't close the bathroom door, and he could hear her, the toilet flushing, water running, then a few moments later the soft whoosh of the fridge opening. She returned with two bottles of water, hers already a quarter empty. He didn't realize how thirsty he was until he'd gulped several mouthfuls.

She'd also brought a bottle of oil, and when she climbed back onto the bed and stretched out on her stomach, she said, "Okay, that back rub you promised."

He went to work on her hands, arms, neck, and shoulders, along her spine, every muscle. She moaned and groaned almost as if she were climaxing all over again. His cock stirred. He massaged her buttocks, her thighs, her calves, the soles of her feet. The oil scented the air, perfumed her body, filled his head. Lavender, like the color of the room.

By the time he was done, he was throbbing again, hard, his balls aching with need. She might have fallen asleep. She didn't open her eyes as he reached for the second condom on the side table. She didn't protest as he spread her legs and entered her from behind. She was still slick and hot. The only move she made was to hug the pillow she was lying on. He was slow and gentle this time, taking long minutes to build the tension. She didn't moan, didn't make a sound until the moment he pushed a hand beneath her and found her clit.

Then she gasped, her body contracted around him, and she buried her face in the pillow as he filled her, coming as soundlessly as he did.

Her climax was no less powerful, merely different, not frantic and mind-altering, but somehow just as intimate. Like the way she'd rubbed her face against his chest.

This time he didn't pull out to remove the condom. He simply rolled to the side, taking her with him, put his head beside hers on the pillow, and fell asleep with her in his arms.

HIS SKIN WAS HOT AGAINST HER BACK, BUT HER FRONT WAS cold without the blankets. Charlotte had programmed the thermostat to turn down to fifty-five degrees at ten o'clock. So it was after ten, but the clock was on the bedside table behind her. Behind him. She had no idea how long they'd slept, but they hadn't moved much, and he was still inside her. She felt filled. Surrounded. Sated. It would have been perfect except for the heating, or lack thereof.

She hadn't slept with a man in a long time. She didn't sleep with men she was only casually dating, i.e., men she had sex with. The last time she'd dated seriously—meaning she saw the man for more than sex and might actually consider a relationship with him—had been eighteen months ago. The last real relationship— where she considered long-term commitment and even marriage— had been over three years. He'd also been five years younger than she was, while Lance was ten years older. The boy, which he was compared to the principal, would never have tied her to the bed; she would have tied him. Not that they'd ever done anything kinky, but she would still have liked to be the one doing the tying up. At least she'd always thought she'd want it that way until tonight. In the end, they'd parted company because he had wanted children and Charlotte wasn't ready. She still wasn't, and she was beginning to believe she might never be ready. She'd make that final decision when she turned forty.

Did Lance want kids?

The question shocked her fully awake.

He made a throaty rumble against her hair, hitched her closer, wrapped his arm across her middle and palmed her breast. She started to feel warm again. Comfortable. Too comfortable. As if she'd like to sleep this way all night, securely in his arms.

"I'm cold," she said, her voice too loud in the still room. "And I have to pee." It was blunt, unromantic. He grumbled unintelligibly, but it forced him to release her.

Free at last, she grabbed her robe off the hook on the inside of the closet door and used the bathroom. When she came out, he was in the kitchen. He'd obviously disposed of the condom in the trash and now stood naked, his body beautiful in the dim light from the hall. She had the insane urge to nuzzle her face in the soft hair on his chest like she'd done earlier. But that was before. This was now. The stove clock showed it was ten minutes to midnight.

"I'll use the facilities, too," he said, passing her in the hallway, running his fingers lightly across her abdomen. Her body reacted immediately, tightening, getting wet, ready.

She couldn't remember the last time a man made her feel like this with a single touch. Maybe she'd never felt like this.

In the bedroom, she straightened the pillows at the head of the bed and pulled up the covers. She untied the rope, coiled it, and laid it on the table along with the red silk cuffs.

The first sex had been wild and crazy. But the next, after the massage, had been deliciously sensual, as if it had been one long massage, first on the outside, then on the inside.

He wrapped his arms around her from behind and nestled his face in the crook of her neck. "Mmm," he said, as if it were a word instead of a sound.

"It's almost midnight," she said.

"Yeah." He rubbed his hand on her belly, round and round.

It was easier at his house because she could simply leave. Here, she had to tell him to go. But they needed to stick to the rules. She couldn't sleep with him. She couldn't wake up wondering if he wanted children. She couldn't start thinking about past relationships and him all in the same dreamy state. Since he would always be the one who did the tying up. He wasn't built to do it any other way. Which was fine in the bedroom, but as today had proved, he wanted to lord it over her everywhere, at school and in her practice. She just couldn't allow that. Because for a moment there, he'd made her doubt herself, made her wonder if she'd handled Jeanine incorrectly, and her husband. Even her son.

So he couldn't spend the night. It was simply too dangerous.

"Midnight is when we part company," she said.

He stiffened against her and not in a good way. The belly rub ended. "Perhaps we should bend the rules tonight."

"No." It was unequivocal. It was her safe word.

"Yes. For tonight." He reached down to pull back the covers, making a spot for them.

She tried to pry his fingers off her abdomen, but he clenched. "I will spend the night. You are my submissive and you will do as I say."

"I'm not your submissive after midnight. That's what we agreed."

"Don't be ridiculous. It's midnight. I'm not driving home. I'm staying here."

She wriggled furiously. "Like hell you are."

"You don't have a choice." Holding her tightly with one arm, imprisoning both wrists, he grabbed one of the ropes she'd rolled up.

It had been a sexy fight before, bucking on the bed, fighting him. Seriously, she'd tried to stop him, but she'd enjoyed his triumph over her. This was completely different.

"No. I mean it." She tried to kick back, but he lifted her off her feet and fell down on the bed with her.

It was almost frightening to realize the strength of a man, despite the fact that she knew he would never hurt her. She couldn't pry her hands loose. She couldn't kick him off. In a matter of seconds, her wrists were bound and he'd secured her once again to the headboard. Her robe was up past her waist, and he was hard against her backside.

He reached back to turn out the light, then pulled the covers over them, curled an arm beneath her breasts, and put his lips to her ear. "Now, isn't that much more comfortable than sleeping alone?"

God, it could be good, far too good. "I am seriously pissed," she said.

"Admit it, you wanted me to spend the night. I made it easier by forcing the issue."

That was the worst part. He was right. She wanted him to stay. She wanted him wrapped around her all night long. She wanted to wake up in the morning to the feel of him inside her. She wanted to make him peach pancakes for breakfast.

That was why he had to go.

Except that the principal wasn't going anywhere.

She lay stiff in his arms until his body slackened into sleep, his arm deliciously heavy across her, his length warm along hers. His rhythmic breathing against her neck lulled her.

God, yes, she wanted it. But to have it, she had to accept everything else about him. He wanted to take care of her, protect her, fight her battles for her as if she weren't capable of fighting them herself.

He was a dangerous man. She couldn't control him. He would simply have to go.

LANCE HAD UNTIED HER IN THE MIDDLE OF THE NIGHT. SHE hadn't thrown him out, but she'd gone to the bathroom and returned wearing a pair of sweats.

He'd told himself he would fix things in the morning, but when he awoke, she was gone, leaving him a terse note on the kitchen counter.

I'm at the gym. Please be gone by the time I get back.

At least she was polite. He couldn't believe he'd slept through her leave-taking. Then again, last night had been one hell of a workout.

All right, perhaps he'd made a mistake tying her to her own bed in her own home. It might have worked better in his house. If she hadn't run out, he'd have explained that it was all part of the persona, dom and sub, master and slave, student and principal. It was a game, a role play.

But he knew it wasn't. He'd intended to force the issue. He'd intended to spend the night. And he'd intended to use any means to pull it off.

The mistake he'd made was that it was too soon.

Lance would have stayed to hash it out, but he was sensible enough to realize that if she saw his car out front, she'd simply drive past. Yet it was too demeaning to move it down the street and out of her sight.

No, the best plan was to let her cool down. He'd call her tonight. Or perhaps let her have the weekend and call Sunday night. Yes, that was the better idea.

He would talk her around. After that out-of-this-world sex, he didn't have a doubt that she'd be back for more.

20

"YES, IT WAS A BIT CHILDISH TO WALK OUT AND LEAVE HIM ALL alone," Charlotte agreed.

She'd called Lola for an early morning trip to the gym. Gray had paperwork to finish before Monday, so he'd said it was fine that Lola go. There was something about the phrasing that rumbled in Charlotte's belly, as if Lola needed Gray's permission to do something as ordinary as working out. Then again, Charlotte's irritation could be attributed to her frame of mind, and the real meaning behind Lola's words—and Gray's answer—was simply courtesy.

They were now racing up and down hills on their programmable stationary bikes. Still seething, Charlotte wasn't breathing hard just from the hills. "But he needs to be taught a lesson. He can't just bully me."

"Right, so now you have to talk to him about it later," Lola said reasonably, "instead of getting the discussion out of the way."

Charlotte ignored that. "Here's what really bothers me." She launched into a litany of Lance's transgressions. He wouldn't let her deal with Smith. He ordered her not to talk to Eric. He decided how to handle Melody and Eric without consulting her. He even blamed her for the fact that Eric had shown up at her office as if she'd actually invited the boy there. And he'd tied her to the bed when she told him to leave. She didn't add that he'd made her begin to think she'd mishandled everything.

"I love it when Gray ties me to the bed all night long." Lola smiled, a seductive, inner-directed smile that spoke of all the things Gray did to her while she was restrained.

Despite being a Saturday morning, the gym was close to empty. Charlotte had received a two-week trial membership—with Lola as her guest for the day—but she'd already wasted a week. The place, though, was kind of cheesy, the machines not as clean as she'd like and the odor of sweat hanging like a pall over the big room. In addition, the lone man also in attendance had chosen a treadmill only two machines away instead of on the other side of the room. Somewhere in his early thirties, he had quite an impressive set of pectorals, and his calves weren't bad either, muscles rippling as he ran. Usually, that would be enough to make her slightly wet. Yet the only thing getting wet was her face, perspiration dotting her upper lip and forehead from her workout on the stationary bike. He looked . . . too young. He didn't stand out in a room the way Lance did. Good God, the damn principal was even affecting how she looked at other men.

Though the guy appeared to be watching CNN, the TV wasn't loud enough to actually discern what the newscaster was saying. Charlotte wondered if their voices carried.

Whatever. She didn't bother to tone down. He could eavesdrop all he wanted. "It's not about whether I liked what he did. It's that I asked him to leave and he didn't. And when I insisted, he threw me on the bed and tied me up."

"God, that's sexy," Lola said.

Charlotte made a disgusted sound in her throat. It had been sexy the first time he'd done it last night. Okay, if she was honest, it was sexy the second time, too. But it still pissed her off.

"He did it even though I'd specifically told him that spending the night together was not part of our deal. He manipulated me."

Lola wiped the perspiration off her forehead with a towel. "Did you hate it?"

"No. And you know that's not the point."

Lola shrugged. "I know it. But do you know what the real point is?"

"Of course. He's trying to control me. In and out of the bedroom."

"No. The point is that you can't separate the sex games from the workplace."

"That is absolutely not true." But she felt a twinge. Because a similar thought had occurred to her that day in Lance's office, just before the Wrights arrived.

"I have never heard you complain about the way *Principal* Hutton"—Lola stressed the title—"dealt with some issue at school."

"That's because I didn't have anything to do with him. I've always gone through Alice."

"Yeah, but he still brought down edicts from on high. Like the time that kid was caught in a lie on his admission application. You just wanted to send in a corrected form, but the principal said there had to be consequences for that kind of action, and the school couldn't simply brush it under the rug."

Oh. Yeah. "See, he was a hard-ass even then. That mistake has followed Chris through the rest of his academic career."

Lola gave her a long look. "It wasn't a mistake. He lied. And as I recall, you admitted that the principal was right. You wanted to assist the kid, but you agreed that covering up his lies wasn't helping him grow into a better human being."

The falsified applications had been withdrawn, and Chris didn't get into the university of his choice. But he was accepted into a southern California college that wasn't as expensive and hadn't bankrupted his parents the way the other school would have.

Damn. She should never discuss this kind of stuff with Lola. Because it got thrown back in her face. Lance had made the right call. Charlotte had been too soft.

"But the situation with Eric and Melody isn't the same." Sweat trickled down between her breasts. When was this ride supposed to be over?

"The principal is the one stuck in the middle between you and the school board. When a parent denies you access to a student, don't you have to abide by that? I mean, doesn't he have a point, even a little one?"

Lola was way too reasonable.

"It's the way he's ordering me around that I don't like." Charlotte was sounding childish again.

"Remember when you told me not to throw away this thing with Gray just because I was afraid of a relationship?"

Great. A change of subject. She wasn't the one in the hot seat anymore. "And wasn't I right about that?"

"Totally. But maybe you're throwing away a good thing because you're afraid of giving up even a tiny bit of control."

Damn. It wasn't a new topic.

"If you're worried about your job at the high school, isn't it actually a good thing that he's on your side?"

Charlotte narrowed her eyes, giving Lola a squinty glare. "Who's the psychologist here?"

Lola laughed. "You are. But you always say you can't analyze yourself."

"And you always say I overanalyze."

"Which is exactly what you're doing. Don't dump him yet. Wait till later. Maybe he's not as controlling as you think."

Charlotte glanced at the guy on the treadmill. He was watching the TV now, their conversation obviously boring him since they'd stopped discussing sex.

"All right, fine. The principal gets one more chance," she told Lola. Though she might have to be less available. She wouldn't go to his house whenever he demanded it, or let him drag her to places like the Park and Ride and Lookout Point. She glanced at her program on the cycle's screen. They were on the downhill side of their ride. "Now let's turn the spotlight on you and the coach. When are you moving in?"

Lola groaned. "I don't know. We're still talking." She shrugged. "But we are taking Rafe up to Tahoe for Thanksgiving to do some skiing."

Charlotte gasped, truly surprised. "You mean the ex-wife from hell is going to let Gray have his son for the holiday?"

"They made a bargain. She gets Rafe for Christmas and Gray gets him for Thanksgiving. We're taking Wednesday off to drive up." Wednesday was the last day of school before the holiday and not much of anything happened. Lance always let classes out at noon.

"Wow. Family time," Charlotte said. "How does that feel?"

"Kinda scary. I've never spent this much time with Rafe." She rolled her eyes. "There'll probably be some kind of blowout."

"Don't start thinking that way. So"—Charlotte shot Lola a beady-eyed stare—"are you staying in Gray's room? Or do you get your own, and he and Rafe will share?"

"We sleep together at the house. Gray doesn't hide it. So we're not going to do anything differently up there. I stay with Gray,

Rafe gets his own room. But I am *not* having a communicating door."

"Thank God." There were some limits. "This is a huge step in acceptance, you know."

"I'll tell you about acceptance when we get back. Rafe and I are holding our own so far, but five days might be stretching it."

"Be positive. And call me if you feel like you're ready to implode. I'll talk you down."

With Lola gone, she wouldn't have anyone to talk *her* down. She hadn't even thought about the holiday in terms of the principal. Did that mean she wouldn't see him for five days?

Her heart gave a little lurch. She shouldn't have felt anything at all. It was only five days. Only a holiday weekend. She would spend the majority of it with her family—Mom, Dad, two brothers, two sisters, and assorted nieces and nephews. She wouldn't miss Lance at all. Besides, after the way he'd lorded it over her last night, some time apart would give them both greater clarity. Yes, a short break was in order.

"YOU WANT TO TAKE A BREAK UNTIL AFTER THE THANKSGIVING holiday?" Lance was stunned.

He'd called Charlotte Sunday night to apologize. Well, not *apologize*, that wasn't the right word. To discuss whatever issue she had.

"This is a big holiday for my family. It's not just Thanksgiving Day itself, but lots of activities. We all go to the movies on Friday. And if the weather's nice over the weekend"—which it was forecasted to be—"we'll go down to Monterey. We'll probably do the aquarium. The kids love it."

It all sounded like an excuse not to see him. Dammit, he'd

been making plans as if she were now part of his life, while she was still relegating him to the role of dom. And nothing else.

"Besides," she went on in an almost airy tone, "we don't want to give David Smith any more ammunition right now."

"This is private. Just between us. He doesn't know. No one knows." But Charlotte had a point. With Smith on the warpath, Lance stood a better chance of defending Charlotte if no one knew about their relationship. That was in her best interests for the time being.

"All right," he agreed. "But when I see you again, we'll talk about the overnight arrangements. I'm changing the rules." Said just like the dom he was supposed to be. Charlotte would fight, but he would maintain the upper hand.

She huffed loudly, a sure sign of her annoyance. "We'll see about that, Principal Hutton. Until we speak again."

She was gone. He wasn't done, not anywhere near. He'd wanted to hear her come. He'd wanted to come with her.

A week without her? He'd definitely go into withdrawal. But when he had her again, Jesus, it would be explosive. The wait might very well be worth it.

DAMN. SHE SHOULD HAVE AT LEAST GOTTEN AN ORGASM OUT OF that phone call last night. In her haste to assert control over the relationship by saying they needed a break, Charlotte had hung up on Lance too soon. One tiny little orgasm wouldn't have hurt anything. It would definitely have taken the edge off her nerves, especially when she wouldn't have a sexual outlet other than her vibrator until after the holiday. That bit about overnight arrangements and changing the rules, however, didn't bode well for her retaining control.

To top it off, Charlotte was a little edgy before her appointment with Jeanine. She still hadn't decided on the best tactic for handling her client. Should she coerce her into a couple's session with Smith? Charlotte didn't like the word *coerce*. She simply wanted a chance to mediate between them, an opportunity to understand exactly what Jeanine had told her husband, and to correct any misconceptions. At least to identify why he was so angry. Most likely he was afraid Charlotte was going to tell someone what he wanted his wife to do.

The red light flashed on her phone, and her chance to come up with a firm game plan was gone.

Dressed in what Charlotte could only describe as a power suit— tailored jacket with matching skirt—Jeanine took her usual seat, crossed her legs, and primly pulled the skirt's hem to her knees.

"Thank you for coming," Charlotte greeted her.

Jeanine set her purse on the table between them. "First, I apologize for that scene in the principal's office. I didn't handle it correctly."

"It was a shock." Charlotte would give her that.

"If I hadn't gotten upset, David would have been none the wiser."

This gave Charlotte the opportunity she needed. "Our therapy is confidential and private. I would never divulge anything to anyone. But you have the right to privacy, too." Charlotte encouraged her clients to talk about their sessions with their significant others, but she also counseled that they had a right to keep whatever they wanted to themselves. It was a balance. Some of the frank discussions she had with clients could be hurtful to the other partner.

"I didn't tell him much." Despite her power suit, which Charlotte suspected was meant to give her courage, Jeanine stared at her stylish pumps. "He was angry that I went to a psychiatrist without telling him."

"You have a right to consult with a therapist. The issue that needs to be addressed is why you didn't want to tell him in the first place."

Jeanine gaped. "You *know* why. He's asking me to do something, well, amoral."

"I know that upset you. But my question is more about why you didn't say to him that you were feeling uneasy with some aspects of the relationship and needed to talk out your feelings with a professional." She let the polite words sit for a beat, then added the punch. "Why weren't you honest with him about seeing a therapist?"

"Because he wouldn't have let me do it." Jeanine's voice rose.

"You didn't need his permission." Jeanine needed to stand up for what she wanted.

"It's not about permission. He would have been afraid that I'd tell you everything. Which is exactly what I did."

"I could have assured him that anything said within these four walls stays here."

Jeanine shook her head. "I never would have gotten that far." She set her mouth in a straight line. "And I wanted something for myself. I didn't want to tell him. I didn't want him trying to direct things. I didn't want him coming to see you, telling you his side. This is about *my* side, about how *I* feel."

Well, that certainly was a new perspective. Jeanine had demanded something for herself. "I agree," Charlotte said. "But now it's out in the open. I see no reason why we can't continue."

Jeanine snorted. "Oh please, you're joking. I'll never hear the end of it. And neither will you." She pointed a finger. "He will hound you."

A shiver ran down Charlotte's spine. The man was already hounding her. "Perhaps it would be a good idea if I talked with him, assured him about confidentiality, allayed his fears."

Jeanine shook her head. "Absolutely not. It will only make things worse."

Without Jeanine's permission, Charlotte was out of options. "I'm concerned about you. We still haven't resolved the issues you came to me with in the first place."

"Believe me, he and I aren't talking about sex at all."

"That doesn't mean things are resolved." It meant they were far worse.

Jeanine drew in a deep breath, sat up straight, squared her shoulders. "I'm not coming back, Dr. Moore. There's nothing you can say to convince me. I'll work this out myself."

Charlotte hated failure. And this one was huge. Jeanine was leaving in worse shape than when she'd arrived that first day. Except for that straight back. Perhaps she was a tad less spineless. It could be a good omen for a change in the way she dealt with her husband.

"I want you to feel free to contact me at any time. But before you go, we need to talk about the mistaken impressions your husband has regarding my practice. I'm not a sex surrogate, and I am not advocating that you commit deviant acts."

She would have said more, but she was alerted by a sound out in the waiting room. A glance at the clock assured her it was too early for her next client, yet a moment later, her office door burst open.

David Smith stood on the threshold, his face mottled with anger. "I thought you said you weren't coming to her anymore."

Jeanine jumped to her feet. Charlotte rose with her, heart beating wildly. "Mr. Smith, please calm down."

"I'm not talking to you."

She didn't like his tone. Or his attitude. "But I'm talking to you. Please keep your voice down. There are other offices in this building."

With three big steps, he towered over her. She loved it when Lance did that, but David Smith vibrated with malice. "This isn't high school. I'm not one of your students. Don't tell me to shut up."

All right, she needed to take charge. "Regardless of the circumstances, Mr. Smith, I'm glad you're here. I'd like to talk about any issues you might have. With Jeanine's permission, I'm sure we can alleviate any fears about our therapy."

His voice boomed in the otherwise quiet office. "I'm not afraid of anything, least of all you. We will not be discussing the situation, and I want you to leave my wife alone. Leave my son alone, too." He stabbed a finger at the center of his chest. "Don't you realize I'm chairman of the school board? I can have your job."

He was threatening her. It was unbelievable, like something out of a melodramatic TV movie. "I haven't done anything, Mr. Smith. You can't take away my job."

He dropped his head, glared at her, and lowered his voice. "Wanna bet?"

She didn't like to admit it, even to herself, but the man frightened her.

"If you're not careful, I might even take away your license to practice as well." Then he turned his gaze on his wife. "Jeanine, we're outta here."

He didn't grab her arm or drag her away. He simply turned. And Jeanine followed. The outer office door slammed behind them.

She'd been upset that Lance hadn't let her handle her own problem. Well, she'd certainly gotten her chance.

And all she'd done was make a bigger mess.

21

LANCE SLUNG HIS JACKET OVER HIS ARM. IT WAS UNSEASONABLY warm for Thanksgiving week, especially considering the temperatures and rain the previous week.

"Principal Hutton, I gotta talk to you."

Eric Collins cornered him in the staff parking lot early on Tuesday morning. His hair was wild and his face pale with dark circles beneath his eyes as if he'd pulled an all-nighter. Lance didn't think the boy had even bothered to use a comb before leaving home.

Other faculty and staff were entering the lot, parking their cars, heading up the aisles to the school. A few glanced their way. He thought about telling the boy to come by his office during his study period, but Eric appeared frantic, bouncing on his heels, his pupils large and dark. "What can I do for you?"

"It's about my stepdad." Eric tapped his fingers nervously against his jeans. "Can we talk in your office?"

"Don't you have class"—Lance flipped his wrist to check his watch—"in fifteen minutes?"

"I do, but I guarantee you'll give me a pass after you hear what I have to say."

"I'll be the judge of that." Lance didn't like Eric's ominous sound. Smith was becoming a huge pain in the ass.

He gestured for Eric to follow. They garnered curious stares as they traversed the halls, Eric half a pace behind as if he were a dog Lance had told to heel. Or a kid who was in trouble and being taken to the principal's office.

Mrs. Rivers looked up as they passed through, her eyes seemingly magnified through the lenses of her horn-rimmed glasses.

"Do I have any meetings in the next half hour, Mrs. Rivers?"

"No, sir."

"Good. Hold my calls." He ushered Eric into his office and closed the door.

Eric waited until Lance was seated behind his desk, then took the chair opposite.

Lance leaned back. "All right, tell me."

"It's my parents, Principal Hutton. And Melody's."

Despite Lance's nonchalant pose, his senses were on alert. "What about them?"

"Well, my stepdad had the Wrights over to our house last night, and he was fuming."

"With them?"

"No, at Miss Moore."

His stomach sank. "You didn't talk to her again, did you?"

"No, it was my mom who went to see her yesterday, and my stepdad found out. I guess he and Miss Moore had a fight or something, then he dragged my mom out of there."

Lance gnashed his teeth. Dammit, why the hell hadn't Charlotte told him? Oh, yeah, because they were taking a break from each other. But this was school business, not personal.

Eric twisted his hands together. "Anyway, they were all in my stepdad's study, but the laundry room's on the other side, and if I put my ear up to the wall socket when there's no plug in there, I can hear whatever they say." Talk about cheap construction. How did kids figure this stuff out? It was ingenious. "That's the only way I ever know what's going on around there." A typical kid, Eric rolled his eyes.

"Go on," he said, as if Eric needed permission to reveal what he'd overheard.

"My stepdad was saying they had to put a stop to her—Miss Moore, I mean—that she was a menace to kids like me and Melody. That if there's anything wrong with Melody"—Eric looked at Lance beseechingly—"and there's not, I swear it."

"I know there isn't. She'll be fine. We'll work through this."

"But she won't get through it if she doesn't have Miss Moore." The boy's features were tense, earnest.

Lance wondered how Charlotte inspired this kind of faith. But then he knew, because she cared. She was the real thing. She didn't mouth platitudes or fob off responsibility. She did anything she could to help the kids who came to her in need.

"Melody will get all the help she requires," he promised. "But finish telling me about this powwow last night."

"Well, Mrs. Wright was pissed—I mean angry," he changed the word this time as if afraid *pissed* would be considered profanity. "Anyway, she says that whatever's wrong with Melody is all Miss Moore's fault, that Miss Moore is telling Melody that she— Mrs. Wright, I mean—is abusing her because she's offered to let her have surgery. She says a guidance counselor can't be allowed to turn kids against parents."

"Surgery? What kind of surgery?"

"Breast implants."

Lance drew his brows together and leaned forward. "That woman wants her fifteen-year-old daughter to get breast implants?"

"Yeah." Eric nodded vigorously. "She thinks it'll solve all Melody's problems."

He'd thought acne was her problem. How did they suddenly jump to breast implants? At this point, though, it was academic. There were only two germane points: First, Smith hated that his wife was Charlotte's client, and second, Kathryn Wright thought she was being bad-mouthed to her daughter. Maybe it was the same symptom, the two didn't like what was said about them behind their backs, most of which was probably true.

"Then what happened?"

"They were going on at my mom about what Miss Moore might have said to her, and she just kept saying that it was confidential and she couldn't talk about it."

The truth was that it was confidential only for Charlotte. She couldn't reveal anything, but Jeanine Smith could say whatever she wanted. Dammit, why the hell hadn't the woman defended Charlotte instead of clamming up?

Eric grabbed the arms of the chair and leaned forward gravely. "Then my stepdad starting saying how Miss Moore was probably talking about sex with all those students she has in her office, corrupting them, telling them that it was okay to have sex as long as they used condoms, and maybe she was even encouraging them to have multiple partners and orgies and stuff."

It was so ridiculous, Lance would have laughed. Except that he could hear Smith's voice in his head, pandering to parental fears, whipping up fury.

"And Mrs. Wright was agreeing and Mr. Wright was saying

he didn't want Melody alone with her." Eric lowered his voice. "It was scary, Principal Hutton. Like one of those Salem witch hunts."

Yes, indeed, it was. "What do they plan to do about all this?"

"They're starting a petition to have her fired. Mrs. Wright's going to take it round to all the parents of the freshman class."

Shit. His worst fear.

"My mom said they were getting out of hand. But I don't think anyone was listening to her at all."

A petition. All right, he had time to undo any damage before it really began. "Thank you for bringing this to my attention, Eric. I'll take it from here." Another conversation with Smith was in order. This time, he'd need to make a few threats of his own.

"I talked to Melody and—"

Lance cocked his head. "I thought Melody wasn't speaking to you anymore. Isn't that how this whole thing started?"

Eric's face flushed, whether with embarrassment or something else, Lance wasn't sure. "Yes, sir," he said deferentially. "But this is extreme. So I sent her a text. And she answered. She doesn't like what they're trying to do to Miss Moore either."

It was miraculous. Charlotte had gotten them together without even trying. The two teenagers were putting aside their differences and rallying round her.

"All the kids like Miss Moore, don't they," Lance said, musing almost to himself.

"Yeah," Eric agreed. "Most everyone thinks she's awesome."

"And your parents are going to other parents to get them to sign a petition to get rid of her." Not that he'd let it happen, but a little help never hurt. "Perhaps those parents need to hear another point of view from their kids." He let the idea sink in.

Eric's face suddenly animated. "Yeah."

The seed would germinate. Hopefully when Kathryn Wright started making the rounds with her petition, she wouldn't find a whole lot of signers.

CHARLOTTE STOPPED DEAD JUST BEFORE SHE ENTERED THE quad. She was later than normal because she didn't have an appointment until after the first period.

And there, right in the center of the quad, students streaming around them on their way to class or the library or a lab, stood Melody and Lydia. Good God, Lydia was befriending the girl. Charlotte could have cried. It was the one good thing in a really bad week, and this was only Tuesday, for God's sake. By involving Lydia, at least she'd done something right where Melody was concerned.

She hung back beneath the relative darkness of an awning to watch. Lydia did half her talking with her hands and arms, not to mention a very mobile face. The girl couldn't hide anything; what she thought was written all over her features for everyone to read. When Melody spoke, her arms stayed at her sides and her body exhibited very little movement, as if she kept everything buried deep inside. Her brown hoodie and blue jeans were like the dead leaves of winter versus Lydia in all the vibrant colors of New England trees in fall. The utterly amazing thing, though, was that Melody talked. The girls weren't fighting. Melody hadn't stomped on Lydia's shoe or poured the contents of a Coke can over her head. They were talking. Lydia nodded. Then Melody nodded. They parted company, and Lydia grabbed the arm of one of her BFFs— Lydia had many—and dashed up the steps. At the opposite end of the quad, Melody rounded a corner and disappeared.

Charlotte stood there for at least another minute and pondered the meaning. She could have kissed Lydia. Then again, maybe she needed to find out what was going on. A sly question or two to Melody in their session today would draw out the answer. As she finally moved on toward her office, she could only hope this was a good thing. But it seemed a little too fast. She was suspicious of huge turnarounds in a short space of time. Still, it was a good beginning. It had to be.

She was on tenterhooks through her first two appointments of the day, both of which concerned course planning to facilitate acceptance into the schools of choice. One was an Asian girl interested in high-level computer languages, the other, her brother, a year older, who had structural engineering on his mind. She often found that Asian students of immigrant parents chose career paths early and were very focused in their goals.

Melody was a horse of a different color, so to speak, but this morning as she entered the office, Charlotte felt there was the slightest buoyancy in her step that hadn't been there last week. Though that might be wishful thinking.

She started with something innocuous. "How was your weekend, Melody?"

"Fine." The girl toyed with a loose thread on her sweatshirt.

"Did you do anything fun?"

"Watched some movies on cable."

Okay, this was sounding like a repeat of last week. "Did you try any of my suggestions?"

Melody crossed her ankles and drew her feet back beneath the chair. "I haven't seen a new pimple since yesterday."

Staring at herself in the mirror looking for new pimples wasn't exactly what Charlotte had in mind. The difference here was not that Melody looked in the mirror, but that she was sharing what she considered was a triumph.

"That's good. Maybe you're feeling a little less stressed." Charlotte could only hope.

"Not really."

After a pause in which Melody added nothing, Charlotte decided it was time to bring up Lydia. Melody had isolated herself. She needed friends, activities.

"I wanted to—"

But Melody talked right over her. "I saw Eric yesterday."

Charlotte's heart started to beat faster with anticipation.

"And I didn't kick him, slap him, bite him, or dump a beaker of sugar water over his head." Melody smiled. It was sheepish, a bit self-deprecating. But it was a smile, and she was actually poking fun at herself.

Charlotte wanted to punch the air. Instead she merely said, in keeping with the humor, "You didn't spill Coke on his shoes either?"

Melody rewarded her with another smile.

Fabulous. Things were looking up. Yet Charlotte didn't think she'd had a thing to do with it.

LANCE ASKED MRS. RIVERS TO CALL SMITH'S OFFICE. HIS SEC-retary said he hadn't been in yet this morning. So Lance had Mrs. Rivers call the Smith home. No answer there either.

He knew something bad was coming his way. He just wasn't sure what exactly, or when.

The *what* and the *when* arrived at eleven o'clock in the form of Smith's posse, which included his wife and the Wrights. Lance was ready for them. He wasn't about to bullied. No way was he firing Charlotte.

They bypassed Mrs. Rivers and barged into his office en masse, Smith with his chest puffed up, Kathryn Wright in a chic black suit that had cream-colored panels down the front of both the jacket and skirt. The outfit was two inches too short and tight for a woman her age. Her husband stood back a pace, looking as if he'd dressed for the golf course. Jeanine Smith faded into the background as though she were simply another piece of furniture in his overcrowded office.

"To what do I owe this pleasure?" Admittedly, he sounded sarcastic. He also didn't care.

To his surprise, Kathryn Wright took the first shot. "I do not want Miss Moore counseling my daughter. She's a sex therapist, and she has no business talking to Melody. Or any of the other kids in this school, for that matter. You should have told us *that* before you issued your orders the other day."

He ignored the sneering tone. "Charlotte Moore is a family therapist whose practice includes dealing with sexual trauma and related psychological maladies. But at this school, she deals with career planning and common teenage issues, and she is not counseling your daughter on anything sexual."

Kathryn leaned forward and pointed as if she could reach him over the desk. "What she's doing is telling my daughter that I'm a crappy mother and that the things I'm trying to do for Melody are bad. She's undermining my relationship with my daughter."

"Yeah, she's undermining our authority," Steven Wright piped up as if he were his wife's backup singer.

"She's a bad influence," Smith said, speaking for the first time.

"She demonizes parents," Kathryn added.

"She says we just throw money at the problem," Steven finished.

Jeanine Smith contributed nothing at all.

"The *chairman* of the school board"—Kathryn gave the title an air of reverence—"says you can't force Melody into counseling if we object. You don't have the right."

Lance eyed the woman. "I offered counseling in lieu of suspension or expulsion." He shot a look at Smith. "I do have the authority to suspend or expel any student who breaks school rules." He turned back to Kathryn Wright. "Which would you prefer?"

"I—well—" She started to sputter.

"We just don't want *that* woman counseling her," Steven Wright said, for once having a voice when his wife didn't.

Smith stepped forward, obviously feeling the meeting was moving beyond his control. "We want her resignation. She doesn't fit in here. The parents don't want her."

They couldn't possibly have gotten a petition signed this quickly. Smith was bluffing. Of course, the chairman could simply bring the matter before the school board. With support, he could do just about anything he wanted.

Lance wouldn't let it come to that. "There is no basis for firing Miss Moore."

"Nobody wants her here," Smith countered.

"The students love her."

He looked pointedly at Jeanine Smith. She was the key to this whole thing. Her husband didn't like the idea that she'd talked to Charlotte. Maybe she'd revealed something, and he was afraid of it getting out. Lance willed her to say something, to defend Charlotte. Yet she stood mute, her eyes downcast.

"I am not standing here debating this with you," Kathryn Wright interjected. "I have the right to choose my daughter's counselor. And I don't want that woman. I know Melody's meeting with her right now, and I want her out of there."

"Right now," Steven echoed her sentiment.

So that was the reason behind the timing of the meeting. They'd staged a dramatic show. They were correct about one thing: He did not have the right to force Charlotte on them.

He also knew Charlotte. More than anything, she wanted to help Melody. This would break her heart.

22

CHARLOTTE WAS SURE IT WAS A BREAKTHROUGH—SOMETHING
major. They were on the verge. True she didn't trust quick turnarounds, but there were things at work in Melody, and maybe all
the girl had needed was Eric's acceptance. Or rather to acknowledge it, because she'd always had his acceptance. She'd simply
never taken it.

"Would you like to tell me what you two talked about?"

Melody parted her lips. Charlotte crossed her fingers the girl
was ready to reveal everything that was on her mind.

And the office door opened. No knock. No voice requesting
permission.

First in was Principal Hutton. Then the Wrights. And behind
them, the Smiths.

Damn, damn, damn. Charlotte stood. They'd ruined everything. The moment with Melody was lost forever. "What's
going on?"

"Mr. and Mrs. Wright would prefer that Melody speak with

another counselor." Lance looked at her without a flicker of emotion. He was every bit the authoritative principal.

Charlotte felt as if an invisible band encircled her chest tight enough to cut off her breath.

Melody jumped up, out of character for a girl whose usual pace rivaled that of a snail. "But I don't want to talk to someone else. I want Miss Moore."

Charlotte secretly cheered, despite what was actually happening in the office. This was another breakthrough. Or maybe Melody was just fighting her parents. Whatever the reason, in the face of the principal's heartlessness, the girl's support warmed Charlotte.

Kathryn Wright tried placation first. "But she isn't good for you, sweetie."

"We'll find you someone more in line with our thinking," Mr. Wright added like a punctuation mark.

Melody's lips tightened. "I don't want someone you choose. I want someone on my side."

Mrs. Wright pouted. "We're on your side, honey."

"I'm the chairman of the school board, young lady." David Smith stepped farther into the room, shoulders back, chest out. Like the cock of the walk. Charlotte felt like plucking his tail feathers right there in front of everyone. *You can't get it up, so you want other men to screw your wife for you.* What would they all think of that?

"You'll have to talk to someone else now because Miss Moore won't be working here much longer."

His words chilled her. She looked at Lance. All he said was "This isn't the place to fight your battles, Smith."

They weren't particularly comforting words.

"What do you mean she won't be here?" Melody's eyes flashed from her parents to the principal and finally to Charlotte.

Mrs. Wright held out a hand. "Never you mind, sweetheart. We're taking you home."

"I'm not a child." Melody stepped back, avoiding her mother's touch. "And I'm not going home. I have classes. I want to go."

"But you said you hate school," Mrs. Wright cajoled.

"I don't want to miss my classes. I'll never catch up," Melody said stubbornly.

Her mother backed down. "All right, fine, but you're not talking to this woman ever again." She narrowed her eyes on Charlotte. "I'm going to make sure you don't undermine any more parents from now on. The chairman will see to it."

"Mrs. Wright—"

The woman held up her hand and turned her face away in a teenage talk-to-the-hand gesture.

In the doorway, Jeanine Smith stared at Charlotte, then slowly mouthed, "I'm sorry."

Why didn't she speak up, tell them Charlotte was a good therapist? But she knew why. Jeanine's husband. Jeanine's fears.

"You don't have any grounds on which to fire me," she stated the issue aloud, just so everyone understood.

"I totally agree," Lance said. She felt him suddenly inches closer to her.

"We don't need grounds," Smith said, his eyes hard as he stared at her. "We only need to tell people what you do in your outside practice."

"Oh yes, you do need grounds, Smith." Lance's voice was deadly. She'd never heard quite that tone out of him.

The man stepped closer, crowding the principal, but Lance didn't back off.

"Remember that offer I made to you at lunch, Hutton? Well, it's off the table if you haven't taken care of things by tomorrow."

Offer? What on earth was he talking about?

Lance was an inch or two taller, but right now, his air of dominance seemed to add five inches over the chairman. "That offer was never on the table as far as I was concerned. And if you want her gone, then bring on your proof. *You* have until tomorrow." He glanced at his watch. "Shall we say ten thirty? School's out by noon for the holiday."

"You'll be sorry you crossed me, Hutton." David Smith shook his finger, his face a danger-zone red, then he turned and marched out of the office. In the hallway, he simply expected Jeanine to follow. Which she did.

"Melody." Mrs. Wright held out her hand. Melody didn't take it, but she did follow her father into the hallway. She gave Charlotte one last look before she disappeared around the doorjamb.

"I'm not letting them fire you," Lance declared. "Only I have that authority, not them."

"Yes, but I see you allowed them to take Melody away." That, more than anything, made her stomach drop. "We were right in the middle of a breakthrough."

"I'm sorry."

His face was impassive. She didn't think he looked sorry at all. "That's just a platitude."

"They are within their rights to request another counselor."

She knew that. She was disappointed for Melody. Or was this really all about Charlotte herself? Because she'd failed Melody in some way.

Lance closed the door, leaned back, his hand on the knob. "Now tell me what's going on with Smith. This is all about your therapy with his wife. I want to know what it is, then we can nip this whole thing in the bud."

"You know I can't tell you that."

He stood straight, towering over her the way he had David

Smith. It reminded her too much of the way Mr. Smith had towered over her yesterday in her office.

"I know all about your confidentiality. But that's mitigated when these people threaten your job. I need ammunition."

"I'll handle this myself."

"How? By *talking* to Jeanine Smith again and *asking* her permission?"

She flared her nostrils at his tone. "Yes."

"That hasn't worked. You need a new tactic."

"You know, I'm not totally incapable. I'll figure one out." She could confront Smith in his home. But that would only antagonize him more. And she still couldn't say anything about the therapy. So honestly, what ammunition did she really have?

Lance stepped into her, forcing her to back up until her butt was against the desk. "My dear Miss Moore," he said, his lips only an inch from hers, "I know what's needed here." He slid a hand down her belly, fitted his fingers between her legs.

Despite herself, her breath was suddenly fast and hard in her chest. "Stop it. Anyone could walk in."

"I locked the door." He stroked, pushing deeper into the vee of her thighs.

Charlotte swallowed, put her hands on his arms to push him away, but somehow didn't end up doing that at all. "Someone could see in the window."

"The blinds are closed."

Oh. Yeah. She'd closed them to protect Melody, shutting out prying eyes. "I'm already in enough trouble. This isn't going to help."

He nuzzled her neck, licked her ear, blew a warm, tantalizing breath on it. "I can help. Just tell me a tidbit. Something I can use against him. I'll fix everything."

Between his lips and his fingers, she was sliding down a very slippery slope. "No. I can't. It's unethical."

Removing his hand from between her thighs, he palmed her butt cheeks and held her against his cock. He was hard. "Then let's both go to Smith's house and confront him. We'll scare him into thinking you told me." He tongued her ear.

It damn near drove her mad with desire. "That's as bad as actually telling you. And it'll make things worse for Jeanine." She was breathing hard, her head lolling back as she let him do anything he wanted.

"Then I'll talk to Jeanine. Get her to see the light." He gathered her skirt in his fingers, started pulling it up, up, up.

This was absolutely crazy. They were in her office in the middle of the day. And he was trying to seduce her into telling him Jeanine's secrets.

This time Charlotte pushed hard, getting her hands between them, shoving his chest. "Stop. It."

She managed to make him stumble back, far enough for her to scramble away from the desk and put a chair between them. "Stop trying to mesmerize me with sex."

His chest heaved. He was breathing as hard as she was, and his pants were tight over his groin. "All I'm trying to do is help you. Smith is a menace. I know him better than you do, and the nice tactics you're employing aren't going to work on him."

She narrowed her eyes. "What was that offer he made you? Are you keeping something from me?"

He waved a dismissive hand. "He proposed helping me get elected to the school board. I don't want the job." He pointed a finger. "All I'm trying to do is make sure you don't lose yours."

"I don't like how you're going about it. Taking advantage of me in my own office. You wanted to bend me to your will. And you were using sex to do it." It was appalling. Especially since she'd almost succumbed.

He spread his hands. "I was using sex because I wanted to touch you."

"You're such a liar. This dom-sub role play has totally gone to your head. I'm not your sub. You can't order me around or manipulate me in my work environment."

He met her glare for glare. "I'm trying to save your job."

"Thanks a lot for your support. But if you weren't screwing me, you wouldn't be trying to get all this information out of me about Smith." She took a step closer, narrowed her eyes. "I bet it's more than saving my job. It has something to do with his offer."

"I told you I'm not interested in anything from him. I'm only trying to protect you."

"Well, I don't need it."

"Yes. You do. You need me."

He was always pushing for more. When she said she wouldn't spend the night, he forced himself into her house and tied her to the bed so she couldn't kick him out. When she didn't tell him what he wanted to know, he tried to use sex against her. The other night, hadn't he said he was going to change the rules on her? Yes, he was taking over, first in the bedroom and now in her job.

"I don't like this arrangement anymore, Principal Hutton. In fact, I'm canceling it."

"What the hell does that mean?"

"It means," she stated flatly, "that I'm not playing the game anymore. I'm done. I'm your employee, and that's all. If you want to fire me for that, then go ahead. Otherwise, get out of my office."

He cocked his head. She was reminded of a TV show on Animal Planet where the predatory panther tipped his head just that way, right before he pounced. "I don't think you really mean that."

She stalked around him, opened the door, held it for him. "Thank you for coming, Principal Hutton. I appreciate your support in this matter. I will see you at the ten thirty meeting tomorrow."

They weren't alone. Out in the hall, a couple of faculty members were deep in conversation. Lance couldn't argue. He couldn't do a thing. Except leave the way she'd demanded.

He eyed her a moment longer. Until finally he moved, passing through the open door. "I'll see you at the meeting."

Charlotte closed the door and leaned back heavily against it.

God, it was a mess. They were taking Melody away from her just when the girl was starting to open up, and Charlotte had gone and kicked out the one person who might be able to help her. The problem was that Lance had decided the only way to help was by forcing her to betray a confidence. She couldn't do it. She wouldn't, but that meant she would ultimately fail Melody. It also meant she might soon lose her job at the high school.

And now she'd made sure she didn't even have the principal to lean on.

IT DIDN'T MAKE SENSE. YES, HE'D TRIED THE DOM THING ON HER, using sex to coerce her into revealing what Jeanine Smith told her. But sex was how they best communicated. All he'd wanted to do was make her see that she needed help dealing with Smith and that he was more than willing to do whatever was necessary to make the problem go away. Why couldn't she accept that? Dammit, she simply couldn't end things this way. He wouldn't allow it.

Yet that very statement in the depths of his mind was the

essence of the problem. He'd taken to the role of dom so easily because he was in fact domineering. Authority was part of his job, his career, his soul. But it was possible he'd taken it too far in his relationship with her. Good God, was it even the reason for his failure at marriage?

He was authoritative and dictatorial. That's who he was. And that's exactly what Charlotte had come to him for. She wanted to experience spanking, dominance, submission.

Obviously she hadn't liked it as much as he had. But he didn't need to have sex that way. He could take it any way she wanted.

Lance didn't call Charlotte on Tuesday night. He didn't show up on her porch with cuffs, rope, and condoms in his pocket. He wanted to let her calm down. Besides, he needed to think no less than she did. He had to figure out exactly where he'd gone wrong.

The Wednesday morning conference required more official surroundings than the original parent meeting. Lance had Mrs. Rivers prepare the coffee and show the Wrights and Smiths to the conference room. He would not be waiting for them. He would enter later, flanked by Charlotte and Alice Sloan, thus taking the upper hand. It was an us-against-them strategy.

After a brief tap, Mrs. Rivers opened the door enough to stick her head in. "They've got their coffee, Principal Hutton." She was well aware of the strategy.

He met Alice and Charlotte in the hall. He'd already strategized with Alice who was in full agreement with him: They were not firing their best guidance counselor. He'd left it to Alice to appeal to Charlotte for her cooperation, not that there was any way Charlotte would reveal even one word of what was said in her therapy office.

She wore a sweater dress that hugged every curve and stole his breath. It emphasized her mouthwatering breasts. High heels showcased her shapely legs. She was perfect. Christ, he ached to touch her, literally ached deep in his bones. But the dress certainly didn't tone down her sexuality. It was almost a statement: She wasn't going to deny or justify.

She glared as if daring him to pick a fight about her choice. The fight he wanted wasn't with her—there were so many other things he wanted to do with her, over and over—so he simply opened the door and flourished a hand for them to precede him. "Ladies."

In a power-play move, Smith had taken the head of the table. There were, however, two heads. Lance took the other and indicated for his staff to flank him in the two chairs, Charlotte facing Jeanine Smith, who sat at the other end of the table next to her husband. Of course, this put Charlotte on the same side as the Wrights. Which might be a good thing.

"Thank you for coming," Lance opened the meeting diplomatically. "As we discussed yesterday, if you wish to have Miss Moore terminated, we'll need to hear the basis and review its merits." There was an official review process, but he didn't want that to even get started. For now, they were completely off the record, and he wanted to keep it that way.

Smith started with the finger-pointing, aiming straight at Lance as if they were now the two adversaries. "I want you to know I've looked at the school regulations, and since she's only part-time we don't have the same obligations as we would with a fully tenured teacher."

Asshole. But he was correct. "You still need to prove Miss Moore has committed some sort of malfeasance."

Smith puffed up his chest. "All we have to do is show that her personal life is detrimental to the fulfillment of her responsibilities at school."

"This isn't about my personal life," Charlotte said. "It's about my therapy work. And my work has nothing to do with my job at the school."

"Right," Smith snapped. "That's like saying it's okay for a drug addict to teach kids as long as he or she doesn't bring drugs to school."

"Oh, for God's sake," Charlotte said, disgust in every syllable.

"That analogy is spurious, Smith." It also pointed out that Smith didn't have any legitimate arguments to bring up.

"Mr. and Mrs. Wright," Alice interjected, "we've assigned another counselor to Melody. Miss Moore will turn over her file—"

Kathryn Wright didn't let her finish. "I don't want anything she has to say going to Melody's new counselor."

"Mrs. Flannigan will need Melody's history," Alice insisted.

"Fine." Kathryn leaned around her husband and pointed at Charlotte. "But not a thing from her. She's biased toward me."

"Mrs. Wright, I'm not biased," Charlotte started. "But I'd really like to say a few words about Melody—"

"I'm not talking to you," Kathryn Wright said in a silly sing-song voice.

Charlotte closed her mouth in frustration, but there was more written on her face, a line of worry across her brow, something in the deep green of her eyes. Lance could only define it as sadness. His heart turned over for her. He was worried about her job. But she was only concerned for Melody.

"No, please," Charlotte persisted. "I feel we had a small breakthrough yesterday. I'm not saying I have to be the one to work with her, but I really need to let Mrs. Flannigan understand the issues. For Melody's sake."

Smith jumped in as if her words were his cue. "It's for Melody's sake and students like her that we're going to get rid of you and your disgusting influence."

Lance was aware of a noise building outside the bank of chest-high windows at his back, perhaps from the quad, the third period was just ending. He couldn't deal with it now; he needed to answer Smith.

"Whether Miss Moore is part-time or full-time, you need evidence to prove that her extracurricular activities negatively impact the performance of her job. That's what we're here for." He put a hand out. "Where's the proof?"

"I've started a petition for all the parents of the freshman class." Kathryn Wright tapped a paper in front of her.

"We'll go to the rest of the parents, too." Steven. Of course.

"How many signatures do you have?" Lance fired back. The sounds outside were growing in intensity, becoming harder to ignore—was that chanting?—but he stared down Kathryn Wright.

"Well, I've just started," she snapped. Which probably meant the only signatures she had were hers and her husband's. "But when I tell them how she's tried to turn Melody against me . . . " She sniffed for effect without actually finishing the sentence.

"Mrs. Wright, I'm very sorry if my view on surgery offends you—"

"You don't need to apologize, Miss Moore." Lance meant it kindly, yet Charlotte glared at him.

Outside, the commotion had become a dull roar.

"What the hell is going on?" Smith said gruffly.

Then the conference door burst open, and the usually unruffled Mrs. Rivers stood framed in the doorway, panting as if she'd run the length of the hall. "Principal Hutton, you really need to get out here."

Lance rose and moved to the windows.

"Holy hell," he said.

Then he felt her beside him, Charlotte, her scent enveloping him, reactivating the need to touch that he'd felt when he first saw her.

She had to stand on tiptoe to see the full spectacle. "Oh my God."

Then everyone peered out the bank of windows.

The quad undulated with students clapping, chanting, shouting, and waving signs that read "Don't Fire Miss Moore" and "We Love Miss Moore."

Suddenly the chanting had clarity. "We want Miss Moore. We want Miss Moore. We want Miss Moore."

"Jesus Christ," Smith muttered.

Smith's plans might very well be dead in the water. And Lance hadn't needed to do a thing.

23

CHARLOTTE COULD HARDLY BELIEVE WHAT SHE WAS SEEING. Lance had led the way outside, and she was drawn along with him almost as if he had his hand on her. They stood on the quad steps above the crowd of students. On her other side, she could hear David Smith, his breath puffing, either from exertion or rage.

"What is the meaning of this?" he shouted at Lance.

The principal waved a hand across the throng. "You can see what it is. The students support Miss Moore completely." He shot a sharp look at Mrs. Wright. "I don't think you're going to get a single signature on that petition."

Kathryn Wright was, for once, speechless. Which meant her husband was, too.

"I won't be bullied by a bunch of teenagers," Mr. Smith blustered.

Then Lydia took two steps up the concrete stairs. As if the

whole thing had been choreographed, the assembly fell silent, the air pregnant with anticipation.

"Principal Hutton, the student body has heard a rumor that you're going to fire Miss Moore."

Charlotte wanted to cry, her heart melting. Lance moved a step closer, so completely *there* beside her.

"And we're here to tell you that she's the best counselor any of us has ever had."

A cheer rose like a roar from the crowd. Oh God, she was going to cry; really, she might not be able to stop it.

Lydia lifted her hand, and the throng at the base of the stairs parted. Two teenagers moved through the crowd, Melody and Eric, their hands linked.

"Do you see that?" Charlotte whispered without truly meaning to.

Lance heard. "I see it," he answered softly. "I do believe you've worked a miracle."

"Mom," Melody called out.

Charlotte felt Kathryn Wright back up as if she were terrified the student body would maul her like rabid dogs.

"We all want to keep Miss Moore. You don't know what she's done for me."

It was too much to take in. Charlotte covered her mouth.

"She's the best, Mom. Don't let her get fired." This came from Eric. He wasn't speaking to his stepdad, but to Jeanine.

Lance held both hands in the air, waiting for silence before he called out, "Everyone, you don't need to worry. Miss Moore is here to stay if I have anything to say about it. And believe me, I do. I'm not letting her leave any of us."

He glanced down at her, and she was sure there was more in his meaning than just her job.

"Now hold on a minute," David Smith started.

A chorus of shouts came up from the crowded quad, and the principal shifted, his arm dropping as he if might actually backhand the chairman of the school board.

"David, shut up." Jeanine. Standing next to Mr. Smith, Charlotte thought she was the only one who heard, but Lance turned his head.

"What did you just say?" Mr. Smith's brow went up in shock.

"I told you to shut up, David. You will stop this immediately. Because if you don't, I'll tell everyone present exactly what I've been talking to Dr. Moore about in our sessions." Amid the renewed shouting and chanting of the student body, the argument was drowned out except to those closest.

"But, but," Smith began to splutter. "You wouldn't."

"I will. Believe me. I'll tell ev-er-y-thing," Jeanine enunciated, staring him down, her back straight, nostrils flared, eyes narrowed. Good God, she'd become an Amazon. She'd at last found her backbone. "And I'm going back to talk to her as many times as I want. And you're going to pay for it. Do you hear?"

"But—" His *but* became a lot less forceful now.

"Tell them she can stay." Jeanine shot a piercing glare at Kathryn. "Don't you dare contradict him unless you've got some really good proof she's done anything wrong. And it better be able to stand up in court."

If Melody's mom had planned to say anything, she slapped her lips shut on it.

"Tell them, David." Jeanine glared.

With one last look at his wife, Mr. Smith finally turned to the student body. "All right, she can stay," he said softly.

"Louder," Lance demanded.

Mr. Smith shouted for all to hear. "She can stay."

"School is out for the holiday," Lance's voice boomed across the quad. "See you on Monday."

The cheering drowned out everything else.

CHARLOTTE HUGGED ERIC AND MELODY AND LYDIA FOR ALL they'd done organizing the rally.

"You have my endorsement for class president," she whispered in Lydia's ear. "No one else can galvanize a crowd the way you can."

"You're super, Miss Moore." Then Lydia was borne away in a wave of her peeps.

Melody spontaneously hugged Charlotte one more time. This was so uncharacteristic of the girl Charlotte knew, she was shocked. Yet she hugged Melody hard. "Thank you, my dear."

Behind Melody, Eric winked at Charlotte.

It took Melody less than five minutes to get her parents to agree to family counseling with Charlotte. It may or may not work—Charlotte had definitely antagonized Kathryn Wright and they'd have that to work through—but she'd give it her best shot. She could always recommend another counselor if her differences with Melody's mother got in the way of the therapy. But for now it was a triumph.

Eric left with the Wrights instead of his own parents, and while Mr. Smith stalked off to the car, Jeanine stayed behind a moment to tell Charlotte she'd be back for her usual Monday appointment.

All's well that ends well, right?

"We never would have let you go," Alice said, patting her arm, then she, too, left.

Charlotte and the principal were now alone on the steps as the quad slowly emptied, students making their way to the parking

248 • Jasmine Haynes

lots, or curbside to wait for their ride, or heading out to the main road to catch one of the city buses. Due to budget cuts, there were no longer school buses for high school students.

"Thank you for your support," she told him, surveying the dispersing crowd. The words sounded so . . . inadequate.

She could tell he looked out over his student body, too, and not at her. "It wasn't me. It was all Eric. He told me about the petition, and I simply suggested that he and Melody should start a groundswell of student support. They took it from there."

So that's why she'd seen Melody and Lydia deep in conversation yesterday. Charlotte hadn't really done much for the girl at all. It was the principal who'd gotten Eric and Melody together again. It was because of him that Melody had come out of her shell and opened up to Lydia. Melody's big breakthrough was all due to Lance's behind-the-scenes plotting, and nothing to do with Charlotte. He'd fixed everything just the way he'd said he would, while all she'd done was fumble around.

"You did the perfect thing for them," she told him. "Thank you."

"I did it for you," he said softly, "but it seems to have had that added benefit."

"I certainly appreciate it." She had her job. She had her practice. But she'd also lost something, too: her faith in her own abilities. He'd proven she wasn't capable.

"My theory is that Smith was bad-mouthing you in order to discredit anything you might reveal about him."

"That's very plausible," she agreed. It would appear that Charlotte was telling lies about him in order to cover her own butt.

Lance shifted and she could feel his assessing gaze on her. "I don't suppose you're going to tell me what his wife was threatening him with."

Though she didn't look, she could hear the smile in his voice, the teasing note in his words. "No, I still can't tell you."

"Not even if I tied you up and had my wicked way with you?" He kept his voice low, but there was no one close enough to hear anyway.

"Not even if you do that," she answered softly.

"It would be worth a try, Miss Moore. After all, you are my sub."

He thought things had changed, that since he'd solved her problems for her, they'd go back to the way they'd been, to the things they'd done, to the naughty little trysts.

But everything had changed.

Charlotte turned her head just enough to meet his gaze. "That's over. We need to move on."

"Don't be ridiculous. I was joking about you telling me what Smith's wife said."

He didn't get it. She was his sub, completely, his subordinate. She'd failed; he'd had to rescue her. Everything she'd feared had come to pass. She was incapable and she needed a man—an older, wiser, better man—to fix her mistakes. She was not in control, he was. If she kept on playing the games with him, she would never regain the confidence she'd lost today.

Of course, she wouldn't tell him any of that. He'd find a way to refute it. "We said everything there was to say in my office yesterday."

He gazed at her a moment, as if trying to read between the lines of what she said. "But everything's changed since yesterday."

Yes, it most certainly had, but Charlotte didn't let her weaknesses show. "It was a game. I'm tired of playing."

"I'm not."

Which meant it was still a game for him. "Then I think you need someone else to play it with." The thought made her sick. She didn't want to imagine him doing those things with another woman. But she couldn't play anymore. "Since this isn't one of my school days, I assume I'm free to go. Have a nice holiday, Lance." She didn't call him Principal Hutton. That was part of the game.

She simply walked down the steps and crossed the quad, pretending all the while that nothing had broken inside her.

LANCE WATCHED CHARLOTTE DISAPPEAR AROUND A CORNER.

He didn't get it. Unless she was still pissed about yesterday. He fully admitted he'd been out of line, trying to seduce her into giving him the information he wanted. He should have told her that before she walked away. It would have solved the issue. Wouldn't it?

He backed up a step, stopped again. Perhaps he should have told her that it wasn't just the situation with Smith and the Wrights that had changed, but *everything*. He didn't want to play games anymore. Well, of course he wanted to play *games*, but the relationship he wanted with her was no game at all. He wanted something that was far more permanent. He wanted to spend the night. Many nights. All his nights. If she let herself go for half a minute, he knew she wanted it, too.

He returned to his office by way of the hall that passed hers. The door was closed. He knocked, but no one answered. He tried the knob; it was locked. She'd probably turned that damn corner, then run like hell so she could beat him in and out of the building.

Mrs. Rivers was at her post, steadfast as ever.

"You can go like everyone else," he told her.

"Congratulations on a problem well solved, Principal Hutton." She rolled open her lower drawer and withdrew her purse.

He stopped in his doorway. "Thank you, but Miss Moore didn't do anything wrong, so it was easy to defend her."

"Thank goodness she had you as her champion. Or she would have lost her job for sure."

"It wouldn't have come to that."

She tut-tutted. "It was definitely coming to that."

He would never have let it happen.

"Well, I, for one, am glad you stepped in. She's an asset we can't afford to lose. Have a wonderful Thanksgiving, sir." She locked her desk and smiled once more before leaving.

Mrs. Rivers was wrong. Charlotte would have fixed the issue on her own eventually. She was a capable woman. An admirable woman. He had all confidence—

Except that he hadn't shown full confidence. He'd insisted on having a hand in fixing it.

He had a *duh* moment. Of course. He'd taken care of everything regardless of the number of times she'd told him to butt out. He'd decided how it should be handled. He hadn't even told her about Eric's visit. He'd withheld a crucial bit of information and tried to bend her to his will instead.

No wonder the woman was pissed.

All he had to do was explain. Apologize. Even grovel. He didn't have a problem with that. She was worth groveling for.

But she didn't answer her phone. Saying all that in a message wouldn't cut it. Nor would a text. Not even an email. Groveling required face-to-face.

"Call me," he said to the phone. "I would really like to discuss things with you."

There, it wasn't dictatorial. In fact, it was rather pleading. He would *really* like to talk to her. Just the right word for the situation.

Except that she didn't answer any of his calls, and she didn't call him back. Not on Wednesday, not Thanksgiving Day, not the day after. He was home; he traveled at Christmas to see his family in Colorado. He thought about driving by her house, but she'd said she was inundated with family stuff, and sure enough, he never saw a light on in her front window or the car in her drive.

Okay. She'd said she wanted a break until after the holiday. He would give it to her. But Tuesday, when she was back at work doing the job she was so very good at, he would help her see things his way.

"ARE YOU TOTALLY INSANE, CHARLOTTE MARIE MOORE?"

All the way from Tahoe, Lola still managed to sound just like her mother had when Charlotte was a child, using her full name in that exact same tone of exasperation.

Charlotte sagged on a wooden bench in the aquarium's lobby. She loved the wide-eyed amazement of children, how they were curious about everything, asking a million questions, most of them unanswerable, and could stand for hours watching sharks go round and round in the huge tanks. She'd been resting her tired feet for a couple of minutes when Lola called.

"No, I'm not crazy," she said reasonably. "By the way, where are Gray and Rafe?" It was Saturday; Lola should have been out skiing. Of course, it was also a lame attempt at changing the subject.

Lola, not being lame, at least not all the time, didn't fall for it. "You answer that man's calls right now. He is absolutely perfect for you."

"I beg to differ. He's autocratic and dictatorial. Just like Martin was. No, worse than Martin." Because Martin had been wrong. And Lance was completely correct; she couldn't have fixed her problems without him.

She also didn't tell Lola that not answering all his calls and messages was the hardest thing she'd had to do in a long time. Because honestly, she wanted to hear his voice, not in a message, but right there next to her while his hands were all over her.

But she couldn't be weak.

"So what if he took care of Smith? I don't get what's so wrong with that?"

Charlotte had told Lola the story, or at least as much of it as she could without divulging any confidential material. "He's not supposed to step into my work life or my personal life."

Lola snorted. "He's definitely in your personal life."

"He was in my sex life. There's a difference."

"Only you could parse things down to saying your sex life and personal life aren't the same."

Charlotte had to admit she was a bit compartmentalized. "I can even parse my work life between therapy and guidance counselor." It only made sense to do that.

"Answer one thing. Are you tired of him? Is he boring you in bed? Is he boring you out of bed?"

"That's three things." Still, there was keeping thoughts to herself, and then there was outright lying. She couldn't lie to Lola. "But no, I'm not."

"Are you angry with him?"

"That's a fourth thing."

Lola huffed loudly.

Charlotte sighed and answered, "No."

"Does he blow his nose in the shower?"

"I haven't taken a shower with him." She felt a sudden wave of sadness. There were so many things she hadn't done with Lance. She'd never even eaten a meal with him. Or cuddled in the corner of the couch while they watched a chick flick or an action movie, depending on who had control of the streaming queue.

But those were things she'd never asked for. Plus, they were almost as intimate as spending the night with him.

"All right, are you aware of any habits that you hate?"

Charlotte shook her head, then said, for Lola's benefit, "No.

Except the thing about being dictatorial." She'd loved that in the bedroom compartment.

"So the only problem is that you had a disagreement on how to handle the chairman of the school board."

"It was the whole scenario, the way he dictated Melody's punishment, sentencing her to counseling, calling all the meetings, getting Eric and Melody together." Worse, he'd been right about everything.

"That sounds like he was just doing his job."

"No. He was doing Alice's job."

"So it would have been okay if Alice did all those things?"

Well, yes, probably. It would have felt more like she and Alice were solving the issue together. "He only stuck his nose in because we were sleeping together."

Yet Lola brought up a larger question. Would she still have felt like a failure if Alice had helped her instead of Lance?

"You're so terrified of losing control of your life that you can't even accept help without thinking someone's trying to take over."

Charlotte ignored the rest and answered the only thing that mattered. "Taking over is exactly what the principal does." The gut-wrenching issue was that he'd been right. She couldn't handle Smith on her own. She hadn't handled anything correctly.

"Did you ever think that maybe his job was on the line just as much as yours?" Lola ventured.

"Of course it wasn't." But David Smith *was* the chairman of the school board. "You're mixing me up," she said.

"Good. You need to be mixed up so you can start to think clearly."

"That doesn't make a bit of sense."

"I'm in love. I'm not supposed to make sense."

"Does that mean you're going to move in with Gray?"

"I told him I'd give him an answer when we get back."

"Don't be an idiot. Just do it."

"And don't you be an idiot. Call the principal." Lola paused, softened. "You do realize that you're overanalyzing again, right?"

"Yes. But the answer is still the same."

Pigtails flapping, her eight-year-old niece Sasha flew across the aquarium lobby, sliding to a stop in front of Charlotte. "Mom won't touch the bat rays in the touching pool, Aunt Lola. Will you come touch them with me, please, please?"

"Yeah, sweetie, but just a minute." She put a finger on the tip of the girl's nose to hold her still. "I hear the call of the bat rays," she told Lola. "They aren't the stinging kind." Although she wasn't sure if stingrays actually stung. Sasha had probably already learned the answer. She was a sponge for fish facts.

"I'll call you when we get back," Lola said, "and we can analyze the whole thing again until you admit I'm right."

Charlotte didn't need further analysis. With the principal, she wasn't in control, and she never could be.

24

"THANK YOU FOR YOUR SUPPORT LAST WEDNESDAY, JEANINE. I was very proud of you for handling your husband the way you did."

Jeanine had arrived for her regular Monday appointment. She still tended to look at her knees when she talked, but she hadn't brought out the tissues, and they were already fifteen minutes into the session.

Charlotte had great hope for her. "I'm not sure we have a lot more to work on. You needed the confidence to stand up to your husband and you did." It could have gone badly. They might have been on the verge of divorce after the way Jeanine had challenged him. But oddly, David Smith apologized to his wife later that same day. "You've paved the way for having a mutually satisfying discussion on the rest of your issues."

Jeanine's eyes darted up. "You can't leave me yet. I'm going to talk him into couple's counseling if it's the last thing I do, and I can't bring up all this stuff with anyone else now. It was hard enough telling you the first time."

"There's a problem with that." Charlotte had to be diplomatic. "Your husband and I don't have a good relationship, and I don't believe I'm the right therapist to mediate for the two of you." In addition, Charlotte wasn't sure she could work with the man after what he'd tried to do to her.

"I don't want someone to mediate. I want someone to challenge him." Jeanine leaned forward, lowering her voice. "You know his secret."

"About the other men?"

"About the impotency," Jeanine said, eyes widening as if it was patently obvious. "That's what he was afraid you were going to tell."

"He was worried I'd tell someone he suffers from ED?" That's what this was all about, not even the fact that he wanted his wife to have sex with other men? It was mind-boggling.

"Of course. If Principal Hutton knew, he'd have made David a laughingstock."

"That's ridiculous. The principal isn't like that. He's a man of integrity."

"Well, David thinks he's out for his job. He says Principal Hutton fights him at every turn. So he was fighting back." She puffed up her chest and deepened her voice. " 'It's a dog-eat-dog world, Jeanine.' "

Charlotte was taken aback. "Principal Hutton isn't interested in being on the school board. He prefers working directly with the kids."

Jeanine raised one brow. "He strikes me as someone who always needs to be in charge."

"Perhaps. But when it comes to his students, he's always got their best interests in mind."

"It must be hard working for him."

"No, it's very easy." It *had* been easy until that day in detention hall when she'd goaded him into spanking her. Then again, she didn't actually work for him. She worked for Alice.

But they were straying from the point. This wasn't about Lance. Or her. It was about Jeanine and David Smith.

Charlotte turned it around on her. "It sounds like you're transferring all your husband's qualities onto the principal. Isn't David the one who needs to be in charge?"

Jeanine shrugged. "Not really. It appears that way, but that's only because he's been under pressure, feeling that his reputation was being threatened."

Charlotte remembered their earlier discussions, that Jeanine's husband wore two personas, one for everyone at work and a much easier-going side for home. This was the man Jeanine had fallen for, the man she lived with, the man she wanted back.

"Come to think of it," Jeanine mused, "all his current behavior stems from my having threatened his reputation by coming to you in the first place. Actually it's my fault. If I'd told him that I wanted to see someone, if I hadn't kept you a secret from him, then none of this would have happened." She focused on Charlotte's face. "You always encouraged me to come clean. I should have done what you suggested."

She couldn't have Jeanine start playing the blame game now. It would be totally counterproductive. "You didn't tell him because you knew how he'd react. You didn't want to add a fight about our sessions to the arguments you were already having about sex. You had a legitimate reason." And Jeanine was proven correct. David Smith's reaction had been near devastating. "So don't start taking blame yourself for how everyone else reacts."

Jeanine heaved a great sigh of relief that blew out her lips. "Thank you, Doctor. For a minute there, I was actually letting myself get carried away again."

But her own words, in addition to Jeanine's, made Charlotte

stop. She was taking blame for everyone else, too. She was the therapist, so she was supposed to fix them all. If she'd fixed Jeanine, then David Smith wouldn't have started all the trouble. If she'd fixed Melody, then the Wrights wouldn't have started the petition. If she'd handled Kathryn Wright more diplomatically in that first session, she wouldn't have gotten her back up. That had been her thinking since the rally in the quad. Charlotte had taken all the blame. But in reality, they had to fix themselves. She was merely the conduit. Maybe all the weeks with Charlotte were the reason Jeanine had finally stood up to her husband. And why Melody was suddenly holding hands with Eric. Charlotte had given all the credit to Lance and taken all the blame for herself, but they'd all played their roles, and each of them had had an effect.

And really, had Lance done anything horrendous? David Smith was dictatorial simply to protect his reputation, but Lance had used his authority to protect her. Was that such a bad thing? Would he really try to take over her life, control her every action, tell her what to do, belittle her if he didn't agree with her decisions? Or was she basing that conclusion on emotions and fears that belonged to the woman she'd been with Martin?

You're so terrified of losing control of your life that you can't even accept help without thinking someone's trying to take over.

Lola had it right.

"We all let ourselves get carried away with our fears sometimes," she said in answer to Jeanine's comment. "It's learning to recognize it before it does any damage that counts."

She wondered if she'd recognized it before the damage was irreparable. Only Lance could tell her for sure.

FOR THE REST OF JEANINE'S SESSION, THEY'D GONE BACK TO HER original problem: how to approach her husband about fantasizing and setting limits and ground rules. Actually, setting limits had arisen out of Charlotte's rules with the principal.

Did she want any limits? Did they need any ground rules? Or should she just tell Lance she was his submissive, and he could do whatever he wanted? Charlotte wasn't sure what she needed, except to talk to him. She'd think about what to say once she heard his voice.

Jeanine, however, had needed coaching and practice to figure out how to convey exactly what she wanted. She would also work on getting David Smith in for couple's counseling. Charlotte was sure she'd have a difficult time overcoming the hostility between herself and the chairman of the school board. She'd have to do it, though, for Jeanine. It was too much to expect the woman to start over with a new therapist. Jeanine was Charlotte's responsibility.

All in all, it was a good afternoon, her remaining sessions of the day going to according to plan. She would have driven straight to Lance's house, said a dirty word, and received her well-deserved punishment—maybe that was all she needed to say or do—but honestly, she wanted to shower and change. And shave her legs.

Half an hour after she'd gotten home, she stood in only panties and bra amid the chaos of her bedroom. Piles of discarded clothes were all over the bed. And the chair. And the carpet. What was the perfect outfit?

She huffed out a frustrated breath, blowing a wayward lock of hair off her forehead.

Then her phone rang. Her heart leaped. But it was Lola, not the principal. Ah, but Lola could help her pick out what to wear.

She answered with "Hey, when'd you get back?"

"We stayed an extra day and just dropped Rafe off at his mom's. And I've told Gray I'm moving in, so we want you to come over to his house to celebrate with us tonight."

No, no, no, she had to see Lance. He'd had five days to brood about everything she'd said last week, not to mention that she'd ignored all his phone calls.

"Woo-hoo," she said, trying to sound enthused. Honestly, she was happy for Lola.

"We've got a bottle of champagne. And I was hoping you'd help me pack everything up."

"Tonight?" Luckily, her voice didn't come out as a shriek.

Lola snorted. "Of course not. Tonight's champagne, next weekend is marathon packing."

"Sure, I can help." But *tonight* . . . She'd gone on and on for Lola to take this step, so how was she supposed to beg off the celebration? "I'm dying for champagne. What time do you want me there?"

They decided on forty-five minutes. She could move on to Lance's house after she'd toasted Lola on her decision.

What if he'd decided she was too much of a pain in the butt and was already looking for a new sub?

She couldn't think negatively. Instead, she chose the sexiest outfit on the bed.

CHARLOTTE HAD BEEN TO GRAY'S HOUSE SEVERAL TIMES. THE yard was neatly trimmed, edged with manicured bushes that acted as a short fence around the lawn. The front path was trimmed with ground lights, and the porch illuminated by Chinese lanterns on either side of the double doors.

She rang the bell. Gray—the coach, as Lola liked to call him—answered the door, reaching out to enfold her in a bear hug. He was big and tall, making her feel petite in his embrace, just the way Lance did. A few years younger than Lance, with only a few strands of gray in his dark hair, Gray was Lola's perfect complement.

"She's fussing in the kitchen." He waved a hand behind him.

Lola was not a gourmet cook, but since her twin nephews had stayed with her for the summer, she'd been working on her culinary skills.

"How was the snow?"

"White." He gave her a gleaming grin, then ushered her into the living room where the champagne was chilling in a bucket on the brick fireplace.

Lola floated in from the kitchen, a tray balanced on her hand. Cambozola cheese, rice crackers, and pepper jelly.

"Yum," Charlotte said. She'd powered down half a salad out of the fridge before she'd left home, but the cheese was her favorite, and her stomach clamored for a taste.

While Gray popped the champagne and filled three flutes, Lola set the goodies on the coffee table. She was radiant in a slim-fitting black velvet cocktail dress with a scoop neck and long sleeves that tapered to a point. She'd accented the outfit with black nylons and suede high heels.

Charlotte didn't feel underdressed in her ensemble. "You certainly look like the cold weather suited you."

Lola's smile was radiant, too. "It most certainly did."

"For you, my dear." Gray handed a glass of champagne to Lola, then Charlotte. With his own in hand, he raised the flute to toast. "To you, Charlotte, who, I understand, was instrumental in encouraging Lola to move in with me."

"My pleasure." She tapped her glass to his, then turned to Lola.

And almost dropped the damn thing. "Oh my God, an engagement ring." A shot of excitement kicked her pulse rate up. She glanced at Gray, his beaming face, then his fingers holding the champagne glass. One finger in particular, which bore a plain gold ring. "You didn't." Wide-eyed, she checked Lola's hand again. Not only was there a solitaire diamond, but also a matching gold band. "Jesus, you got married." Charlotte could hardly take it in.

"You aren't mad that we didn't take you with us, are you?" The brown of Lola's eyes deepened. "Gray"—she glanced briefly at him—"surprised me."

"I knew if I gave her too long to think about it," he said, "she'd say no."

But had Lola *really* thought about it? For a woman who couldn't make up her mind if she wanted to move in, Lola had certainly made a sudden turnaround. "A leap of faith?" she said softly, her voice rising just enough to make it a question.

Lola touched her hand. "Yeah. I told Gray that you were right. I was crazy for not jumping in with both feet, eyes closed, and nose pinched."

Charlotte made a face. "I didn't say it exactly like that."

"Whatever you said," Gray drawled, "was absolutely perfect."

"I would have done it anyway," Lola said. "Eventually."

It was true. Lola might have been scared, but she wasn't an idiot. She never would have let Gray go. Besides, Charlotte would have beaten her bloody if she had.

"Anyway," Lola continued the matrimonial story, "we had to stay until Monday. We couldn't get the license at the county clerk's office the week before because of the holiday."

"It's down in Minden," Gray explained, "on the other side of the Kingsbury Grade from South Lake Tahoe. We decided to get married right there in the courthouse instead of going back to Tahoe."

"We couldn't find a chapel on the spur of the moment that wasn't just plain cheesy." Lola stifled a giggle with her hand. "But we had to wait for half an hour while the judge finished sentencing a bunch of prisoners."

It sounded romantic in an odd sort of way. "So you just got married this morning?"

Lola bobbed her head. Gray laced his fingers with hers. "Yes."

"How was Rafe with all this?" She regretted the question as soon as it was out. This wasn't the time to put a damper on their day.

"I asked his permission." Gray pulled Lola under his arm, hugging her close to his side. "He said he thought Lola was good for me. He came into the judge's chambers with us."

It was amazing. Three months ago, Rafe had hated Lola. "So you got married this morning and just rushed home?" They didn't even get a wedding night. Although having your son in the next room might not be such a romantic idea anyway.

"Rafe had to be back to school tomorrow." Gray shrugged. "Some project due."

Lola dipped her head to his shoulder. She didn't seem to mind the circumstances at all.

"Group hug," Charlotte said, afraid she'd actually start crying.

In the end, it was a hug for Gray, an even tighter one for Lola. Charlotte went on her tiptoes, since Lola wasn't petite like Charlotte.

"If I'd had time to plan," Lola said softly, "I would have had you there. I swear." She pulled back. "We're talking about doing another ceremony here. Or maybe just a big reception. I don't know. What do you think?"

"I think the ceremony at the courthouse after the prisoner sentencing will always be a sweet memory." Charlotte smiled. "So just do the reception."

Lola glanced at Gray, her eyes shining. "Is that a good game plan, Coach?"

He smiled. The guy was definitely a hunk, and his adoration for Lola gleamed in his gaze. "Perfect game plan. We need a honeymoon, too."

They began arguing about locations. Gray suggested Honolulu; Lola said there were too many tourists. Charlotte listened, tossing out a couple of ideas. The fact that Lola had gotten married without her in attendance didn't bother her. After all, she'd been in the wedding party the first time, and that had been no guarantee of success. She was delighted for her best friend, and the tiny ache beneath her rib cage had nothing to do with their happiness. It was the thought that popped into her head and simply wouldn't pop back out. The thought that Lola had finally found her coach. And maybe Charlotte wanted to be more than just a submissive to the principal's dom. Maybe she wanted to feel the way Lola did.

"How about a sleeper train across the Canadian Rockies?" Gray offered.

Lola rolled her eyes. "If we take a sleeper car, we'll never even get to see the Rockies."

Gray eyed her. "My point exactly.

Lola actually blushed.

Charlotte felt the tiny ache under her rib cage grow in size, sort of like how the Grinch's heart grew when he saw the Whos down in Whoville on Christmas morning.

"If the Rockies don't work, how about the Carlsbad Caverns?" Gray planted a kiss on Lola's forehead.

She wrinkled her nose. "Bat guano is supposed to be romantic on a honeymoon?"

The doorbell rang while they were still far from any agreement.

"Ah, he made it." Gray pointed to a corner cabinet in the dining area adjacent to the living room. "Sweetheart, would you get another champagne glass?"

"Sure, honey."

As they went in separate directions, Charlotte didn't get a chance to ask who *he* was. She'd been to a couple of parties Gray had, but she couldn't have said any of those people would be

someone exclusive that Gray would invite to toast his wedding day.

Yet with the murmur of male voices in the foyer, goose pimples rose along her arms.

Oh God. It couldn't be. Lola wouldn't.

But Lola had.

25

GOD, SHE WAS GORGEOUS. LANCE'S HEART THUMPED IN HIS chest. Her dress was cinched tight beneath her breasts, plumping them. The fitted waist flared out over her shapely hips, falling in soft folds to her knees. Tasteful, elegant, and sexy as hell, hinting at the promise of sweetly scented skin beneath. How deliciously easy it would be to lift the skirt over her delectable ass and have his way with her. Or give her a good spanking.

"Principal Hutton, so good of you to come." Lola Cook held out her hand while Gray filled a champagne flute and began topping off the others.

"Congratulations." Her hand was warm in his. She was a pretty woman, long and lithe, with a silky mane of dark hair. "You can call me Lance."

"Oh no," she said, fluttering her eyelashes with a sidelong glance at Charlotte. "You're the principal and he's"—she pointed at Gray—"the coach." She smiled. "Right, Charlotte?"

"Of course, Lola."

His knees felt weak at the sound of Charlotte's sultry voice. He'd known she'd be here. He'd realized Lola and Gray were matchmaking when Gray had called little over an hour ago and asked him round for a drink to celebrate their nuptials. While he was on friendly terms with Gray Barnett, respected him, and had attended a few parties and faculty functions with the man, he would never have expected to be invited for this particular occasion.

They'd brought him here for Charlotte.

Maybe Gray and Lola thought he needed a kick in the pants to get him to see the light. But Lance had seen it the moment he'd found Charlotte searching for her apple under the desk. When she'd held it up, he was as hooked on her as Adam had been on Eve.

Of course, after the apple incident, they'd been kicked out of the Garden of Eden.

He held up his champagne. "To the two of you and many happy years ahead."

All four glasses clinked in the middle of their circle.

"We're discussing the honeymoon." Gray arched an eyebrow, his gaze on Lance. "I'm voting for a sleeper train over the Canadian Rockies."

"It would be gorgeous in the snow," he mused. "And Lake Louise is beautiful." The things he could do to Charlotte in a secluded compartment. Parts down below stirred with the thought of it.

He didn't realize his gaze rested on her until her face bloomed with color. As if she could see every one of those images playing like movies in his eyes.

"I told you, Lola," Gray said dryly. "There are definite possibilities."

"What do you think, Miss Moore?" No one said a word about Lance's formal address.

She parted her lips, licked them, swallowed, then finally said, "I vote for the Rockies, too."

"I'm outnumbered," he heard Lola say. "Wouldn't it be fun to take the trip together?"

His heart stilled. She was pairing him with Charlotte. She was taking his side, if indeed there were sides in this.

"But we're not even dating," his dear Miss Moore said.

"What if the principal asked you out on a date?" Lola urged, while her newly minted husband looked on indulgently.

Lance was sure the woman knew every detail of every moment he'd spent with Charlotte, all the things he'd done to her, how she'd felt about every single one.

There were so many things he needed to tell Charlotte, so many things she needed to hear, things he couldn't say in front of the Barnetts.

"Say yes," he murmured. "One date." Maybe it was an order. Maybe he was begging. Maybe it was both.

"I recall my first real date with Lola," Gray said, thoughtfully at first, a smile growing.

Lola glared at him. "I remember it, too." Then something passed between them, and the glare morphed to a smile. The heat between them was palpable, almost embarrassingly so.

Or it would have been if he didn't feel the same and more for Charlotte.

She was staring at the newlyweds. "Miss Moore," he said softly, "one date. If it doesn't meet your expectations, you're free."

Charlotte would know he meant that she wasn't his slave or his submissive. That he wasn't issuing an order. He was begging.

He could read nothing in the jewel-bright green of her gaze as she asked, "When?"

"Whenever you like."

"Where will we go?"

"Dinner. A movie. The theater. Your choice."

"Bungee jumping," she said.

"Bungee jumping?" He could only repeat her words.

"So you can jump together, feet first," Lola supplied.

"Eyes closed," Charlotte added.

"Nose pinched," Gray concluded.

It didn't make a lick of sense. "All right, bungee jumping it is."

"Or maybe zip-lining." Charlotte tipped her head. "Are you too old for that?"

"Hell, no," he answered quickly. "Just try me."

She gave him a long look, and he couldn't say he knew exactly what was going through her mind. Bungee jumping, zip-lining. It wasn't a regular date, but Charlotte Moore wasn't a regular kind of woman. With her, he would always have his work cut out for him.

"I most certainly intend to try you," she answered softly.

They weren't done. There was a hell of a lot more to say. But this time, unlike that day on the quad steps when they'd vanquished Smith, she was willing to listen.

IT WAS THE LONGEST HOUR OF HER LIFE. OKAY, THERE'D BEEN longer, like waiting in her office with Alice Sloan before that parent conference with the Wrights and Smiths the day before Thanksgiving. But the length of this hour was way up there.

Not that she wasn't completely over-the-top happy for Lola and Gray. But she was dying to know what Lance's talk about a date really meant.

Would they come out of the closet, so to speak, at school? Would she still be Miss Moore to his Principal Hutton? Or were they more? Hell, they could even be less. How much more did she want versus how much he wanted? God, yes, she wanted those feelings that Gray and Lola shared. But how could she ever have that kind of relationship with Lance and still retain her autonomy? He just wasn't built that way. Would dating mean he'd expected her to confer about every decision she made? Would she have to ask for permission if she wanted an evening out with Lola? And what about . . .

Honestly, Lola was right. Charlotte overanalyzed everything. Give her an hour to think, and she'd come up with umpteen ideas—which was equivalent to one new idea every five seconds, and she certainly wasn't going to calculate that in her head. It was simple. She wanted whatever he offered, she couldn't let him go, and she'd just have to figure out a way to manage the relationship. Yes, *relationship*. Not just casual sex.

"In the car, Miss Moore." Okay, she was Miss Moore, so it was the principal who opened the passenger side door of his car. She felt completely comfortable with that. This was good. Maybe *dating* didn't mean that everything had to change.

"What about my car?" If they left it here, Lola would know they were going to . . . Lola would know that anyway.

"Can I trust you to drive exactly where I tell you to?"

"Yes, Principal Hutton," she said dutifully, her pulse jumping with his nearness. God, she really did love his mastery when they were in the sexual arena. She'd do just about anything he wanted in order to keep it.

"All right." He closed the door. "Don't move. And don't say anything until I'm done."

She remained on the sidewalk beside his car, not backing up a single step as he moved in on her. Could he hear her breathe? Feel her heart racing?

"First," he enumerated, "the reason I felt compelled to handle Smith myself is that I was the one who got us into the mess and I felt obligated to get us both out."

She opened her mouth to say that wasn't true at all. Jeanine had gotten them into it. And Lance wasn't even a part of that.

He put a finger to her lips. She wanted to lick him, taste him. And she forgot everything she'd been about to say.

"Second, I didn't save you. Your students did it because they love you."

The street darkened slightly as Gray's front-porch light winked out. Then the lights in the living room. And finally all the lights along the front rooms of the house.

"Thank you," she whispered. He understood how important her students were to her. "You always want them to love you, but you're never really sure."

"I don't want them to love me," he answered softly. "I want them to respect me enough to listen to what I have to say. It's the only way I can help them. People don't always listen to the ones they love."

This was true.

"I didn't listen to you, Charlotte."

Surely he could hear her heart pounding now. She could read between the lines. Hell, yes, she could. It thrilled her; it scared the heck out of her. She wanted the emotion, she just wasn't sure she could handle everything else. "Can I say something?"

"Yes, you may."

Just as he'd admitted what he'd done wrong, she had to take responsibility for her issues. "When the problems with Mr. Smith started, I wanted to make everything your fault. I took my feelings out on you. I just wanted to think of you as the dictatorial boss so I didn't have to face my inadequacies." Or her fears.

He put a palm to her cheek. "You're certainly not inadequate."

She smiled. "I actually figured that out on my own. But for a little while there, I was doubting myself." Turning her face into his hand, she kissed his palm. "Now we can go back to the way it was. Before David Smith and the Wrights." She looked at him with everything she felt in her gaze. "Like that day in detention hall. When you gave me my first naughty lesson."

He dropped his forehead to hers, closed his eyes a moment before pulling back. "I don't want to be your principal, Charlotte. I want to be your lover." He put his hands on her shoulders, stroked down her arms until he clasped her fingers in his. "I love you."

She rocked into him, wanting, needing, and laid her head against his chest, breathing in the overwhelmingly sexy male scent of him. It was more intoxicating than the champagne with which they'd toasted Lola and Gray. Love. Desire. That sweetness she'd seen pass between them. Her heart ached for it. Hadn't she searched for this feeling in her previous failed relationships? Only to have everything fall apart, a different reason every time.

But she felt it now. There was no way she was letting him go. She could make things work this time. She wouldn't try to control every little thing, and if she ceded control in the bedroom, maybe he wouldn't notice the places she did keep it.

Oh God, yes. She wanted him, needed him. Principal Hutton. Lance. Her boss. Her lover. "I love you, too." She went up on her tiptoes, winding her arms around his neck. "I don't mind if you want to be my dom, too."

SHE LOVED HIM. DEFINITELY A GOOD THING. LANCE COULD almost say it was everything he'd been waiting to hear from her. But she still wanted him to be her dom, not a bad thing on the face of it. He just wasn't sure they were on the same page.

She wanted to go back to the way things had been. He was her dom. She was his sub. That meant they were still role playing. He didn't want the same thing they'd had before. He wanted to expand it.

He glanced in the rearview mirror as he rolled to a stop at the light. She was still following him. Still obeying orders. The light changed and when he pulled away, putting more distance between them, her headlights came up to obscure his view of her in the mirror. She was nothing more than an outline.

How the hell was he supposed to get to her? He'd told her he loved her. She'd repeated the words. He was even sure she'd meant them. Yet she was holding back. Talk didn't work with her. Only issuing orders did. As long as he did it only in the bedroom. As long as it was on her terms.

How could he use that to his advantage?

Turning into his driveway, he punched the garage door opener and maneuvered into his usual spot. She parked on the drive behind him.

Lance didn't wait for her, entering the laundry room off the garage and heading into the kitchen. He threw his keys on the counter, emptied his pockets of wallet, comb, change.

"I closed the garage door." She stood in the laundry room, a silhouette of curling hair and full breasts against the windows behind the washer and dryer.

The darkness was sweet. It hushed everything, turned the atmosphere more intimate. "Go to my bedroom."

"Where is it?"

He'd imagined her in his bed so many times that he hadn't realized he'd never had her there. Not sure she could see him clearly in the light of the moon, he pointed anyway, indicating a doorway off the laundry area. "Down the hall and to the right. It's on the end."

She moved obediently. He followed. By the light of the moon falling through the floor-to-ceiling windows along one side of the bedroom hallway, she made her way to the room at the end. Entering, she passed his closet, then stood at the end of the bed. Latticed windows with low sills filled two walls. On the other side of the bed in a small alcove lay another closet, built-in drawers, and a vanity. To the right of that, divided from the bedroom by the wall behind his bed, was the master bath.

His furniture was dark wood, a Chinese style that was more masculine than feminine. The bedspread was dark blue, with only two pillows at the head. With her in the room, he suddenly realized how girlie it would have been without his furniture. The latticed windows were meant for lace curtains instead of the utilitarian blinds he'd hung. The vanity cried out for a woman's makeup and jewelry, and the built-in drawers had been designed for lingerie. He saw clearly for the first time that it was a couple's room, his and hers.

He'd been missing the female side. No wonder the house had always seemed too big, always a little empty. He needed Charlotte to fill it.

He didn't close the blinds. His fences were high enough to protect against prying eyes. Stepping past her, he switched on a bedside lamp to its lowest setting.

When he turned, somehow the scoop neck of her dress was lower, her breasts plumper, the dusky color of her nipples almost visible. She'd slipped out of her shoes and seemed impossibly petite, irresistible.

"We need some new rules," he said.

"Like what?" Her eyes sparkled in the lamplight.

"Whenever you say no to me, I spank you."

"No," she said quickly.

"Does that mean no, I can't spank you, or no, you want to be spanked right now?"

"You'll have to figure that out, Principal Hutton."

Ah yes, she wanted the spanking. But he wasn't done with the rules. "Outside of business hours, you'll be at my beck and call."

"Yes, Principal Hutton."

"You'll spend the night." He waited for the no on that one. It never came. "Whatever you want, Principal Hutton."

That was an improvement. She wanted to sleep in his bed, to wake up beside him in the morning.

He knew where she needed to be when he told her everything he wanted. When he dropped the role play and begged. When he bared his soul. It was time to get her there.

"Tell me the secret," he demanded, knowing exactly what her answer would be.

Just as she knew exactly what secret he wanted. "No, Principal Hutton. That's breaking my client's confidentiality." She dropped her voice to a whisper. "I'll never tell."

He pointed a finger. "Just remember you're asking for this by your willful disobedience. It hurts me more than it hurts you. Now take off your panties and hose."

She reached beneath her dress and gracefully rolled everything down as if she'd had all the practice in the world, after which she tossed the bundle aside.

"Get on the bed," he snapped. "Hands and knees."

She smiled wickedly, knowing what the sight of her bare legs and plump breasts did to him. "Yes, Principal Hutton."

Once in position, she pulled the dress to her waist without even being asked.

He damn near forgot what he was trying to accomplish. Her round cheeks beckoned to his hand, yet the ripe folds of her pussy begged for so much more. He wanted to sink deep inside her and stay there forever.

He willed himself to follow the plan, as undefined as that plan may be. "Are you going to tell me the secret?"

"No."

He swatted her, hand cupped, fingers connecting with the sweet, moist center of her. She didn't scream. She didn't cry. She simply let her head fall forward and moaned.

"Oh, Principal Hutton," she sighed.

"I'll ask you one more time."

"The answer is the same. No."

He brought his hand down again. She shivered and pushed back, leaving his palm wet with her sweet juice. Lance licked his skin, tasting her. She was right. He would need to play her dom. He would always want this, his hand on her, her moans filling the air around him.

"Say it again," he demanded.

"No. I won't tell. No, no, no."

He spanked her hard for every word. Her rump was red, her pussy wet, her breath fast, and her moans loud. She tossed her head and said it again, "No, no, no," goading him.

"I'm always going to test you," he told her, swatting again. "I'm always going to ask, just so you'll say no. Then I can do this." His cock was long, full, and aching in his trousers. He could have taken her now. But he wasn't done, far from done. "I'm going to tell you to do things so you'll stand up to me and say no."

Charlotte needed to say no. She needed independence. She needed to be master in her own purview. He didn't want to take that away from her.

"No, no, no," she chanted. He gave her what she wanted until her body trembled, until she couldn't form the sound anymore, until she was a creamy dish beneath his hand.

"I'm ordering you," he murmured, not knowing if she was even capable of hearing him, "to defy me. To never let me take over." His hand connecting hard, he felt her shudders communicate themselves up through his arm, to his chest, his heart. "To say no to me."

She gushed for him, cried out, fisted her hands in the bedspread, threw her head back, hair cascading over her shoulders. He kept his hand on her, his fingers cupping her pussy, working her, until finally she collapsed on the bed.

"Oh my God," she whispered, eyes closed. "That was so good." She lifted her head slightly, cracked one lid. "Can I say no again right away?"

He smiled. "Yes." But had she understood what he was giving her?

He'd told her he loved her, but he hadn't bared his soul for her yet. If he wanted her, he was going to have to give her everything.

CHARLOTTE FLOATED IN ORGASMIC BLISS. SHE'D LOVE TO SAY NO again, but she honestly didn't have the strength to move. She could barely open her eyes when she felt him stretch out beside her.

His voice rumbled somewhere close to her ear. "I'll probably always give you my opinion, Charlotte." He gently pulled her dress down over her hip. "But you can always say no to whatever I suggest. You should know I respect your work. Always have, always will."

She could feel the thump of her heart in her chest, its rhythm slowing as she came down off the high. He was not a dom now. He wasn't the principal. He was a man. And he was telling her the things she needed to hear. He was telling her he understood. That he knew her. That her fears had meaning. They weren't just something a silly woman felt.

She opened her eyes, searched his face, read his sincerity in the darkness of his gaze. "My work is important."

"I know."

"The decisions I make can't always be understood without sitting through session after session, without hearing everything a client or student says to me."

"I understand."

She bit her lip. "But I'm afraid of being wrong. And I don't like to admit that."

He didn't touch her beyond his hand resting on her hip. "I didn't fall in love with you because you were perfect."

She hadn't fallen in love with him because he was perfect for her, either. He was exactly what she didn't want. But maybe he was everything she needed.

She put her fingers to his lips. "We never listen to the ones we love," she said softly. "But maybe I can turn over a new leaf and at least discuss something without feeling that you're telling me I'm wrong."

"I'm a controlling asshole," he said.

She leaned in to nuzzle his cheek, touching her mouth lightly to his. "Not that I'm discussing patient confidences with you, but a client recently discussed his or her significant other in those terms, and I have to say that you are far from being a controlling asshole when compared to that person." She tipped her head back to meet his gaze. She'd told many of her clients that sometimes you have to give up something to get something. Relationships were always a compromise. She'd never listened to her own advice. If she compromised just a little bit more, she could have the whole man. She could have everything. "I might be willing to admit that I've been too hasty in judging the things you say to me. I'm going to have to change that. I might even be willing to listen to you."

He brought her hand to his lips, kissed the tips of her fingers. "I'm willing to admit that I overdid the role playing and issued too many orders. I'm going to have to change that."

"I like orders." She blinked, smiled. "I like the spanking. I like it when you throw me down on the bed, fall on top of me so I can't move, and tie me to the headboard."

He glanced up. His bed didn't have a headboard. There were shelves and cubbyholes, stacks of books, the clock, a reading lamp. But no posts to tie her to.

"Looks like I'll have to buy a new bed." He held her chin in his big hand. "Because how will I make you spend the night if I don't have anything to tie you to?"

"You don't have to tie me up," she said softly. "I'll stay the night."

"How many nights?"

"As many as you want."

"How about all the rest of our nights?"

She held her breath. She didn't know exactly what that meant. Was he proposing? Or was this just moving in? Or was it . . .

Damn, she was overanalyzing again. "Yes."

His eyes glittered. "But if you say no to me about anything, I can still spank you."

"No," she said emphatically. "No, no, no," she went on as she pushed him back on the bed and began removing his clothes.

26

CHARLOTTE WAS ASTOUNDED. DURING EACH OF THE LAST SIX weekly sessions, she'd encouraged Jeanine to bring her husband. Even if it was for one meeting. Charlotte just hadn't figured that David Smith would ever agree.

Yet here he was, taking time off work on a sunny mid-January day. As far as winter months went in the San Francisco Bay area, January was usually gorgeous. In fact, she and Lance had gone for a hike on Saturday up at Castle Rock.

Funny how he'd entered her thoughts about every hour or so of every day in the six weeks since they'd officially started dating. He'd taken her to Colorado for Christmas to introduce her to his family. She'd passed muster, thank God. Here at home, the entire student body had been ecstatic at that turn of events. Charlotte suspected they had Lydia, Eric and Melody, and probably Alice Sloan, too, to thank for the groundswell of approval. No one knew they were practically living together, though. Lance figured they'd give people three months to get used to the dating thing before they made the rest known. Charlotte was already looking for a renter.

Of course, the most important person they had to thank for making their relationship run smoothly was the chairman of the school board. He could have made a huge stink, claiming that a guidance counselor couldn't date the principal she worked for, that it was against the rules, blah, blah, blah. Even if Charlotte did report to Alice. But Lance had tackled that problem with sly aplomb, crediting David Smith for opening Lance's eyes and bringing them together, all's well that ends well and so on. The chairman couldn't backtrack and say he'd tried to get her fired.

Well, he could have, but he'd probably been a little afraid that if he made too big a fuss, his little secret might come to light.

So here he was in her office.

"I'm glad you could come, Mr. Smith."

"I'm doing it for Jeanine." His voice was gruff, semi-irritated, but at least he was here. Since she'd last seen him, his face was less florid, and he appeared to have a lost a few pounds, not a dramatic difference, but enough to be noticeable. This was a good sign. He looked healthier. "And this better be completely confidential."

"Of course it is," Charlotte said without offense. She had decided to forgive him for trying to get her fired. She was going to put aside the past and make this all about solving her clients' issues.

Instead of sitting in the chairs by the window, the positioning of which would have the effect of making him the odd man out, she'd pulled three chairs into a triangle in the middle of the office. Upon sitting, he'd immediately hiked a pant leg and crossed one foot over the opposite knee. It would have been a relaxed pose except for his fists bunched on the arms of the chair. Next to him, Jeanine sat with her knees primly together.

With his statement, Mr. Smith had given Charlotte the obvious place to start. "Counseling works best if there's willingness on both sides." For him, she avoided the word *therapy*.

"Don't push your luck," he said like a sullen schoolboy.

His attitude wasn't the greatest, but she'd known it was something she'd have to deal with and diffuse. "Regardless of what brought you here, you *are* here. Why don't you tell me what you hope to get out of it?"

"To make her happy." He pointed at Jeanine.

The finger-pointing was a tad rude, but Charlotte didn't admonish him as if he were the schoolboy he sounded like. Instead, she changed tack completely. "Eric tells me that you've planned a family outing with the Wrights over the holiday weekend." It was Martin Luther King Day the following week.

Mr. Smith had lifted the ban against seeing Charlotte, and Eric dropped by every couple of weeks. He was already discussing colleges and career planning. Right now, he was vacillating between forensic psychology and being a medical examiner. Charlotte figured he'd been watching too much *CSI*, and his thinking would change over time.

"We're all going up to Alcatraz," Jeanine said. "Our two youngest have never been. Neither has Melody. Eric went on a school field trip, but Melody was sick that day."

"It sounds both educational and fun."

Jeanine smiled. Mr. Smith harrumphed and said, "It'll be crowded as hell on a holiday weekend."

"Yes, dear," Jeanine said sweetly, "but you said you couldn't take a day off, and a weekend would be too busy. So we picked the holiday instead."

"I don't really need to go, do I?" It was a question, not a statement.

"Eric and Melody want all of us to go," Jeanine insisted.

Charlotte was proud of the way she spoke, with determination but no acrimony.

"I said I'm going," Mr. Smith grumbled.

According to Melody, she and Eric had started hanging out together again, but they were *not* boyfriend and girlfriend. Eric, on the other hand, was a teenager who knew what he wanted. Charlotte had the feeling he would turn out to be an amazing man. She credited him for the changes she saw in Melody. All right, the girl hadn't suddenly turned into Miss Popularity, but she occasionally had lunch with Lydia and her peeps. She'd even been seen around a few of her old friends from middle school. She hadn't dumped a soda or a beaker of sugar water on anyone. She hadn't gotten into any fights. Her breakouts seemed less severe and of a shorter duration. And, miracle of miracles, she'd thrown out the brown hoodie and sometimes pushed her hair behind her ears to show her face. Her parents had decided not to switch her over to Mrs. Flannigan, so Melody still met with Charlotte twice a week, and her parents attended weekly. Mr. Wright was still his wife's second voice, and Kathryn Wright had obviously had a fresh injection of Botox because her face simply did not move. Not to mention the puffy collagen-enhanced lips. Charlotte had a hard time not staring at them. Maybe they'd settle down in a few weeks and look a bit more normal.

Whatever, she wasn't going to fix the Wrights, she knew that. But they'd stopped urging surgery as a solution to every problem Melody mentioned, and they were talking with their daughter, *really* talking. And listening. Now this, a family outing. Things were definitely looking up since last November.

"It shows great progress that you and the Wrights are willing to work constructively together for the sake of your children."

He harrumphed again. "Don't get me started about that woman."

Of course, he'd been willing to use Kathryn Wright when he was trying to get Charlotte fired. Now she'd become *that woman*. She probably had been before the incident as well.

"You've shown incredible restraint, dear," Jeanine said, once again without acrimony.

Mr. Smith glanced at his watch. "Look, this is time and money. Let's not waste it talking about that woman. Let's get to the issues."

Charlotte resisted the smile. She'd been intending the little conversational diversion to lead into the point that people needed to work together to solve problems. But trust the cost of something to get to David Smith first. In that, he was just like Steven Wright.

"That works for me. Tell me why you're here."

"We all know why I'm here. But for the record, I never meant Jeanine should actually do it, just that we could fantasize about it."

It was getting harder to resist the smile. Using sex with another man as a fantasy had now become his idea. Jeanine had finally broached the subject with him a couple of weeks ago. Last week, when she'd call to say that he'd agreed to a counseling session, she'd made it abundantly clear that Charlotte should leave out the part about his sexual problems for the time being. Another thing Charlotte found funny, or odd. He was more willing to discuss his wife and other men—or fantasizing about it—than he was to admit he had erectile dysfunction. She would get around to the issue eventually, but for now she'd decided to go along with Jeanine's wish.

Charlotte, however, would call him on his avoidance tactic. "If that were the case, Mr. Smith—"

"Oh please, call him David," Jeanine said, and this time there was a note of exasperation.

Charlotte raised a brow. David Smith nodded. And she went on. "If that were the case, David, you didn't make it clear to your wife that it was only a fantasy. Our entire therapy has been predicated on the fact that she thought you actually wanted her to be with someone else, then come home to tell you about it."

His jaw tightened. He didn't like being pinned down, in addition to the fact that Charlotte had voiced exactly what he'd wanted.

"I don't remember how I said it." His voice rose slightly.

"I remember," Jeanine said, calm in the face of his irritation.

"Communication is key," Charlotte said. Communication was their biggest problem. She hoped to introduce exercises that would help them improve those skills. "You both need to be clear about what you want and what your limits are."

Jeanine's gaze shot to her face. "You're not saying I'm supposed to do it?"

"Of course not. What I'm saying is that you need to make rules that fit the two of you. If, in a healthy relationship, you want to discuss spicing things up in different ways, then I'm all for trying alternative"—she smiled meaningfully—"approaches."

David Smith merely gaped. Jeanine started to smile. Perhaps she'd figured out where Charlotte was going with this.

"I'm not judgmental," she went on. "Getting a little kinky can be quite fun." Oh yes, she knew all about that. "You can experiment with all kinds of things. Toys. Role playing. A little bondage. Dirty talk. Spanking." She could certainly attest to how good spanking was. She'd also used a lot of dirty words over the last few weeks to goad the principal into giving her a well-deserved punishment.

David's face began to redden. He opened his mouth, but couldn't seem to get a word out.

"However," she went on, "your fundamental relationship needs to be sound before considering anything like adding another partner or even swinging. You need to have ground rules. Both of you have to agree. There can be no coercion."

David made an odd noise, as if he were choking. For a moment, she was worried. In the next, he let out a guffaw that bounced off the walls. "You're putting me on, right?" He wiped at his eyes. "This is a joke."

"I'm perfectly serious." But she liked his reaction. It was something she could work with.

"But you really talk about sex with your patients. I wasn't actually sure what you did."

Yet he'd accused her of being a bad influence on the students she worked with. She had, however, put that aside. If she couldn't, she wouldn't have agreed to counsel them both.

"We talk about emotions," she corrected, "in relation to sex." Though she had to admit she didn't normally dive in the way she had with him. It was the history between them. She'd wanted to shock him into being honest. "But let me make this clear, I'm not recommending that you and your wife bring anyone else into your relationship."

"But we can use whips and chains," he said, still laughing hard enough to make his eyes tear up.

"Whips and chains might be a bit much. Why don't you start with silk scarves for binding? A feather teaser might be nice, too." Very, very nice. She should know.

He looked at Jeanine. "I'm supposed to tie you up, or are you going to tie me up?"

"I haven't considered that yet," Jeanine said, her expression thoughtful. "But I think I'd like to do the tying up."

He guffawed again. "I can't believe you're actually suggesting this, Dr. Moore."

She didn't correct him on the title. "I'm simply throwing out ideas. But my real point in all this is that the two of you need to talk about what you want. I can mediate for you here. And I can give you homework."

"Homework?" he echoed.

"What's the first assignment?" Jeanine asked, her words quick, laced with excitement.

"You each write down a fantasy. Then you let your partner read it. There should be no judgment about the fantasy. You both promise the other that you won't get angry. Discuss why it turns you on." She smiled. "Then quickly shred the pages so the kids can't read them."

They both laughed with her.

"If, however, you don't feel you can read the fantasy without making a judgment or getting hurt, then don't exchange. Bring them here, you can read them with me present, then we'll discuss how you each feel about them in a nonjudgmental atmosphere."

The homework wouldn't solve their problems. It was simply a tool to begin the dialogue.

"Do you think you can read the fantasies without judgment?" she asked them both

"No," Jeanine said.

"Yes," David answered just as quickly.

"Since one of you says no, then bring them here for your next session. Don't read them ahead of time."

They both agreed. Charlotte put them in her calendar for a week from Wednesday because next Monday was the holiday. Things were going exceptionally well. The first step was that David had actually agreed to see her. The second was that he'd laughed.

But the best part? She liked her own advice. She wanted to try it with Lance. He'd gone totally wild the night she'd spun that fantasy about having sex with another man while he watched. A little fantasy could work wonders. The wonderful thing about Lance was that he was old enough to appreciate a good fantasy. Younger men just couldn't get into it. They didn't get that the mind was as powerful a sexual tool as the body. How could she ever have thought that younger men were the better way to go? A real man like Principal Hutton was absolutely perfect.

She finished her notes in the Smith file, and before the red light flashed to indicate her next client had arrived, she dashed off a quick text to Lance:

> I've got a fabulous idea, Principal Hutton. Wanna play a new game?

She was already thinking about the fantasy she'd write for him. It had to do with a sleeper train. In fact, the fantasy had been growing in her mind since Lola and Gray had booked their honeymoon ride for mid-February. Charlotte and Lance had decided not to go despite the talk that night. After all, a honeymoon was only for two. Sex on a train. Very hot. She could come up with a really good fantasy about that.

Maybe they should send their fantasies as private emails. That was a sizzling idea. It would take some time to write. She wanted the fantasy to sound perfect when he read it. They needed to read them alone, so maybe she'd go to her place first, send it from there. Get him all worked up so that by the time she got home—

Her phone chirped. She read his message.

> Hell yes, I wanna play. Tell me the rules.

They didn't need rules. They didn't need limits. They didn't need a safe word. She trusted him completely, with her heart, with her soul.

And she told him how to play the new game she'd just made up.

Keep reading for an excerpt from

THE PRINCIPAL'S OFFICE

By Jasmine Haynes
Now available from Heat Books

PROLOGUE

THE PRETTY BLONDE STARED INTO THE REFRIGERATED JUICE section, like a child in front of a candy store window seeing the very thing she wanted and knew she couldn't have.

She was perfect.

Rand was relatively new to the area, having moved here to start a job last fall, five months ago. But even so, he didn't prowl grocery stores early on Saturday mornings looking for women. He'd needed a couple of items and didn't like waiting in line, so he'd stopped after his run along the canal.

Then he saw her. It was fortune smiling down on him, the law of attraction at work.

Her blond hair fluttered just past her shoulders. Her pretty profile showcased full ruby lips and long lashes several shades darker than her hair. The tight white T-shirt outlined mouthwatering breasts that were more than even his big hands could hold, and her jeans hugged the delectable curve of her ass. She wasn't too thin, yet was well taken care of. Best of all, there was no ring on her finger. He never amused himself with married women. He came from a long line of players, marriage being no barrier whatsoever between them and the objects of their desire. He wasn't about to be like any of them.

She was no sweet young thing, but closer to his age—forty—or possibly a couple of years younger. He preferred his partners to be older, seasoned, more sure of themselves, of who they were and what they wanted. Women who were old enough to appreciate trying something new, something daring.

He was as staid as they come during work hours, with a position that required a quiet, unwavering authority, steadfast diplomacy, and a hell of a lot of psychology. But after hours, his life was his own business. After hours, anything goes.

He smiled as she finally made up her mind and reached for the fridge door. Her breasts plumped with the movement.

Oh yeah, he'd love to get daring with her.

RACHEL STARED AT THE ROWS AND ROWS OF JUICE BOTTLES. SHE was a frugal shopper, buying only what was on sale, because in her mind, the sale price was the real price, and anything else meant you were overpaying. She lived for coupons. Penny-pinching was the only way she could make ends meet. Sure, her ex paid half the boys' expenses since they had dual custody, but the cost of living in the San Francisco Bay Area was astronomical, gas prices had once again skyrocketed, and cable TV and high-speed Internet, not to mention the boys' cell phones, just might bankrupt her. She had a full-time job she enjoyed, with excellent medical benefits, but she was a receptionist. Her salary barely covered standard monthly expenses. Her ex, an accountant, was the real breadwinner. Their house was underwater so they hadn't been able to unload it during the divorce settlement, and they were still waiting for the market to recover. In the meantime, she lived in it. The boys were with her every other week; teenage boys could eat you out of house and home. For the most part, she made healthy home-cooked meals and only occasionally brought home fast food. It would have been cheaper to buy soda for the boys to drink, but she did her damnedest to make sure they learned good eating habits.

So she wanted that juice, which was on sale at half off, plus she had a coupon. Wouldn't you know, though, the last bottle had twisted at the top of the rollers, stuck fast, and there wasn't a grocery clerk in sight to help her out. Well, she was *not* going to be bested by a damn juice bottle. Yanking open the refrigerator door, she put a foot on the rubberized track, grabbed the edge of the shelf, hauled herself up, and stretched until her fingers just brushed the plastic bottle. If she could knock it a little, dislodge it . . .

"Let me help."

The male voice was deep enough to send a delicious shiver down her spine. She would have gotten out of his way, but she felt him along her side as he leaned into the fridge door with her. His hand on the small of her back set a flame burning low in her belly. She couldn't have moved if her life depended on it. Oh no, this was too good to miss. With barely a stretch, he straightened the bottle and set it rolling down the tracks to her waiting hand.

She was breathless when she turned to look up, and up some more. He was close enough to make her eyes cross, and she couldn't focus sufficiently to take in more than cropped blond hair, piercing blue eyes, and a square, smooth-shaven jaw.

"Thank you" was all she could manage. She didn't want him to move. It had been so long since she'd felt a man this near, breathed in his pure male scent, musky with testosterone and clean workout sweat.

He stepped back out of the fridge slowly, his body caressing the length of hers for what seemed like an eternity, until his heat was replaced by the cool blast of refrigerated air.

"My pleasure," he said in that deep voice, setting her blood rushing through her veins.

She was so used to her ex's average height that, even though she was five-foot-five, this man made her feel petite. Tall and broad, he was a Viking who'd just stepped off his ship. Except for the all-black running outfit. Tight black jogging pants encased his muscled thighs, and the black Lycra shirt framed his powerful chest. She was staring, probably even drooling. In days of old, yeah, he'd have been a Viking or a knight. These days, a cop or a fireman. Or a corporate raider.

The man made her remember how long it had been since she'd had sex. With the divorce and all the stuff that went before, it had been two years. Two *years*. She'd been so busy and worried, she'd hardly noticed. Until *this* man had stood close to her, awakened her.

She realized she must have been staring at him like he was an ice cream cone she was dying to lick.

Too bad she couldn't afford a relationship right now.

"Well, thanks again." With great effort, she tore her eyes away and grabbed her shopping cart. A man was the *last* thing she needed in her life. She had enough trouble managing her sons—teenage boys were murder—not to mention her ex. No sirree Bob, she did not need a man.

Yet she allowed herself one last glance over her shoulder as she wheeled her cart down the meat aisle. He was watching. His gaze turned her hot inside and out.

No, she didn't need another man in her life. But she sure

wouldn't mind a little casual sex. At the very least, the Viking was something to fantasize about.

EVERYTHING HAPPENED FOR A REASON. HE'D COME TO *THIS* store at *this* time; it had to be to see her. He was a believer in the law of attraction. If you wanted it badly enough, it would come to you, whatever it was. He'd felt the sizzle of her body against his, sensed her desire in the quickening of her breath and the perfume of her hormones. So, when he started his engine as she was exiting the grocery store with her full cart and a young clerk trailing in her wake to load the haul into her minivan, he didn't feel any need to get her phone number or give her his. Law of attraction: He'd find her again.

Or she'd find him.

1

RACHEL DELANEY TUCKED THE GROCERY RECEIPT IN HER accordion file on the kitchen counter. She hadn't broken the piggy bank, but who the hell would ever have thought that canned kidney beans with no added salt would cost three times as much as beans *with* salt? Fewer ingredients costs more to manufacture? Wasn't it just a matter of keying a different recipe into the assembly line? Whatever, her goal was making sure the boys ate healthy when they were with her because they sure didn't when Gary had them.

They were still sleeping when she'd arrived home, so Rachel had carted the groceries in, put them away, and started breakfast. She didn't like wasting the weekends she had with the boys on chores, so she rose early to get the grocery shopping out of the way. She certainly didn't need to go to a gym before they woke up either; she got all the aerobic workout she needed running around at breakneck speed so she could accomplish everything and still have time with Justin and Nathan. She and Gary had dual custody, one week on, one week off. She'd have the boys until Sunday after supper, at which time she'd drive them over to Gary's. He had an apartment only a couple of miles away. Wherever they were staying, the boys were close to school.

It was a gorgeous day. January in the Bay Area was usually sunny, though this January had seen its fair share of rain. But on this last Saturday of the month, the sun streamed through the kitchen window as she whipped up the eggs and vanilla for French toast. Okay, not such a healthy breakfast, but it was a once-a-month-only treat. Sometimes you had to give kids a treat or they rebelled against anything that was good for them.

Just as she knew it would, the scent of cooking that wafted down the hallway soon garnered sounds from the bedroom end of the house. In his horrific *The Walking Dead* zombie pajamas, Justin led the charge like a bull elephant rather than with a zombielike shuffle. His short brown hair was askew, his face still creased with sleep lines from his pillow. At thirteen he was the shortest in his eighth-grade class and hated it.

"Did you get maple syrup, Mom?"

"Yes, honey. It's on the table." Rachel flipped a thick piece of French toast. Maple syrup was god-awful expensive, but what was the point of eating French toast without it? If you were going to be bad, do it with gusto.

In sweats and a torn T-shirt, his identically cut brown hair as mussed as Justin's, Nathan shuffled into the kitchen with a typical zombie growl. He should have been the one wearing *The Walking Dead* pajamas. He'd had a growth spurt over the last summer just before he started his sophomore year in high school, and he now topped his father's five-foot-ten frame. She hoped the same would come for Justin.

She slapped two pieces of French toast onto their plates. Justin grabbed his, and Nathan did the same, though at a much slower pace.

"You're welcome," she said.

"Thanks, Mom," Justin answered as he slid into his place at the table on the other side of the kitchen island.

"Thanks," Nathan echoed, albeit grudgingly.

Rachel told herself his attitude was due to still being half-asleep, even at just past nine in the morning. But she knew that wasn't the reason. Since the divorce, Nathan had become difficult.

She set another batch of egg-and-vanilla-coated bread in the hot pan. The boys were on their second helping by the time she sat down to eat her first.

"Dad said that if I kept my GPA above a three-point-five," Nathan said around a full mouth, "and I pass the driver's test with no errors, he'll let me have his car in the summer when he buys a new one."

"Please don't talk with your mouth full." The response was automatic, and not for the first time, she cursed inwardly at her ex. Sure, Gary offered the car, but he expected her to pay half the cost for the driving school and the insurance. She'd asked him *not* to talk to Nathan about it until she'd figured out where she'd come up with the extra money.

Nathan would be sixteen at the end of May, but they still hadn't gotten his driver's permit. She was putting it off as long as she could.

"You know, it would take a load off you, Mom. I could run Justin around so you wouldn't have to."

She almost laughed out loud. Right. As soon as he got that license and his dad's car, he'd be off with his friends.

"Honey, thanks very much for the offer, but it's only a

ten-minute walk to school. Justin doesn't need you to run him around. I already told you that I can't afford the class and the insurance yet. I need to get more settled in my job."

Another zombie growl rumbled low in Nathan's throat.

Before the divorce, which had become final at the beginning of September, she'd been a homemaker. She didn't have a college education or the computer skills required for something higher paying, but she'd managed to find a decent job as a receptionist at DeKnight Gauges, which was only a short drive from the house. There was opportunity at DKG; she was honing those computer skills she was lacking in. But right now, ends didn't always meet. Thank God Gary paid the mortgage and half the expenses for the boys or she didn't know what she'd have done.

Nathan didn't seem to understand how tight things were.

"Come on, Mom. All the other guys are getting their permits. It'll be six months before you have to start paying insurance anyway."

"Nathan, you can wait a little longer."

"Mom—" he started.

"Let's have a nice breakfast," she cut in. "Who wants another slice?"

"I do," Justin piped up.

Nathan simply muttered something unintelligible. She made him one anyway.

"I won't be able to hold my head up if I start my junior year without a license."

Rachel sighed. He got his drama from his father. "Why don't you get a summer job to help pay for it, then?"

She could hear his teeth grinding all the way across the kitchen. "I can't get a job if I don't have a license to drive there."

"There's the bus," she said calmly. "Or you can look for something close by. You could even do some yard work for the neighbors."

"Do I look like a gardener?" he muttered.

The egg coating sizzled in the pan. She didn't answer his question, sure it was rhetorical. When she was his age, she'd done babysitting, hours and hours of babysitting, to be able to afford extras. Saying that, though, was tantamount to the old I-had-to-walk-five-miles-through-the-snow-to-get-to-school story and meaningless to kids these days.

"We're living in the dark ages," he went on. "I can't even text, and I have to watch every minute I'm on my cell phone. You know, that's why Dad *bought* us these phones for Christmas, so we could *use* them."

They had a family plan. She believed cell phones were for keeping in contact with family, making arrangements for pick-ups, and yes, so she knew where her boys were. They didn't have unlimited minutes or unlimited texting or Internet access, and thank God they didn't or everyone would be texting at the dinner table instead of talking.

Since the divorce, everything was her fault because Gary promised them things for which she couldn't afford to pay her share. There was polo for Nathan and soccer for Justin, the cell phones, the *this*, the *that*. Gary's stock phrase was "If you can convince your mom." She always ended up being the bad guy.

She didn't, however, spew any of that. "Here you go." She slid their plates onto the table, too tired to prompt for a thank-you.

"Everything's about money with you, Mom. You make me crazy with it, just like you did Dad."

It was the closest Nathan had come to saying the divorce was her fault. But he thought it, oh he thought it, every day.

"Let's be pleasant at the breakfast table, Nathan."

"I'm not hungry," he muttered, shoving his plate away. He stomped out of the kitchen and half a minute later, the slam of his bedroom door rocked the house.

Across the table, Justin shoveled another bite of French toast slathered with maple syrup into his mouth. At least he swallowed before he said, "Can I go over to Martin's house?"

It was on the tip of her tongue to say they should spend the day together, doing . . . something. But the fact was, her sons didn't want to spend time with her. They were pissed that she'd driven Gary out of the house, that she nitpicked about every dime she had to spend, that she denied them unlimited texting, and that if they went over on free minutes, there was hell to pay.

"Sure," she said, hearing the weary edge in her voice. "Go to Martin's." She didn't tell him to be home by lunch. Martin's mom would feed him.

Alone in the kitchen, she gathered the plates, scraping the wasted French toast into the garbage.

Maybe she was a hard-ass. Maybe she should work harder to pay her portion of the things they wanted. She hadn't gotten her driver's license until she was eighteen, but it was different for a girl. The other boys at school would make fun of Nathan, call him a kid, tease him. He deserved a mother who understood those issues.

"What happened to us?" she whispered.

For Christmas, the boys had gotten her a dress from the local thrift shop, the tags still on it. She'd loved the leopard print. She'd liked that they were learning the value of money. But there'd been something in Nathan's eyes. Something that wasn't . . . nice. As if the gift was a punishment. She'd pushed the thought out of her head, but sometimes, like this morning, it came back. Her eldest boy was starting to hate her. Her heart turned over in her chest every time she thought about the widening gulf, but she had no idea how to breach it.

Justin called out indistinguishable words, maybe a good-bye, then slammed the front door on his way out. Two minutes later, it slammed again. Nathan. She'd have to call his cell and find out where the hell he was going. He'd been hanging around some guys from the basketball team, going to the games with them. He'd tried out but hadn't made it onto the team. He was determined to give it another shot next year. Rachel hadn't managed to meet these new friends yet, so she didn't have a home number to call just in case.

Sometimes she wondered how much more she could take. Everything was falling apart. Nathan hated her, and while Justin didn't seem perpetually angry, she felt him drifting away during the weeks they weren't at home with her.

For a moment, standing at the kitchen sink, a dirty plate still in her hand, she thought about the man in the grocery store. She thought about what it would be like to drop everything, right this very minute, and sneak out to see him. To see a lover. To have hot, fast sex in the backseat while parked in the far corner of a shopping mall lot. Then dashing back home to finish the cleaning before the boys got home. How utterly sexy. How perfectly delicious. Like running away from it all. Even better for relieving stress than soaking in the tub.

Inside, she felt warm and liquid. She'd never been one to daydream a lot, but right now, she sure could use a fantasy Prince Charming to take her away for a little hot nookie. Just like kids needed treats every once in a while so they didn't rebel, she needed a treat, too. An orgasm. More than one. A lot of them. The Viking had certainly awakened her. She could definitely go for having a vibrator in her drawer for moments like this, when she was suddenly, unexpectedly very much alone.

Hmm, was a sex toy in the budget?

ABOUT THE AUTHOR

With a bachelor's degree in accounting from Cal Poly, San Luis Obispo, Jasmine Haynes has worked in the high-tech Silicon Valley for the last twenty years and hasn't met a boring accountant yet! Okay, maybe a few. She and her husband live with numerous wild cats, one of whom has now moved into the house. Jasmine's pastimes, when not writing, are speed-walking in the Redwoods, watching classic movies, and hanging out with writer friends in coffee shops. She is the author of classy erotic romance and the popular Max Starr paranormal romance mystery series, and also writes quirky, laugh-out-loud romances as Jennifer Skully. Visit her at jasminehaynes.com and jasminehaynes.blogspot.com.